"What about

"The orphanage
the one who fou
responsibility." T
arm. Before Rebecca or Heidi could stop him he
grabbed the basket and headed for his horse.

"Besides, you don't fool me. You don't know any more
about caring for the baby than I do. At least I have
my ma at home to help."

Rebecca stared at the retreating back. Technically
the child was not her responsibility. But she couldn't
let him go. She shared something with the child—
abandonment. She wanted to give the baby the care
and love he deserved.

"Wait."

He stopped, and turned slowly. "I'm taking this baby
home."

"I accept your offer. I think it would benefit us both to
work together."

He continued to study her without any change in his
expression. Then he nodded. "Very well. Come along,
then."

Rebecca picked her way across the rough ground. Was
it possible she'd agreed to work with him? Live in his
house?

ORPHAN TRAIN:
Heading west to new families and forever love

Books by Linda Ford

Love Inspired Historical

The Road to Love
The Journey Home
The Path to Her Heart
Dakota Child
The Cowboy's Baby
Dakota Cowboy
Christmas Under Western Skies
    "A Cowboy's Christmas"
Dakota Father
Prairie Cowboy
Klondike Medicine Woman
*The Cowboy Tutor
*The Cowboy Father
*The Cowboy Comes Home
The Gift of Family
    "Merry Christmas, Cowboy"
†The Cowboy's Surprise Bride
†The Cowboy's Unexpected Family
†The Cowboy's Convenient Proposal
The Baby Compromise

*Three Brides for Three Cowboys
†Cowboys of Eden Valley

LINDA FORD

lives on a ranch in Alberta, Canada. Growing up on the prairie and learning to notice the small details it hides gave her an appreciation for watching God at work in His creation. Her upbringing also included being taught to trust God in everything and through everything—a theme that resonates in her stories. Threads of another part of her life are found in her stories—her concern for children and their future. She and her husband raised fourteen children—four homemade, ten adopted. She currently shares her home and life with her husband, a grown son, a live-in paraplegic client and a continual (and welcome) stream of kids, kids-in-law, grandkids and assorted friends and relatives.

The Baby Compromise

LINDA FORD

⟨H⟩ **HARLEQUIN**® LOVE INSPIRED® HISTORICAL

Special thanks and acknowledgment to Linda Ford
for her contribution to the Orphan Train miniseries.

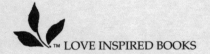

™ LOVE INSPIRED BOOKS

Recycling programs
for this product may
not exist in your area.

ISBN-13: 978-0-373-82968-2

THE BABY COMPROMISE

Copyright © 2013 by Harlequin Books S.A.

www.LoveInspiredBooks.com

Printed in U.S.A.

I can do everything through him who gives me strength.
—*Philippians* 4:13

This story challenged me. It was because of the help of my critique partner, Debora Dale, that it has structure. Debora, with her wonderful grasp of story and her ability to sort out the tangled elements, lent her hand and guided me through the morass. I owe her a debt of gratitude. I can't wait to see her stories published and on the shelves for all of you to enjoy.

Chapter One

Evans Grove, Nebraska
Late May, 1875

One day. He could spare one day away from home. He owed it to the people of Evans Grove to help with the construction of the town's new orphanage. A single day wasn't much, but it was something. The orphans rescued from the clutches of Felix Baxter deserved a safe place to call home.

But still, twenty-eight-year-old Colton Hayes paused at the door as he planted his favorite black cowboy hat firmly on his head.

"Ma, Pa, you'll be okay until I get back?" He didn't like to leave them alone.

"Those poor children need the orphanage as soon as they can get it," Pa said. "You go do what you can to help."

"I'll try to make supper." Ma had her long-suffering tone down to a fine art. Not that she didn't have cause. Bearing him late in life had overtaxed her heart. From a young age, he'd done all he could to ease her burden.

"Don't worry about it, Ma. I'll make something when I get back. You two just take care of yourselves." He'd be hungry after a day of work, but he had pork chops in the icebox. He'd learned long ago to boil potatoes in their jackets to save time.

"Pa, you need anything?"

"I'm fine, son." And to prove it, he pushed up from his chair.

Before he could hobble more than a step, Colton leaped forward to take the cup from his trembling hands. Since his accident three years ago, Pa lived in constant pain that made walking almost impossible.

Knowing his stupidity had caused Pa's injuries twisted Colton's insides. He silently vowed yet again to take care of him the rest of his life.

Colton filled the cup and carried it back to the table beside Pa's chair. "I've left soup on the stove. Ma, can you see that Pa gets a bowl of it?" He really should stay home and make sure they were both safe.

Ma sighed. "I 'spect I can manage, though I've been feeling poorly these past days." She pressed a hand to her chest.

Colton studied her. Did pain deepen the lines on her face?

She waved wearily. "You go ahead. We'll be fine."

"I'll be back later." Still he hesitated, torn between his parents' needs and the building project. "Seems we should help the community as much as we're able," he said, reminding himself why he'd made the commitment away from home. "After all, God spared us from the devastation of the flood." A storm in the spring had caused the nearby dam to break, flooding the town, damaging many of the homes and businesses, and causing several deaths. Then, in hopes of ensnaring more children for his child-labor schemes, Baxter had started a fire that destroyed the school. Thankfully, his attempt to implicate the local orphans so the citizens of Evans Grove would send the children to Greenville had failed. The townspeople were pulling together to rebuild. Colton owed it to them to lend a hand.

Pa settled back in his chair with a muffled groan. "God truly spared us." He lifted his hand in a half wave. "You go help out where you're needed."

Colton closed the door quietly, then turned toward town. One day to work. Then he'd be back home, taking care of his responsibilities.

He swung into the saddle and rode the few miles to town. He passed familiar homes, called a greeting to Mr. Gavin as he passed the general store. Like many of the homes and businesses in town, it still bore the mark of the high water of the flood.

He continued onward to the raw frame of the orphanage. Once it was finished, it would be a two-story structure with bedrooms upstairs for the children and staff. Rooms on the main floor would be used for daytime activity.

Strange. No one had arrived to work yet. He understood that men had volunteered and were scheduled to show up on specific days. Just as he had signed up to work today.

He studied the shell of the building. Wasn't there supposed to be a stack of lumber nearby? Bought and paid for by the generous, yet anonymous, donor funding the project? The gift had everyone talking and guessing as to who the donor might be.

It would be interesting to know who had enough money to fund two building projects—both the orphanage and the school. But unless men showed up to work, the money would benefit no one.

He slipped from his horse, tied the reins to the nearest post and continued his inspection on foot.

As far as he could tell, there'd been nothing done since his last visit to town three days ago. He scratched his head. Moreover, it appeared as if someone had tried to knock out part of the framework where the front door would be. Was there something wrong with the work? He examined the braces and could see no flaw in the construction. Strange.

He circled the building to the back and stared. Someone had left a basket in front of the doorway. Laundry, by the look of it. Who would do that? And why? This whole thing was beginning to feel wrong.

He crossed the distance and squatted by the basket. Looked like… He lifted the first item. Bedding? Small bedding. What on earth?

The laundry in the basket moved. He jerked, almost losing his balance. Sucking in air to steady his twitching nerves, he gingerly plucked at the items. A cotton flannel square and then a quilt wrapped around—

Colton stared. A baby? He jolted upright and gave the surroundings an intent stare. Where was the mother? He saw no one nearby except Mr. Gavin sweeping the sidewalk in front of his store. Colton opened his mouth to call to him and demand if he knew anything, but he was too far away.

The baby made a mewling sound.

Colton squatted by the basket again. "Who are you?" He'd never seen such a tiny human before. He didn't know much about babies—anything, really—but he suspected the infant couldn't be more than a few days old. He touched the incredibly small, pink cheek. So soft. So warm.

Who did this baby belong to? He poked his fingers around the swaddled infant, looking for clues to the young one's identity. He found a bottle full of milk, but nothing more.

Nothing except—

He examined the quilt bundled around the baby and realized that he recognized this pattern. No one made it but his grandmother. She said she'd dreamed it after Grandfather died. She called it "flowers of life." Triangles of dark fabric formed the bottom half of the diamond and then a maze of bright fabric formed the top half. He had no idea how she managed to create such a beautiful design—one that looked like flowers growing from dark soil. No one else had ever managed to duplicate the pattern accurately. She had made this quilt—and she only gave quilts to family. That meant the baby belonged to the Hayes clan. He considered the relations who lived nearby.

Cousin Amelia lived in Evans Grove, but she was in Kansas visiting her sister. Although she had put on weight lately, he'd seen no indication that she had been expecting a baby. She certainly hadn't mentioned anything to anyone. Colton might not get into town very often, but news like that would have reached him no matter what. Children were something to celebrate in Evans Grove, especially after so many had been lost to the flood. No, the child couldn't be Amelia's.

He had cousins in Ohio. Perhaps one of them had come to visit and something had happened. If Ma and Pa had been healthy, the mother might have left the baby with them instead of at the unfinished orphanage.

A fierce protectiveness filled his chest. He would take care of this little one until the parents returned. He reached into the basket, thinking to scoop the baby up, then hesitated. Wasn't there a special way to hold tiny babies? He'd heard women mention it when they handed their infants to others, but he couldn't recall their exact words. Something about holding its head. But *how* should he hold it? Up? Down? To the side? Was he meant to hold the baby from the head or support it from the neck? He pulled his hands back to his knees. He knew how to care for baby calves and foals. He'd seen baby kittens born, watched brand-new puppies. Once he'd even saved a nest of pink mice, only to watch them grow into troublesome rodents. But a human baby! He had no idea what to do.

Standing, he again looked around, hoping the mother had

slipped away on an errand and would now be returning on hurried feet.

But only a pair of cowboys rode down the street. A wagon approached from the north side of town. Somewhere he heard a door slam. And distant voices laughing.

"Hello?"

The only answer came from the basket, a little squawk.

The baby's face wrinkled up like a prune and a thin cry came from the tiny mouth.

Colton's heart turned warm and soft. This lost or abandoned or forgotten baby was somehow connected to Colton and, as such, would receive all the care Colton could provide. Remembering the admonition to watch the head, he cupped his hands under the bundle and lifted it to his chest, hoping for the best.

"You're safe now, baby. Don't cry."

The wee face smoothed. The lips puckered into a little rosebud, and the baby opened watery blue eyes to consider Colton.

Colton's protectiveness grew fierce. Whatever had happened to this baby's mother, he would find her. In the meantime, he would protect the baby and take care of it.

At that moment, the baby screwed up its face and cried—a sound like a mournful cat. So weak and pitiful Colton wondered if something was wrong.

"Don't cry." He cradled the baby against his chest and jiggled the little bundle.

"Don't cry. Please, don't cry."

But the wails intensified. The baby sounded distraught.

What was he to do with such a tiny baby? Colton remembered the bottle and grabbed it. Stuck the nipple in the crying mouth.

The baby choked.

Colton's face turned cold. His heart forgot to beat. In his ignorance had he drowned the wee mite?

Twenty-three-year-old Rebecca Sterling reminded herself to keep a cheerful smile and a hopeful heart as she headed down the street toward the orphanage. She was the one who had received the anonymous check, so she was the one in charge of the orphanage-building project, and she was determined to make it a success.

True, she knew nothing about building, but a year ago, she had known nothing about finding homes for orphan children, either. Her assignment with the Orphan Salvation Society— a New York–based organization that rescued orphaned city children from the streets and found families for them out West—had changed that in a hurry. Now all but one of the orphaned children placed in her care had been settled with families. The last child, ten-year-old Heidi Strauss, was at her side as they crossed the street to the orphanage building site. Half a block later, Rebecca's heart sank and her smile faltered when she could see that no lumber had been delivered.

"No more wood," Heidi announced.

"So I see." No lumber. Things gone missing. Boards destroyed and made to look like an accident.

Someone didn't want her to succeed at getting the orphanage built. Rebecca fought against her feelings of frustration. They were running out of time. The specially appointed U.S. marshal would soon return with the rescued orphans who'd been forced by Baxter into virtual slave labor for unscrupulous miners and farmers all over Nebraska territory.

The children deserved more than rescue. They deserved a warm place to live where they would be welcomed and protected. She intended to see that they got it. The orphanage would be built. Somehow.

She tucked her chin toward her chest in a sign that anyone who knew her would recognize as a sign of stubbornness. Whoever was at the root of her troubles would soon learn that Rebecca Gwendolyn Sterling expected people to do as she asked.

Her chin sagged. Here in small-town Nebraska, the name Lawrence Sterling III didn't carry the weight it did back in New York. Few people here had heard of her father. Fewer knew or cared that he was a rich importer of European goods.

She again drew her chin back. She would not accept defeat.

Through the framework of the building, a dark figure lurched from side to side.

"Someone's there," Heidi whispered as she tugged on Rebecca to stop her.

Rebecca jerked to a halt and clung to Heidi's hand. Was he the one responsible for the mischief at the site? Or was he there to help?

Realizing that she was alone except for the small girl, who squeezed her hand hard enough to numb her fingers, Rebecca glanced around, but saw no one. No one to help her…but no one to aid the intruder, either. There was only one of him, after all. No reason to be all trembly inside. She'd had enough of delays. If his intention was anything but working on the building…

A horse whinnied as she and Heidi trod past him.

A cry reached her ears. A thin wail. She stopped and listened. "What is that?"

Heidi listened, too. "It sounds like a baby."

"Must be coming from an open window." She moved on until she reached the corner of the framed building, where she paused to study the man. A big man, broad at the shoulders. Something stirred within her. A sense of recognition and more—a sense of eagerness and curiosity.

Nonsense. She pushed away everything but caution and

determination. Whoever he was, whatever he was up to, she had a job to do on this building. It was time everyone involved realized that she was in charge and would not relent until her job was done.

"Come along," she murmured to Heidi, who hung back, afraid of the man. Rebecca led her forward.

At that moment, the man turned.

Rebecca recognized him—Colton Hayes, a cowboy she'd seen in church, in the store, riding down the street, driving a buggy with an older man and woman she'd been informed were his parents.

Her admiration of the way he gently helped his parents from the buggy was her justification for why she'd studied him so intently. Noted his strong build, his thick black hair. The few times she'd seen him without the black cowboy hat he now wore, she'd noticed that his hair dipped in a wave. Today he wore a soft-looking blue shirt and denim trousers faded across the thighs, darker at the seams.

Surely he wasn't the one responsible for the mischief.

Not a tall, handsome man like that.

He considered her across the distance. Too far for her to see the color of his eyes, though she knew they were as green as emeralds.

Rebecca Gwendolyn Sterling, have you taken leave of your senses? Staring shamelessly at a man? What would your father say? She scolded herself in her mother's voice and words. Her mother had died seven years ago, yet Rebecca still heard her and listened to her. But that was not to say that she always followed what she knew would be her mother's advice. If she heeded her mother, she would demurely approach the man and speak quietly and gently. Perhaps ask if he needed assistance. Instead, she lifted the hem of her navy blue skirt and stepped quickly and confidently across the rutted ground. She circled the corner and approached the man. Heidi followed on her heels, trying to be invisible behind Rebecca's skirts.

"Am I ever glad to see you," the rancher said at their approach.

She jerked to a halt. Confusion clouded her thoughts. What on earth did he mean? And what did he have in his arms? Something alive, if the movement inside the quilt indicated anything. The cry she'd noted before came from that bundle. The squalling intensified.

"What *is* that?"

His crooked grin seemed both amused and desperate, which didn't make any sense. She couldn't imagine this big, bold man uncertain or desperate about anything.

"It's a baby." His voice carried a definite note of tension. "A crying baby. I tried to give it a bottle but nearly choked it to death."

"I see." She didn't. Why did he have a baby?

"Perhaps you can help."

"Me?" Her voice squeaked and she swallowed hard, forced calmness to her words. "What would you like me to do?"

"I don't know. Something. Anything."

She closed the remaining distance and looked at the small, scrunched-up face. Two little fists quivered beside the red cheeks. "It's very tiny."

"I figure it can't be very old."

"Is it a boy or girl?"

He shook his head as he continued to jiggle the infant. "I don't know."

"How can you not know?"

He chuckled. "Maybe because I haven't seen anything more than the bit that's not wrapped up."

"You mean to say—"

"I found it here in that basket. Can't you make it stop crying?"

He expected her to know what to do? Of course he would. After all, as an agent for the Orphan Salvation Society, she was deemed an expert on children. Only one problem. Until her father had signed her up for this trip, she'd had very little to do with children except in the company of their mothers or older sisters. Never had she even seen a baby so tiny.

Still she told herself, *I can do this.*

She *would* do this. She'd prove to her father and everyone else—herself included—that she wasn't simply a fancy lady from New York. She was capable.

He held the crying infant out to her.

Her heart thumped so hard she thought he might hear it. She sucked in a steadying breath. Hoping her arms wouldn't shake noticeably, she took the baby. It was incredibly tiny. Somewhere deep in her being, a protective ache made itself known and she cradled the bundle close.

Heidi stood on tiptoe to peek around Rebecca's shoulder. She pulled aside a corner of the quilt to look at the baby. "Oh, sweet," she whispered. Then, as she realized Colton could see her, she ducked back out of sight.

Colton heaved a sigh that Rebecca took for relief. Obviously, he thought she could take care of the little one.

"Very well." She could do this. "What does it need?"

He shrugged, though it seemed more like a gesture of uncertainty than lack of concern. "Beats me. But I suppose it's hungry."

"Then hand me the bottle, please." She indicated the nursing bottle he held in one hand.

He did so. His fingers were long and firm-looking. A workingman's hands. Hands that would grip life with an unrelenting grasp.

She pulled her thoughts back to reality and the heart-wrenching wails of the infant in her arms. She rocked. "Shh.

Shh." But the cries did not abate. What was wrong? What should she do? Steeling her face to reveal none of her fears, she shook the bottle then tipped the nipple into the open mouth.

The baby choked.

She jerked the bottle away. *Oh, dear God, please don't let this little one die.* At that moment she wished some of her deportment lessons had been forgone for instruction in child care. But, of course, she was expected to follow her mother's example and let her future children be raised by wet nurses and nannies. Rebecca recalled her nanny from when she was about five. When Miss Betsy left, she remembered crying for days until her mother had forbidden any more tears. Then she'd cried in private, often disappearing into a closet and shutting the door, hiding in the darkness.

Her arms tightened around the baby. No child deserved to know such loneliness and isolation, if it could be avoided. A child belonged in a home where he or she would be loved and valued.

Heidi tapped Rebecca's shoulder and whispered so softly Rebecca strained to catch her words. "Maybe the baby needs a dry diaper."

Rebecca stared at Heidi. How did this child know more about infants than she, a grown woman, did? She stilled a sigh. Because Heidi had been taught from an early age to be practical rather than ornamental.

The girl smiled. "Maybe there's one there." She indicated the basket, but didn't move.

Rebecca understood that Heidi didn't want Colton to see her. The poor girl was terribly self-conscious about the burn scars on her face and arms, especially after they'd kept her from gaining approval from any of the families looking to take in one of the Orphan Salvation Society children. But their time together had left Rebecca feeling very close to Heidi and very protective of the sweet, quiet girl. If she couldn't find a home for Heidi, the child would live in the orphanage and Rebecca would have to return to New York once she was done here. If her father would allow it, she would take Heidi back to New York and keep her so she wouldn't have to go to the orphanage. But even if Father did approve, the Society would insist the child be placed in a two-parent family. And anyway, her father would absolutely refuse. Rebecca prayed daily for a loving home for the child and did her best to ignore the ache in her heart at knowing she must say goodbye to Heidi.

She edged toward the basket to consider the contents, letting Heidi follow in her shadow.

Thankfully, Heidi reached around her and searched through the items. "I found one." Her voice remained low, not wanting Colton to hear her. "And here's a note." She handed the piece of paper to Rebecca.

Her heart quivering, Rebecca unfolded the page.

I'm so glad there's going to be an orphanage where my little boy can be safe. Please take good care of my darling. His name is Gabriel.

She pulled the baby close to her heart. The orphanage wasn't ready, but she'd take care of this child until it was. But now she had Heidi and the baby in her care. And an orphanage with stalled construction. The baby cried and she jiggled it in a vain attempt to soothe it.

It was a lot to manage. She drew in her chin. But she would do it.

Chapter Two

Rebecca handed the note to Colton, felt his concern even before he read the words.

Heidi tugged at Rebecca's arm. She bent to catch the child's soft words. "What does it say?"

She told Heidi that the baby had been left behind.

Little Heidi's big brown eyes filled with shock. "His mama and papa are gone? Are they dead?" Sorrow hollowed out each syllable.

"I don't know what's happened to them." A number of possibilities came to mind, but none she wished to share with a ten-year-old, especially one who knew all too well the agony of losing her parents.

"Poor little baby." Heidi reached out and tenderly stroked the tiny cheek.

The baby stopped crying long enough to swallow hard, then began again. He sounded so distressed that Rebecca's heart threatened to weep in response.

Heidi offered her the diaper.

Rebecca simply stared.

"You want I should do it?" Heidi's voice carried more eagerness than Rebecca had heard since shortly after they left New York. At that time Heidi had been full of hope for a new, loving family. But at every stop, people had seen her scarred face and turned away.

Perhaps helping care for the baby would ease Heidi's hurt. "If you'd like."

Heidi didn't have any younger siblings, yet she knew what to do. Were some people born with that knowledge? If so, what was she born for? Her mother's voice answered, *Rebecca Gwendolyn Sterling, there is no greater privilege than to run a home, entertain guests and be an asset to your father's station in life. And when you marry, provide the same for your husband.*

The lessons she had learned about maintaining flawless etiquette, organizing superb dinner parties and dressing to the most fashionable degree were all well and good in New York, but here they proved utterly useless. She couldn't help but wonder if those lessons were truly any more useful in the big city. Certainly her fiancé had found her lacking, despite her rigorous training to be a high-society hostess. She shoved the thought away. She'd vowed not to think about Oliver once she boarded the train on this trip.

At her father's request—insistence, really—Rebecca had left New York two months ago with thirty children. As an agent under the auspices of the Orphan Salvation Society, she had assisted the late Mr. Arlington in placing children at the various towns in Indiana, Illinois, Iowa and Nebraska. They had been on their way to Greenville—the final stop on their itinerary—when tragedy struck.

She tried to stop the horrifying memories from filling her mind, but they came with brilliant sharpness. The holdup of the train. The bandits making impossible demands. The children crying. The chaos that broke out when the thieves couldn't open the safe and then the shock of a gunshot echoing through her head and heart. Her mouth still grew parched at the memory. Poor Mr. Arlington. His life ended a few miles from Evans Grove. But good had come even from the darkest of days, since the loss of Mr. Arlington had caused her and the children to settle—temporarily at first—in Evans Grove. If they'd gone to Greenville, most of the children would have ended up in Felix Baxter's orphanage, farmed out for slave labor. Instead, nearly all the children had found good homes in Evans Grove. All but Heidi, who looked as happy as Rebecca had ever seen her with little Gabriel to care for.

Heidi spread a blanket on a clean board and indicated that Rebecca should put the baby down.

Colton moved closer, peering over Rebecca's shoulder as Heidi tenderly folded back the quilt until the baby lay exposed in a white flannel gown.

Rebecca could not believe how tiny he was.

Colton whistled. "You ever see such a small baby?"

Heidi jerked back at his voice. She gave Rebecca a pleading glance before the baby's cries drew her attention back to him. Rebecca let out a gust of air, thankful that Heidi hadn't gone into hiding the way she often did with strangers.

She answered Colton's question. "Never." A fierce protectiveness filled her heart. She tore her gaze from the baby to Colton's face and blinked at the way his green eyes glistened. As if he found the sight of the baby as incredible as she did. For a heartbeat she let herself share the sense of pleasure and possibility with him. Though she couldn't have explained either if anyone asked.

She shifted her attention back to Heidi, carefully memorizing everything the child did. Rebecca might be inexperienced when it came to caring for babies, but she had proven over and over that she could learn new things very quickly. She'd learn how to care for this tiny newborn and provide for his every need.

Heidi put a dry diaper on the baby, then swaddled him in the quilt. She pulled at Rebecca's skirt, urging her closer so she blocked Colton's view. Then she sat cross-legged on the board, took the bottle from Rebecca's hand and began to feed the baby. She indicated that Rebecca should lean closer and she did. "You have to wait until he stops crying so he won't choke."

Rebecca filed that information alongside the steps on changing the baby and swaddling him in a blanket. Then her brain raced with all the things she needed to do. "He's going to need fresh milk. I'll speak to Mr. Gavin about it. At the same time I'll ask where the building supplies are. I'll arrange for a crib or cradle to be put into our room at the hotel." Somehow she'd care for the baby and oversee the orphanage construction at the same time. How hard could it be? She turned back to Colton to assure him that she could manage.

But she did not see approval in his face. She saw resistance. He opened his mouth, but she wouldn't let him voice his argument. She might be a city girl, but she could handle a lot more than people gave her credit for.

"The orphanage should have been finished by now. That's obviously what the mother of this little boy expected." She tipped her head toward the note he still held. "As the person responsible for the building project, it's only reasonable for me to care for him until he can be safely sheltered under this roof." She indicated the building under construction.

He shook his head. "Not this baby."

She stared at him. What did he mean? Was he suggesting that she wasn't up to the challenge?

She tipped her chin and rallied her defenses.

"This baby belongs with me." Colton forced himself to ignore the shocked hurt in Rebecca's eyes.

Her cheeks flared pink. "He's your son?"

His face burned and he hoped he didn't turn the color of a bonfire. "No."

"Then I don't understand what you mean."

"You see the quilt?"

From the way she looked at him, he knew he wasn't making any sense.

"It's my grandmother's. Or rather, my grandmother made it." He stumbled over the words. When had he ever had such a hard time explaining a simple thing? Never. But with Rebecca's wild-flax-flower blue eyes on him, he could hardly think straight. He felt clumsy and way too big before her daintiness. Though she was tall for a woman, she still had to tip her chin to meet his eyes. Which she did, her expression was patient, serene and yet downright challenging. No doubt she wasn't used to having her decisions disputed.

She might be a rich, city girl and he only a nothing-special kind of cowboy, but this baby wasn't going to an orphanage if he had anything to say about it. "The quilt proves he's connected to the Hayes family, and I aim to take care of him." He let out a sigh of relief when she didn't point out that the quilt might have been passed on to someone outside the family, though he detected a flicker in her eyes that might indicate she wondered at the possibility.

"I'm sorry, but I have to ask how you intend to care for a baby. You're a——"

"A cowboy. I know."

"When I got here a few minutes ago, you didn't know what to do with him. You appealed to me to help make him stop crying."

"True. But I'm sure I can manage. My ma will help." At least, she'd be able to give advice. "He's family. I have an obligation." Caring for a baby would stretch his time to the limit. Already he struggled to keep up, always torn between the demands of the ranch and the care of his parents. But he'd find a way to make it work. He wouldn't accept any other possibility. He had a duty to this child, and he was determined never to fail in his family duties again.

She smiled, making it even more difficult for him to figure out his thoughts.

A tiny thread of suspicion made its way up to his brain. Was her smile meant to disarm him?

"I admire your sentiment." Her tone didn't quite match her words. "But it's clear as glass that the mother intended the baby to be cared for in the orphanage. That means I am the one who should care for this baby until the building is finished."

"Then what?" Surely there was more in the baby's future than being raised in an institution. There were already too many children who didn't have loving homes. A fact that tore at his insides. He wouldn't leave an abandoned kitten to fend for itself, and the thought of abandoned, orphaned children seemed as wrong as a yellow sky. He couldn't take in all the children who would eventually come to stay at the orphanage...but he could take in this one.

"He could be raised in the orphanage or maybe placed in a foster home or adopted," Rebecca replied.

A moment ago he'd feared that his face was turning red. Now the blood rushed from it. "No. I'll take him home. He'll be safe with me." He wouldn't contemplate the baby going to strangers.

Little Heidi had fed the baby the milk and burped him. He now slept in her arms, the fingers of one hand curled around her index finger. Asleep he didn't look like such a challenge.

Heidi saw him watching her—or, more correctly, the baby—and ducked behind Rebecca's back. He understood Heidi's shyness, having seen the scars on her face. They marred an otherwise beautiful child, but he didn't find her appearance off-putting, especially given her sweet way with the baby. Since she hid behind the curtain of her saddle-brown hair and kept her face turned down, he guessed she thought otherwise. Someone should tell her to let people see her big brown eyes more often and they'd forget about her scars.

He returned his attention to Rebecca. The pretty blue eyes had become brittle granite. He took a step backward and tried to sort out his thoughts. He didn't know the rules of arguing with a pretty city girl. All he knew was that he intended to personally see to the care of this infant and he'd brook no argument.

She turned to the little girl. "Come along, Heidi. We'll go to the store first."

Before she could take a step, he planted himself in her path. "Now, wait just a minute." He tried to form a plan, mount a convincing defense, but her steady consideration of him and the way she held her head high left him scrambling for reason. "Look, maybe we can work something out."

She quirked an eyebrow. "What do you have in mind?"

He didn't have anything concrete planned, but perhaps they could share the responsibility. The idea immediately appealed to him. "There's plenty of room at the ranch. You and Heidi and the baby could live there. I could help care for the baby and make sure he's okay." As he spoke, the idea took shape in his mind. "You wouldn't have to stay at the hotel any longer."

Rebecca smiled, though the brittleness remained in her eyes. "That's a lovely idea."

He heard the *but* before her smile faded.

"But I have to stay in town to see why the materials haven't been delivered. I have to make sure this building is complete before the orphans come to live here. Wyatt will return any day with children." Wyatt Reed was the newly appointed U.S. marshal charged with tracking down the orphans Baxter had hired out. The marshal had recently married Charlotte Miller and they'd adopted Sasha, one of Rebecca's young charges. If

Wyatt hadn't discovered how Felix Baxter was getting rich by hiring out orphans from earlier trains, those poor children would still be suffering. "It makes me angry to think how the children have been mistreated." Felix had robbed those children of any chance at a normal life.

Colton jerked his attention to the frame of the building beyond her shoulder. The only thing he could offer was his help. "I came here this morning to pitch in on the construction." An idea took root and blossomed. "If you take care of the baby at the ranch, I could do more work on the orphanage."

The doubt that clouded her eyes did not clear.

He had to convince her. It was the only way he could think to get her to give up or at least share the care of the baby. "I'll take over supervision of the construction work. Personally see that this building gets completed in a timely fashion." Surely a few words in the right ear and an occasional trip to town would be sufficient. The task wouldn't require much time away from the ranch. It was the ideal solution.

But she shook her head. "I am not prepared to abdicate my task to someone else."

He got the clear feeling that that was her final word on the subject. Was there anything that could be said to change her mind?

Chapter Three

"Miss Sterling."

Rebecca barely managed to bury a sigh at the imperious tone of the woman approaching her. She'd avoided her at the hotel dining room, but it didn't look as if she could escape her now. Miss Beatrice Ward was not a woman to be ignored. From the beginning, she'd opposed the presence of the orphan children in Evans Grove. Every time Rebecca encountered Miss Ward, with her helmet of silver hair and steely-gray eyes, she had to endure yet another lecture about the folly of keeping the orphans in the community.

"Riffraff," she'd said in a public meeting. "Mark my words, we'll suffer a rise in crime rate with these hooligans around." And every time something went awry, she blamed the orphaned children. The idea of constructing an orphanage to provide for even more orphaned children had sent her into a frenzy. But this time, she'd changed her strategy. Instead of speaking out against the children directly, she sought to block the building instead, saying there needed to be ordinances and building codes in place first. She insisted that Evans Grove should aim higher than basic wooden structures. Delay after delay ensued, thanks to Miss Ward.

Now her plan of attack had shifted to questioning God's

approval. Honestly, if Rebecca once again heard the woman warning, "The lack of success is surely a sign from God that the plan should be abandoned," she would forget her polite upbringing and tell the woman exactly what she thought of her constant interference.

As Miss Ward neared, Heidi clutched the baby to her chest, bolted to her feet and pressed herself to Rebecca's side, as if hoping she could disappear into the folds of Rebecca's skirt.

The poor little girl was certain everyone stared at her scarred face. Over and over again, Rebecca had assured her that people would love her despite the burn scars. But they'd seen plenty of evidence to the contrary on this trip. At each train stop, the children had been examined and several chosen. Heidi had started the journey with her brother, Jakob. The sturdy fourteen-year-old boy had been an ideal candidate for placement, but he had stuck stubbornly to his sister's side, wanting them to be placed together. Each time couples would approach the pair, the sight of Heidi's disfigurement drove them away. It had reached the point where Heidi tricked her brother into getting placed on his own so that she wouldn't hold him back from finding a family. Now she was all alone and still without a family willing to give her a chance.

Rebecca shot a glance toward Colton. What did he think of Heidi's scars? She couldn't bear to see this child rejected time and again because of something she had no control over.

Colton watched Heidi as she shivered at Rebecca's side. Was it her imagination or did his expression reveal tenderness? Tenderness that made her heart tug at its moorings.

"She's frightened of Miss Ward," he whispered.

Rebecca nodded. She wanted to pull Heidi into her arms and reassure her, but she'd learned not to offer Heidi too much in the way of comfort. The child simply withdrew. It had grown worse since her brother, Jakob, had been placed with a family in Iowa. Heidi herself had arranged for the other children to keep Jakob and her apart until someone chose to take him. It wasn't until the train pulled away that Jakob realized his little sister wasn't staying with him.

Rebecca would never forget the silent tears that streamed down Heidi's cheeks as she watched her brother standing alone on the platform calling for her as the train with the remaining orphans pulled away. Rebecca had hugged her and tried to console her, but since that day Heidi—shy and self-conscious even with her brother at her side—had pulled back even further into herself.

"Miss Sterling." Beatrice Ward steamed closer. "We need to talk."

Rebecca glanced toward the store. Perhaps she could hurry away to find out why the materials hadn't been delivered.

The older woman stepped directly in Rebecca's path, making escape impossible.

Little Gabriel whimpered.

Miss Ward's eyes narrowed. "What is that I hear?"

Colton took the baby from Heidi. Rebecca felt the little girl trembling at the man's nearness.

Colton moved to Rebecca's side, the baby ensconced in his arms. "Miss Ward, meet little Gabriel."

"Gabriel?" She squinted at the bundle and sniffed. "I don't recall anyone around here having a new baby by that name." She shifted her gaze, stared at the basket nearby and swallowed hard enough to be audible. Slowly, as if it hurt, she brought her gaze back to Colton and the baby. "He's a foundling, isn't he? Another one. Soon this town will be overrun with the likes of these." She swept her hand to indicate the baby and Heidi, who pressed into Rebecca's back. "It has to stop."

Rebecca smiled gently, hoping it would disarm the woman, even though what she really wanted was to unleash the onslaught that burned at her throat and scalded her tongue.

"Evans Grove is fortunate to have these children in their midst. Each of them has proven to be an asset."

"They are street urchins."

"All with good hearts."

Miss Ward sniffed. The older woman fixed Rebecca with a scowl. "They don't belong here, and neither do any other ruffians. You must cease construction on that…that poorhouse."

Rebecca gasped. "It's not a poorhouse. It's an orphanage."

"It's the same thing, isn't it?"

"Not at all. And I will not order the construction stopped on your say-so." Not that it required an order from her. The construction had ground to a halt of its own accord. Or as a result of someone else's efforts. She suspected that Miss Ward might be behind it, but she had no proof.

Miss Ward looked ready to eat Rebecca for a midmorning snack. "I suspect they do things differently in New York. I don't suppose they give consideration to what others in the community want. Nor do they consult God in their plans. That's the only reason I can think that you haven't considered all the warning signs God has sent your way. This is not His will. Shouldn't you heed such things?"

No matter how many times she heard this warning repeated, it never made any sense. "I don't think I should blame God for vandalism, mischief and the failure on the part of man to deliver supplies as agreed upon."

"Mark my words. If you refuse to listen to God's warnings, nothing but disaster will follow. And if you suspect monkey business, perhaps you need look no farther than the hooligans you brought to town."

Rebecca could do nothing but stare.

"Miss Ward." Colton spoke softly. "It might interest you to know that I've offered to supervise the building of the orphanage. Miss Rebecca and I were discussing the details of our agreement when you came along."

Rebecca gaped at Colton. Realizing that her mouth hung open, she forced it closed.

Miss Ward sniffed again. "It's plain that she's hoodwinked you. But don't think you can manipulate God to your own desires." She stormed away.

Rebecca stared after her. If only she could avoid ever seeing that woman again. Unfortunately, she and Heidi were forced to run into her every day, since Miss Ward also lived at the hotel as she waited for her house to be repaired following the flood. How nice it would be to live where Miss Ward and others couldn't stare at Heidi as she took her meals.

Mr. Hayes was offering her a way out, but she couldn't take it, could she? No, of course she couldn't. Supervising the orphanage building was her responsibility, and if she couldn't fulfill it, how could she ever prove to her father—and herself—that she could complete a difficult job?

"What about it, Miss Rebecca?" Colton asked, trying to read her expression. It remained calm and unruffled, giving him no clue to her state of mind.

"The funds for the orphanage building were sent to me. Overseeing the construction is my responsibility."

"I'm only offering to help you."

"I prefer to see my obligations through. That includes personally seeing that this building is finished. I'd do better to simply take the baby and stay with him at the hotel."

Heidi tugged Rebecca's skirt. "Oh, please, Miss Sterling. Do we have to stay there?"

Colton shook his head. "The orphanage may be your responsibility, but I'm the one who found this child, and that makes him *my* responsibility." The baby nestled in the crook of his arm. Before Rebecca or Heidi could stop Colton, he grabbed the basket and headed for his horse.

"Besides, you don't fool me. You don't know any more

about caring for the baby than I do. At least I have my ma at home to help." Best thing he could do was take little Gabriel home to her now. He'd only come to town to help with the orphanage building, and given the lack of materials, it was clear that no work on that could be done today.

As he rounded the corner, he saw again the damaged door frame. He knew it was deliberate. Would the person or persons responsible take the vandalism further? Did Rebecca know she faced opposition that resorted to this kind of destruction?

If he left her to deal with this on her own, would she get in over her head?

He clamped down on his teeth. He couldn't babysit her. He had his hands full. Literally. But if harm came to her, he would live with it hanging around his neck.

Just as he did with his pa's injuries.

Rebecca stared at the broad back of Colton Hayes. Technically, the child was not her responsibility. But she couldn't let him go. Yes, she wanted to prove herself capable, but that was only part of her reason. She wanted to protect the child. Not from the big-booted cowboy. Colton also wanted to protect the baby. But she'd seen how crippled his parents were. Who would hold Gabriel and rock him? Who would kiss away his tears? Could they? Would they? Her heart squeezed out an answer. Even if they did, she shared something with the child—abandonment. She was grown-up, yet it hurt beyond words to be rejected. Her fiancé had eloped with some seamstress just days before their wedding. This baby had been abandoned by his mother. Neither was right, and she would do what she could to make it better for Gabriel. She'd give him the care and love he deserved.

"Wait." The word rang with more pent-up emotion than she normally revealed.

He stopped, turned slowly and regarded her through the framework of the building. "I'm taking this baby home."

"I accept your offer."

He snorted. "I might have changed my mind."

"A gentleman would not do that."

"I'm no gentleman. I'm a cowboy."

Although his words were softly spoken, she didn't miss the harsh note. Did he intend to make her beg?

She considered her predicament. On one hand stood her father with his high expectations. Would he see it as a failure on her part if she let someone oversee the day-to-day construction work on the orphanage? On the other, there was this helpless baby. If the construction of the orphanage had been finished on time, there'd be a safe place for him to stay. It was her fault that there wasn't—and that meant it was up to her to see to his care, whether the cowboy saw it that way or not.

Very well. She'd prove to everyone that she could handle any challenge. "I think it would benefit us both to work together. An infant would be a lot of work for your mother. I'll help—" She practically choked on the word. "I'll help with the baby and accept your help on this building."

There. She'd spoken the words with as much apology and pleading as she could. And never before had it taken so much effort. "A business arrangement. But I insist on being involved in all decisions regarding the orphanage." She saw his protest coming and hastened to add, "Just as I'm sure you wish to be involved with all the decisions regarding Gabriel."

He continued to study her without any change in his expression. Then he nodded. "Very well. Come along, then. We'll go to the mercantile first."

"Finally," Heidi murmured. "I was afraid you'd let him leave."

Rebecca took Heidi's hand as they picked their way across

the rough ground. Was it possible that she'd just agreed to work with him? To live in his house?

"So how will this work?" she asked the cowboy. "How will we divide the responsibilities?" she clarified when he looked at her questioningly. "I expect to do my share."

"I would expect nothing less. You can take care of the house while I get this building up. It benefits us both. I can be in town working here without worrying about my parents. And I can keep Gabriel safe."

"You mean *we* can keep Gabriel safe." She fell in step at his side as they returned to the street.

"Of course." He struggled to hold the baby and the basket as he reached to untie the horse. The animal didn't care for the arrangement and tugged back on the reins.

"Whoa," Colton ordered. "Settle down. It's just a baby and his bed."

His words did nothing to calm the horse.

Rebecca let Colton struggle for a moment, enjoying his predicament. If this provided any indication of how well he'd manage on his own, he should be thanking her for agreeing to join forces with him.

He shot her a look.

She saw no gratitude in the way his eyes flashed, nor in the hard set of his mouth.

"You're enjoying this, aren't you?"

She wiped all amusement from her face. "I'll take the baby." She reached out to do so.

He drew back.

"I thought we were going to work together," she reminded him.

"That's what we agreed."

My, my, didn't he sound gracious? But she took the infant without further comment, leaving him with the basket.

He quickly untied the horse and they began the journey toward the store.

He walked so close at her side that it made her aware of his size, his rolling gait and something beyond the physical. A sense of strength and confidence. Her skin felt his nearness in a way that alarmed her and she moved aside.

"You aren't planning to run away with the baby, are you?"

She sniffed, realized it sounded like Miss Ward and vowed never to do it again. "Oh, yes. It's always been my dream to be chased down by a horse-riding, big-booted cowboy."

He stopped, lifted one foot and examined it. "My feet aren't that big."

"If you say so." She continued on her way. It took him only two steps to catch up.

"You're just sore that you didn't get your way."

He made her sound like a spoiled child. "I am not."

Heidi giggled. "You're quarreling."

Rebecca clamped her lips together and shot Colton a look that dared him to continue this.

He grinned. Did that glint in his eyes suggest a challenge?

They turned down Victory Street. A lone cowboy rode past, greeted Colton by name and tipped his hat at Rebecca.

Something burned at her thoughts and wouldn't be quenched, despite her best intentions. Was he like her father, doubting her abilities? "Do you think I can't manage on my own?" If so, she would prove him wrong.

He raised an eyebrow at her, but didn't answer. His eyes were like hard bits of rock chiseled from a quarry. Only an accident of birth made them the unusual green color.

"Just because I'm a city girl doesn't mean I'm incapable of caring for a baby."

"Don't recall saying you were."

They reached the mercantile, forcing her to keep her retort to herself. Besides, as Heidi had pointed out, this was childish quarreling.

She shifted the baby to one arm and brought her thoughts to the task at hand—getting the building supplies delivered as promised. No workers would come unless there was material—though she suspected Miss Ward had been spreading her belief about God's displeasure with the project among the townspeople. Perhaps some of them believed her.

Oh, and getting a regular supply of milk for the baby. See, she wasn't a bit incompetent.

With Heidi clinging to her side, Rebecca stepped into the store. She breathed in the smell of coal oil and leather. From past experience, she knew that when she moved closer to the counter she'd catch the scent of licorice and cheese and hundreds of other things more pleasant to the senses.

Colton paused to tie the horse to the hitching rail and set the basket on the bench outside the door, but he reached her side before she made it to the counter. She stuffed back annoyance. Did he think she couldn't handle things without him?

Without giving him a chance to take over, she spoke to Mr. Gavin. "Sir, I thought we had an agreement. You promised that the supplies would be delivered to the building site this morning." He'd given his word several times, but something always prevented him from keeping it. "I was just there, and there are no supplies."

Mr. Gavin raised his craggy eyebrows and gave little Gabriel a look rife with curiosity. She saw the flash of inquisitiveness in his eyes before he thought better of asking about the baby and turned his attention back to her.

"Miss Sterling, I'm doing my best. Unfortunately, I'm at the mercy of the suppliers in Newfield."

Rebecca understood that. Newfield was the largest town to the east. A distance of approximately twelve miles, if she wasn't mistaken. She could have walked that far and carried the boards back one by one in the time since she'd placed the order. "Is there not a regular train?" The question was rhetorical. Everyone knew there was. And although Evans Grove wasn't a regular stop, whistle stops could be scheduled whenever deliveries needed to be made. Furthermore, she knew supplies regularly came from Newfield by wagon. "The work cannot proceed without lumber."

Mr. Gavin made noncommittal noises. "I'm not responsible for the delay."

Colton leaned on the counter, all relaxed-looking, as if he had no concern about this stalemate.

So much for working together.

He shifted slightly, turned his attention to the storekeeper. "Guess there's not much you can do about it, then?"

Mr. Gavin shook his head. "Not a single thing."

"Suppose I could take a wagon to Newfield and bring back supplies. Likely I'd have to make more'n one trip." He spoke in a leisurely, unconcerned way. "Come to think of it, I could buy up supplies for the ranch at the same time."

"I'm sure that won't be necessary," Mr. Gavin all but sputtered. "I'll send a wire again today. Whatever the reason is, this delay is unacceptable." He turned back to Rebecca. "Your supplies will be here tomorrow. I personally guarantee it."

Colton banged a fist on the counter. "Good doing business with you." He considered Rebecca, dropped his gaze to the baby. "We'll be needing a few other things."

Rebecca would not let him take over. "We need a regular supply of fresh milk for little Gabriel here."

"You got another child?" Mr. Gavin asked. "How'd that happen?"

Rebecca silently sought Colton's advice. They hadn't discussed how to handle this situation.

Colton grinned.

She blinked. The man could charm the paper off the wall with a smile like that. Then her caution sprang to life. What was he trying to charm from her?

But he'd turned back to the storekeeper. "Found this baby on the doorstep of the orphanage. He's only a few days old. You haven't seen any woman around town who might have given birth, have you?"

Mr. Gavin's mouth hung open. He managed to shake his head without bringing his lips together.

"I suspect the mother is ill or injured, unable to care for the baby."

Rebecca hoped the explanation was that innocent. But she knew of many other possible reasons. A baby out of wedlock. A runaway young woman. But she understood Colton's desire to protect Gabriel from gossip and speculation, especially if he truly believed the little one was related to him.

The storekeeper continued to shake his head.

Again, Colton dropped a fist to the counter. "Well, let us know if you see anyone like that. Now, about the things we need for the baby."

The man scurried to get the milk that Rebecca asked for. "There's daily delivery so it's always fresh."

"We won't be needing more than this bottle," Colton said. "I can provide milk at the ranch."

The storekeeper looked disappointed at the loss of a daily sale.

Colton must have noticed. "The baby will need a few other things." He glanced around, as if looking for baby supplies. He spotted a nursing bottle and grabbed it. "Put it all on my bill."

"Excuse me." Rebecca kept her attention focused on Mr. Gavin, afraid that if she looked at Colton her annoyance would boil over in a most unladylike way that would shock her father if he could hear. "I am the agent for the Orphan

Salvation Society and as such am authorized to pay for expenses on behalf of children in my care. Therefore, you may add it to *my* account." She pulled the bottle closer.

Colton straightened like someone had jammed a steel rod down his spine.

She would not pay any attention to his indignation, nor would she let his size intimidate her. Just because she'd agreed to their compromise did not mean he would always get his way. She'd stay at his house, as they'd decided, but she'd pay her own way...and Gabriel's, as well. She turned and headed out the door, clutching the bottle of milk in her hand.

Heidi followed.

"Rebecca Sterling." Colton's voice carried a large dose of command.

Rebecca saw the uncertainty in Heidi's face. She almost relented simply to ease Heidi's worry. But neither that nor the echoing voice of her mother inside her head reminding her to always act like a lady was enough to induce her to respond to Colton's call.

As she reached the wide step, she heard his boots clatter across the floor toward her.

On the nearby bench she sat beside the baby's basket, pulled Heidi down on her other side and, with a rigid spine, waited.

Colton Hayes had to be the most annoying, most domineering man she'd ever met. But nothing he said would make her change her mind. She would not relinquish her measure of control in this situation to live on Colton's charity. She'd pay her way when money was called for, and when it wasn't, she'd figure out how to earn her keep. Everyone would sooner or later acknowledge that Rebecca Sterling was a capable young woman.

The door opened with a squawk of protesting hinges then slapped shut.

She did her best to pretend she wasn't aware of Colton standing a few inches away, though the air pulsated with his annoyance. Instead, Rebecca kept her attention on the tiny baby in her arms. He was so sweet and innocent, filling her heart with a protectiveness like nothing she'd ever felt before.

She wouldn't let him down. She *wouldn't*.

Colton stared down at Rebecca's bent head. Her shiny blond hair had been wound into some kind of roll around her face, allowing him plenty of chance to admire her slender neck. Though how he could so dispassionately do so while his insides boiled defied explanation. "Has anyone ever mentioned how annoying you are?"

"Never." She didn't even dignify her response by glancing his way.

"Well, someone should have." Though he supposed rich girls were allowed to act any way they wanted without incurring correction. "Seeing as he's a member of my family, I will pay for this baby's needs."

She lifted her head and fixed him with one of those hard blue looks.

He tried again. "We agreed to share the work."

She lifted one shoulder in a dismissive gesture. "Yes, we did."

He let his breath out in a long, exaggerated sigh, hoping she would understand how difficult she was being.

She ignored him.

Smiling, Heidi sat on the edge of the bench, glancing from one to the other as they talked. She'd forgotten to hide her face. The kid was enjoying the quarreling, as she called it.

He caught Rebecca's eye and tipped his head to indicate Heidi.

Rebecca gave a slight nod to inform him that she saw, and for a moment Colton forgot his annoyance, lost in the pleasure of Heidi's amusement—and something as fragile as butterfly wings that hovered between himself and Rebecca.

Then he noticed the baby bottle in the basket, and all he could think about was the discord between them.

He leaned against the hitching rail and studied the three people he'd invited into his life—Rebecca, who seemed bound and determined to challenge him at every opportunity; little Gabriel, who was tucked into her arm as content as anyone had a right to be; and Heidi, who suddenly ducked out of sight behind Rebecca's shoulder. Fierce protectiveness clutched at his throat, and he was filled with the sense that none of the three had anyone but him to watch out for them.

Nonsense, of course. He'd heard tell that Heidi had a brother trying to track her down, and he imagined that Gabriel's ma would come back for her son sooner or later. He also knew Rebecca had family back in New York. And she'd made it abundantly clear that she did not welcome anything from him. So why did he feel that it was his job to look after them all? Why would he *want* to, with all his responsibilities to the ranch and to his parents?

Even trying to see to their needs would be difficult. He already recognized that sharing the care of the baby at the ranch could prove to be more difficult then he'd initially thought. Would Rebecca resist every move he made, demand to be in control? His skin crawled at the thought.

"We're in this together," he said with as much patience as he could muster. "That's what we agreed. Why don't we cooperate and make it a pleasant arrangement?" She should find the idea appealing, but he knew when she looked at him that she had no intention of cooperating.

"If you mean I should give in to all your suggestions, the answer is no."

"No? Just like that?"

"Mr. Hayes, I did not come west to sightsee. I came with a job to do. And I am determined to do that job. I will not turn my responsibilities over to a—" She paused as if to consider what to say and her gaze drifted toward his boots. "Anyone."

"A dusty cowboy with big feet, you mean?"

A smile tugged at the corners of her mouth. "Admit it." She lifted toward him one dainty foot, clad in a beautiful brown leather ladies' boot. "Yours are pretty big."

In comparison to hers, they were gigantic.

Heidi's muffled giggle came from behind Rebecca.

Colton threw up his hands in mock defeat. "Okay, I have big feet. But that doesn't mean we can't cooperate."

She nodded, amusement making her eyes flash a brighter blue. "I don't mind cooperating, but I am not relinquishing my duties."

It didn't feel like cooperation to him. More like arguments about everything and nothing.

Baby Gabriel started to fuss.

Rebecca glanced at the bottle of milk from the store. "I'll pay for the child's needs. You're already providing shelter for all of us, room *and* board for Heidi and me—so I can cover the rest of Gabriel's expenses. That's a fair division, don't you think?" She didn't wait for a reply. "Now, if you don't mind, I'll take him to Holly and Mason's house." She rose. "Heidi, can you carry the basket?" They headed away without so much as a by-your-leave, the basket bumping against Heidi's legs.

He called after them, "I'll get a buggy to take us home."

She jolted to a stop and faced him. "Home?"

"The ranch."

"Oh. Fine. You know where I'll be."

She continued on her way, Heidi at her side.

He stared after them. This was not turning out at all well,

and he hadn't even gotten her to the ranch yet. How would she react to living so far out of town? How would his parents respond to having her and the two children in their home? He lifted his hat and rubbed his head. If not for his concern for baby Gabriel, he'd be sorely tempted to change his mind about this arrangement. But no, he couldn't shirk his responsibility. Particularly not his responsibility to family.

His gaze shifted to the orphanage.

And, he reluctantly admitted, one other thing stopped him from rescinding his offer—concern about Rebecca's safety, since someone was clearly trying to destroy the place.

He slammed his hat back onto his head. His concern would always, first and foremost, be his family. That meant his parents and now Gabriel. Heidi and Rebecca would temporarily be part of his family, as well.

Sure, Rebecca was a rich girl with a father, but he was back East and Colton was right here. So he would give her the help and protection she needed. Even if she resisted.

Chapter Four

Rebecca resisted the temptation to glance back at the cowboy. She ignored the way the skin on the back of her neck twitched, as if aware of his stare. If she encouraged him in any way, he would run roughshod over anything she suggested. She couldn't allow that to happen.

Heidi bounced along at her side. "Are we gonna keep the baby?"

"Until arrangements can be made."

Gabriel's fussing swelled into desperate wails.

"He's hungry. We got to hurry." Heidi broke into a jog, the basket dragging against one leg.

Rebecca lengthened her stride as her heart alternated between determination to prove she could take care of the baby and fear that she would fail.

Failure was not an option.

Her hurried steps bounced the baby and he stopped fussing.

When they reached the Wrights' house, the teacherage that was spared in the fire that destroyed the school, they were greeted by Holly and Mason's son, who was playing outside. Redheaded Liam was one of the boys Rebecca had brought from New York. As soon as he'd arrived, he'd quickly grown close with both the schoolteacher and the sheriff, who had officially adopted him just days after their recent wedding.

"Hello, Miss Sterling," he called. "Hi, Heidi. Whatcha got?" He indicated the basket at Heidi's side.

"A baby." Heidi pointed to little Gabriel in Rebecca's arms.

Liam ran to Rebecca's side. "A baby? Where'd you get him?"

Holly came to the door. "Did I hear you have a baby?"

Rebecca nodded as Gabriel wailed. "His name is Gabriel and he's hungry."

"Bring him in." Holly ushered them into her small living room. The whole tiny house was not even the size of the ballroom in Rebecca's father's home, and yet it comfortably housed three very happy people. Rebecca marveled again at how little it took to satisfy this sweet woman. There was no doubting her happiness. She seemed to glow from within.

Rebecca bounced to quiet the baby, but he wouldn't be lulled.

"What do you need?" Holly asked.

"There's milk and a bottle in the basket."

"I'll get it ready."

Heidi handed Holly the items. "Can I go play with Liam?"

"Of course." Rebecca knew the girl missed the other orphan children, who had all been placed.

She and Liam ran outside.

Rebecca watched Holly carefully as she washed the bottle and rinsed it with scalding water from the kettle simmering on the back of the stove. Then she filled the bottle with milk and set it in a bowl of hot water. "Why do you do that?"

"You've never cared for a baby?" Holly asked.

"No."

"I'm warming the milk so he doesn't get a tummyache." She took the bottle from the water, wiped the outside dry and shook a few drops of milk onto her wrist. "I'm checking to make sure it's the right temperature. Here, let me show you."

Rebecca held out her arm and Holly dropped milk on her wrist.

"Does it feel comfortably warm?"

Rebecca nodded.

"Then here you go." She handed Rebecca the bottle. "Make yourself at home." They both sat on the couch.

Rebecca remembered everything that she'd seen Heidi do and rubbed Gabriel's little cheek. He turned toward her finger and she offered him the bottle, grinning as the baby sucked eagerly.

"How do you know about caring for babies?" she asked her friend.

Holly chuckled. "Aren't schoolteachers supposed to be experts on everything? Besides, I helped care for babies when I was younger. Now tell me about this little fellow."

Rebecca repeated the story of Colton finding him at the orphanage site. "Gabriel was crying when I came and Colton begged me to make him stop." Strange how they had gone from him asking for her help to him trying to take over. Apparently, she'd made a bad impression when she hadn't realized the baby needed a new diaper. Now he didn't seem to think she was capable of doing anything useful.

A quick knock sounded on the door and Charlotte Reed burst into the room. "What's this about Rebecca finding a baby?" The woman's strawberry blond hair was a bit windblown and her porcelain skin was flushed. Clearly, she'd rushed over as soon as she heard the news.

"How did you hear?" Rebecca jostled Gabriel, who had stopped eating after only a few ounces.

"Likely he needs burping," Holly said.

Rebecca knew what to do from watching Heidi. She cradled the baby to her shoulder and patted his back. He rewarded her with a gentle burp. She could do this. She could care for this baby. She turned back to Charlotte and repeated her question.

Charlotte chuckled. "I stopped at the store. Mr. Gavin told me. His wife was all atwitter about the news." She bent over the baby. "He's so sweet."

Rebecca smiled down at Gabriel and her heart gave a strange tug. Would she ever have a baby of her own? Once she'd dreamed of it. Before she was left at the altar with her hopes dashed.

"Where's Sasha?" Holly asked.

"She's playing with the others."

Charlotte had fallen in love with the raven-haired four-year-old orphan the moment she laid eyes on her when Rebecca and the children had first come to town. She'd persuaded her husband, Charlie Miller, to agree to take in the child, but then he'd died suddenly, leaving her a widow and Sasha's placement in jeopardy—the policy of the Orphan Salvation Society didn't allow for a single woman to foster a child on her own. Fortunately, Charlotte had persuaded Wyatt Reed, a new arrival in town, to marry her so she could keep the little girl. It hadn't taken long for Wyatt to fall in love with this quiet, gentle woman—and with the little girl they had formally adopted. In fact, Wyatt had become so committed to the cause of helping orphans that he'd taken on the appointment as U.S. marshal so he could track down and rescue the children Felix Baxter had endangered.

Rebecca allowed herself a moment of rejoicing in knowing all the children she'd brought west had been placed in good homes with loving families...all, that is, except Heidi.

"Give us all the details," Charlotte said, bringing Rebecca's thoughts back to the present.

Rebecca repeated her story about the baby.

"Are you going to keep him?"

Both ladies leaned closer, waiting for her answer.

"The note his mother left asked for him to live at the orphanage, so I'll care for him until it's finished. Though it would be ideal if we could locate his mother and help her."

The pair nodded. "So you'll take him to the hotel?"

"No. I've agreed to go to the Hayes ranch."

Charlotte gasped, "Why?"

Rebecca laughed at her friend's surprise.

"See this quilt?" She repeated Colton's story. "He's convinced it means the baby is part of the Hayes family and insisted that, as a relative, he would care for the baby." She shook her head. "We'll share the baby's care and he'll help with building the orphanage."

Her friends stared at her in disbelief.

Then Holly chuckled. "You're going to live with that big, handsome rancher?"

Rebecca's cheeks burned. "Not in an indecent way. His parents live in the house, too."

Holly's cheeks flushed red. "Of course. That's what I meant." She brightened. "But Colton Hayes? By my calculations the man is twenty-eight years old and not married. It amazes me. I would think every mother in the county would be parading their daughters before him."

Charlotte asked to hold the baby, and Rebecca relinquished a now-content Gabriel to her. Charlotte snuggled him close. "I guess Colton has his hands full with his parents. Neither of them is well. Have you noticed how gentle he is with them when he brings them to town?" She sighed expansively. "He's so devoted to them. Such a sweet man."

"Not that sweet," Rebecca muttered. Her friends turned to stare at her. "We argued," she said.

"About what?" Charlotte asked.

"He thinks he has to tell me what to do. That I'm nothing but a spoiled little rich girl."

Holly patted her hand. "Well, you are a rich girl."

"My father is rich."

"Same thing." Holly waved her hand in a calming gesture. "But that doesn't mean you're not capable. You've done a good job of looking after the children and getting them placed."

"All except Heidi." How could she leave this child in the orphanage? For that matter, how could she leave her behind? Over the weeks of the trip west, she'd grown close to the child who had lost her parents in the fire that left her scarred. Despite her misfortunes, Heidi had a sweet spirit. But she had grown extremely shy, her tender heart wounded by the horror and shock many didn't bother to disguise when they saw her face.

"I wish I could take her back to New York with me. I might be able to persuade my father to give her a place in the household, even if it is just as a helper in the kitchen. At least she'd be with someone she knew rather than in an orphanage full of strangers." It wasn't what she wanted for Heidi. The child deserved to be part of a loving family. "But I'm sure Jakob is trying to find her." Rebecca had been opposed to separating the pair, but Mr. Arlington had dismissed her concerns. And Heidi had been so determined for her brother to find a family. She hadn't had the heart to tell the girl about the telegram that had reached her, informing her that Heidi's brother had run away from the family they'd placed him with so that he could rejoin her.

Booted steps sounded in front of the house. Even before he knocked and Holly opened the door, Rebecca knew Colton had arrived to take them to his ranch.

A frisson of doubt skittered up her spine. Why had she agreed to this arrangement? Her alarm swelled until she almost choked. How would his parents react when she arrived with Heidi and the baby?

"Good day, ladies." Colton favored them all with a smile that brought in sunshine and joy.

"Colton Hayes," Holly said. "You take good care of this baby and be nice to my friend."

"Yes, ma'am."

Rebecca didn't know how to interpret the look he gave her. Was it challenging? She bristled at the thought. "We're working together." She hoped everyone understood her meaning. She would not let Colton order her around, make her decisions or take away the chance for her to finish the task she meant to complete.

"Heidi is out playing with the others," she told him. Maybe he would take the hint and go call her.

"Yes, ma'am." He ducked out the door.

Charlotte kissed Gabriel then tucked him into the basket. "Goodbye, sweet baby." She hugged Rebecca.

Holly hugged her, too. "If you need any help, remember that I'm the teacher. I'm an expert on most anything."

The three women laughed as they headed out the door to where a buggy waited. As soon as Rebecca stepped outside, Heidi ran to her and grabbed her free hand.

Colton took the basket holding Gabriel and set it on the ground, then faced them.

Rebecca turned to Heidi. "Honey, we have to get into the buggy."

Heidi looked up, her eyes wide with fear and uncertainty.

Rebecca caught the child's chin. "I thought you wanted to go."

Heidi nodded, but the way her eyes darted toward Colton, Rebecca guessed she hadn't realized that they would have to ride in a buggy with him.

"Come along. I'll help you up." She eased the little girl toward the buggy and helped her onto the backseat. Heidi hunched down in the corner farthest from the driver.

Rebecca turned to find Colton at her side, offering his hand to assist her. To refuse would be rude and surely cause her friends to wonder why she wouldn't accept this gesture of goodwill. But his nearness made her insides flutter. Only because he was so big, she told herself and placed her hand in his. It was a work-hardened palm. He held her hand gently as he helped her up and tucked her skirts inside. He smiled. All normal. What any gentleman would do.

But her heart swelled, caught at her lungs and hung on for dear life, making it difficult for her to breathe.

She checked on the baby, using the time to will her heart-beat to return to normal, then sat up straight and waved to her friends and the children.

But despite her efforts, her heart continued to beat in a rapid tattoo and her breathing required far more attention than normal.

Colton lifted his hat to the ladies, then flicked the reins. "We'll go by the hotel so you can pick up your belongings."

"Of course. Thank you." She'd been so consumed with other things that she had not even thought about the logistics of moving to the ranch. Now she shifted her thoughts to what she needed to do. She'd lost most of her possessions in the fire at the school where she and the children in her charge had stayed as they waited for more permanent arrangements after the train robbery ended their journey. The ladies of the community had kindly provided her and Heidi with the ne-cessities and a few dresses. The skirt and shirtwaist she wore had been given to her. Charlotte, an expert seamstress, had tucked and adjusted each item until it fit perfectly. Her best dress was an emerald-green one Charlotte made. The woman was a wonder with a needle. She was making plans to open up a seamstress business.

They reached the hotel, a simple wood-framed, two-story

building. Nothing like the places she'd stayed in with her parents on their travels, but it had proven adequate.

Colton jumped down and hustled around to help her. Then he reached up for Heidi. But the child shrank back.

He studied her for a moment. "I won't hurt you."

But when she continued to withdraw, he dropped his hands. "Have it your way."

He lifted the sleeping bundle from the basket.

Heidi waited until he stepped aside before she climbed down.

Rebecca reached out to take the infant.

He shook his head. "I'll watch the baby while you get your things."

"I can manage."

He sighed heavily. "Are we going to have this argument every time I try to help?"

Some perverse little corner of her mind wanted to say yes. But she realized how childish that would be. "Of course not." She turned toward the hotel. Was that Miss Ward in the lobby? Her neck muscles twitched. Could she possibly avoid her?

At least when they were at the ranch, Miss Ward wouldn't be able to follow Rebecca around, terrifying Heidi and dispensing her litany of complaints and concerns.

She waved to Miss Ward as they crossed the lobby, pretending she'd interpreted the older woman's imperious gesture to wait simply as a greeting. "Come, Heidi, let's get our things."

Heidi clung to her hand as they rushed up the stairs to their room and collapsed on the bed.

Heidi bounced down beside her. "I'm glad we're leaving this old place."

"It's not very old."

"I don't like it." Heidi bounced again to emphasize her dislike.

That bounce unbalanced them both and they fell backward, laughing.

"It's not the hotel you don't like. It's all the people you have to see." As often as she could, Rebecca assured Heidi that everyone wouldn't stare rudely at her, but the girl remained unconvinced and, as a result, was always uncomfortable in crowded places.

For a moment, Heidi didn't respond. Then she said, "Mr. Colton's parents might not care for me to live in their house."

"Mr. Colton offered. We'll trust that he knows what his parents would think."

"He doesn't stare at me. Why don't you like him?"

Rebecca sat up and stared at the girl. "Who says I don't?"

"You quarrel with him."

"I suppose I do. How strange. I don't normally argue with anyone."

Heidi studied her as if waiting for more of an explanation.

"We're simply sorting out our—" *Balance of power?* The phrase sprang to her mind. She wondered what prompted that. "We're sorting out how to share responsibilities."

Heidi sat up, her face upturned toward Rebecca. "You don't hate him?"

"No." Though she found him annoying and overbearing. "There are things about him that I admire."

"Like what?"

His smile. His steady strength, which she'd had glimpses of. His defense of little Gabriel. "The few times I've seen him with his parents, he's always been so kind. I would guess he's loyal and trustworthy."

Heidi jumped to her feet and began to fold her clothing. One of the townswomen had given them a small trunk. It wouldn't take long to pack.

Rebecca rose and did the same, but Heidi's question continued to play through her mind. Would Colton's parents welcome them? Inviting three strangers into their household seemed like a lot to expect. She would have to prove to them that she could pull her weight…but what did she know about how to be helpful on a ranch?

"I'm done," Heidi said.

Rebecca checked the room for overlooked items. "I am, too." She closed the trunk and left it to be brought down, picked up her satchel with the paperwork for the children and left the room.

At the top of the stairs, she paused. Miss Ward and Colton were directly below. She stopped by the desk to settle her bill and request that her trunk be brought down and placed in the buggy, hoping Miss Ward would move along. But she stood her ground as if she'd grown roots through the soles of her shoes.

"I understand your concern about this abandoned infant," Miss Ward said to Colton, no sympathy in her brisk words. "But doesn't our town have enough of this sort already? Send him back to New York with Miss Sterling. I understand that she is to leave in a matter of days."

Rebecca couldn't recall ever saying how soon she'd be leaving, but Miss Ward was right. It would only be a matter of days. Father hadn't expected her to be gone quite so long. His last communication had suggested that she let someone else oversee the construction of the orphanage and return immediately. She'd replied that she couldn't leave until she'd finished her work, but it was only a matter of time before he would get more demanding, reminding her of her duties back home. Those duties paled in comparison with caring for Heidi and now Gabriel.

Colton appeared unmoved by the thinly veiled order. "This

baby won't be going to New York. He belongs here. He's part of my family."

"So you say. But nothing changes the facts. You're a single man. Your parents are not in good health. The child will need more care than you can provide. That leaves the baby homeless."

"So you've said, but as long as I live and breathe, this baby is not homeless. Nor will he be going to New York, a foster home or an orphanage."

Rebecca fought an urge to shoo the woman from the premises. *Be polite. Never show your ire.* Her mother's voice. Her mother's words. But how would Mother respond to this situation? Rebecca knew she would just pretend that it didn't exist.

Rebecca has no such intention. She tucked her chin in and prepared to join the pair.

Miss Ward adjusted her pristine white gloves. "I can't imagine what this town is becoming. Misbegotten children. Children bearing the mark of judgment." Her gaze slid toward Heidi.

Rebecca swept across the carpeted floor, her heart thudding hard. "Miss Ward."

Miss Ward jerked around to face her, lines of disapproval deepening the tangled wrinkles in her face.

Colton turned at the same time. Their gazes crashed together with such force that Rebecca jerked in a tiny gust of air.

Beatrice Ward stepped directly in Rebecca's path, making escape impossible. "This town is overrun with the likes of these." She swept her hand to indicate the baby and Heidi, who pressed into Rebecca's back. "It has to stop."

Rebecca did her mother's memory proud with the smile she pasted on her face. "Gabriel and Heidi will be out at the Hayes ranch for now, so I'd say things have already changed. As to God's judgment, might I remind you that we are warned against judging others for we will ourselves be judged? Good day, Miss Ward." She nodded politely and swept past the woman, Heidi clutching her skirts.

Colton followed. As soon as the door swung shut behind them, he let out a low whistle. "So that's how it's done in New York."

"I have no idea what you mean. I was nothing but polite." She spun around to confront him. "How dare she say such awful things?" She almost sniffed, but caught herself just in time. Heavens above, the action had a solid hold on her.

"I'm glad Gabriel is too young to understand." He shifted his gaze just enough to indicate that he understood Heidi wasn't.

Rebecca's anger fled as she turned and pulled the child around to face her.

Heidi hung her head, hiding her face in the curtain of her hair. Rebecca tucked the hair behind Heidi's ears and gently lifted her face toward her. "Honey, I wish I could say it doesn't matter what people say about you, but I know it does." She herself had felt the sting of disapproval in words or expressed in long sighs and sad looks. Her jaw muscles clenched. Not to mention the shame of being left by her fiancé like so much wasted produce. There was no way she could pretend it didn't hurt. Thankfully, her tears had finally subsided. "But someone saying something unkind doesn't make it true. You are a beautiful little girl with a sweet spirit."

Heidi clung to Rebecca's gaze, her eyes full of hope. Then sadness slumped her shoulders.

Colton put the baby back in the basket. "Come on. Let's go home." Colton caught Heidi around the waist and, before she could utter a protest, lifted her into the buggy.

Heidi, her eyes big and round, gasped, then she ducked to hide her face.

He released her, but rested his hands on the back of each

bench. "Heidi, Miss Rebecca is right. You're a beautiful little girl. Never let anyone tell you otherwise. Do you hear me?"

Slowly, Heidi lifted her head enough to steal a glance at Colton.

"Do you hear me?" he repeated gently.

She nodded and hope lit up her eyes.

Rebecca couldn't believe what she'd seen. She was so bemused by how Colton had reassured the child that she didn't hesitate when he held out a hand to help her into the buggy.

She was silent as they headed north through town.

She'd been right about one thing. Colton was kind. She expected she was right about more than that. He was likely as domineering as she thought, too.

Out of appreciation for his kindness to Heidi, she would do her best to overlook that trait. Or, at any rate, she'd *try*. Only time would tell if she'd succeed.

Chapter Five

Colton couldn't remember the last time he'd felt such a burning anger toward anyone. He knew it was wrong, but when Beatrice Ward self-righteously said such nasty things about Gabriel and Heidi, including Rebecca in her attack, he saw a flare in the back of his eyes.

Beatrice might rail against the orphanage and Rebecca, but Colton Hayes would not stand back and let her do so unchallenged. But though he'd been ready to leap to her defense, he couldn't help but be proud of the way Rebecca had defended herself and Heidi. Without raising her voice and with a steady smile on her face, she'd cut Beatrice Ward right down to size.

His anger waned as he escorted Rebecca and Heidi to the buggy and helped young Matt, who worked at the hotel, tie the trunk to the back.

And then they were on their way, north past the town square. They drew abreast of Miss Ward's damaged house and he stopped the horse.

"That's what's left of that woman's house."

They stared. The roof had been badly smashed.

"I know," Rebecca said. "Holly showed me."

"The businesses and homes near the creek took water

damage in the flood. But this house is beyond where the water came. Nope. This is wind damage. If disasters are a sign from God, I wonder what message He was trying to send her."

"Do you believe that?"

He couldn't tell from her guarded tone which opinion she held. So he gave his answer careful consideration. After a moment, he spoke. "I think we too often decide that a man's neglect or meanness is God's hand. I don't believe it is."

"Exactly. The delays at the orphanage are being caused by men. Not God. And I get mighty weary of Miss Ward suggesting otherwise." Her shoulders rose and fell in a way that made him wonder if she grew tired of her struggles. He wanted to assure her that he would take care of vandals and delays, Miss Ward and her interference.

But he didn't want to prompt a reaction from her, so he kept his thoughts to himself.

On second thought, it was kind of fun to see her get all huffy. But before he could speak, Heidi leaned forward to whisper in Rebecca's ear.

"She wants to know what a hooligan is," Rebecca said.

He guessed she was trying to keep the emotion from her voice, but she failed. She sounded ready to explode. He'd spare her the pain of explaining the word to Heidi.

"A hooligan is a person who does bad things to hurt others."

Heidi hung her head. "She doesn't like me."

"Do you hurt people?" he asked softly, turning toward the child.

"I try not to."

"Then you're not a hooligan."

She tipped her head, hiding her face behind the curtain of her hair. "It's 'cause I'm ugly."

He scooped the hair aside and studied her scars. "You are

not ugly. Ugly is something that happens on the inside. Not on the outside."

Slowly, Heidi lifted her face to him and glimmers of trust dawned in her eyes. "I don't want to be ugly on the inside." Her voice dropped to a whisper. "Like Miss Ward."

Rebecca faced the girl. "Heidi, we should not speak ill of others." But her voice bore no trace of scolding and she favored Colton with a smile full of gratitude.

Now, if she could be this pleasant all the time, life at the ranch would be as easy as pie.

He urged the horse onward. They traveled north for another mile, then turned east.

"I should tell you about my parents. Ma's heart isn't as good as it used to be. She doesn't get around much anymore. And Pa had an accident three years ago." He hated to even talk about it. He hero-worshipped his big father. Never saw him as old. Never expected to see him laid up and in pain. "He's pretty crippled."

Heidi leaned forward and whispered in Rebecca's ear. He heard enough to guess she'd asked about Pa.

"I'm right here. You can ask me." He lifted his arms and looked at them. "Unless I've become invisible." He grabbed Rebecca's hand in mock alarm. "I'm not, am I?"

Heidi giggled.

Rebecca's eyes rounded and her mouth formed a rosebud.

He jerked his hand away. "Sorry." He hadn't meant to touch her, but despite the embarrassment between them, he didn't regret it. He liked discovering the cool silk of her skin. "It's just I got so scared thinking I'd disappeared."

Heidi muffled another giggle. "You're still here."

"Oh, good. Then you can talk to me."

She met his gaze, her brown eyes measuring him.

He let her look, hoped she saw that he liked her and didn't think she was ugly.

"What happened to your pa?"

"You mean his accident?"

She nodded.

He snapped the reins and gave far more attention to the road than it required as he sorted his emotions from the facts. When he'd achieved a reasonable amount of success, he spoke. The emotions didn't leave entirely, tightening his throat so his words sounded strangled. Perhaps the others wouldn't notice.

"We were driving cattle and something spooked them." That something had been Colton calling out a greeting to the neighbors passing by, including the family's pretty daughter, who had caught his eye on more than one occasion. So he'd waved his hat and whooped loudly. At the same moment a deer bolted from the brush. Together, it was enough to send the herd of cows racing for the wide-open spaces. Pa had tried to turn them. Colton closed his eyes as he saw it all in slow motion, felt every agonizing heartbeat. Pa's horse had fallen, tossing the man into the midst of the thundering hooves. By the time Colton got to him, he was barely alive. And wishing he wasn't. "Pa got trampled in the stampede. He's never recovered."

Pa didn't complain, but ever since then he could hardly walk and had never again ridden a horse. The man who had lived to ride. And every day Colton faced the reminder of his own stupidity. He had been no green kid. He had been twenty-five at the time. Old enough to have a few smarts stored up.

He felt Heidi and Rebecca watching him and pushed aside his regrets.

"Maybe they would like someone to help them." Heidi sounded as if she might like to be the one to do so.

Colton could think of nothing better, but he was never certain how Ma would react, and with Pa...well, it kind of depended on how much pain he was in. But he didn't know how to explain those details to Heidi, or Rebecca. "We have a fairly big house."

He studied Rebecca. "Probably not what you'd think of as large, but there'll be room for us all."

She spent a few seconds studying the landscape, then looked at Colton. He saw the doubt in her eyes and wondered at the cause. But he didn't have long to wonder.

"Will I have a private bedroom?"

Some perverse part of his brain made him answer, "You and Heidi *could* share with Ma. Her bed is… Well, I'm sure you'll manage. She don't snore too loud. I can barely hear her two rooms away." It was all true.

Her eyes filled with horror.

"Pa can bunk with me if necessary. Though I might decide to sleep on the floor, rather than risk bumping him and causing him pain. But don't worry. I've slept on the ground lots of times when I'm out with the herd. Or even just for fun. I'll be fine. Just fine." Again, still true.

Rebecca stared at him. She swallowed loudly and looked away. Her fingers plucked at a fold in her skirt. Faster and faster. She swallowed again and pushed her shoulder back, then faced him, determination branded on each of her features.

"Mr. Hayes, I fear I have misunderstood you. I don't believe this arrangement will work."

He laughed. He hooted. He tried to control his merriment, but every time he started to speak, chuckles rolled up and could not be contained.

She considered him. At first she was surprised, then confused. Then she grew concerned, no doubt wondering about the state of his mind. As he continued to laugh, she grew annoyed. "I fail to see what's so funny."

He held up a hand, signaling her to wait. "I'm trying—" He swallowed back a laugh. "Let me explain."

"I think that would be a good idea."

He nodded, stilled his chuckles, but couldn't hold back a grin. "I was joshing."

"About what?"

"About you and Heidi sleeping with Ma and me sleeping with Pa. We have two unused bedrooms. Pa built big. He said there was no point in being mean about the size of one's house."

Rebecca's eyes narrowed.

"You and Heidi can each have a room if you want. Or you can share. You can have the baby in the room with you or I can keep him with me." He waited for her reaction. She didn't disappoint him.

"He'll share a room with Heidi and me."

"The offer is open if you change your mind."

"I won't." She faced straight ahead.

He chuckled softly and repeatedly.

"You think it's funny to play tricks on someone?"

"Hugely funny."

The way she considered him, he wondered what she had in mind. But perhaps she only meant to inform him that she didn't like his sense of humor. Or worse, maybe in her fancy life back East she was expected to be serious at all times. Now, wouldn't that be a contrast to the informality of Evans Grove?

What a shame if she didn't know how to laugh. But he'd soon teach her how.

Now, that was something to look forward to.

They turned down a laneway.

"We're almost there." He might have announced impending disaster the way Rebecca straightened and Heidi pressed into the back of her seat.

"Relax. They're my ma and pa. You both know how nice I am. They're every bit as nice."

Rebecca snorted. "What an interesting concept."

He simply grinned. Time enough to prove it.

Rebecca set aside her feelings about how Colton had tricked her. Not that she could even say what she felt— annoyance, disapproval…or pleasure at how he'd laughed, a big, noisy laugh that tickled her insides.

One thing was certain, however. She would find a way to get even, though she had no idea how. Her life up to this point had not included this kind of nonsense. But she would think of something.

Right now the uppermost thought in her head was that they'd reach the ranch house in a few minutes. And his parents.

She looked about her, amazed and surprised at how pretty the area appeared. The buildings were in a little hollow, surrounded by trees in their spring finery. A clean scent filled her mind with joy. She picked out smatterings of color in the verdant grass. Wildflowers. She'd like to see them up close and inhale their scent. Would she have an opportunity? The buildings consisted of a hip-roofed barn, several smaller buildings in a neat row and the house. She had no idea what to imagine, but the house looked inviting. Low and rambling. Painted white with red trim. Windows on either side of a brown door. More windows down the side. Were these the bedrooms Colton had mentioned?

"It looks real nice," Heidi said, her voice full of awe and a bit of longing.

Rebecca sighed. All this child wanted was a home. And her brother, though she bravely said she was glad Jakob had a home of his own. Rebecca would never let her know that she heard the child crying out Jakob's name at night. She'd reach out and touch Heidi's shoulders, and that always calmed the child. She wanted to do the same now— reassure Heidi that she'd be safe here. But as she stared straight ahead, her heart thumped rapidly.

In a moment she would begin an adventure.

She only hoped it would be an adventure and not a disaster.

I can do all things through Christ, she repeated over and over in her head.

But nothing eased the sense of dread and anticipation, and her chest began to hurt.

"Ma and Pa will be happy to see you." Colton's words were meant to encourage, but she detected a note in his voice that wasn't as convincing as his words.

She squared her shoulders. She'd always been a welcome visitor, an asset at any house party. But this wasn't a party and she was an uninvited guest.

He pulled the buggy to the front of the house.

Rebecca sucked in a deep breath, meant to stiffen her resolve, and almost choked. "What is that smell?"

He looked surprised. "What smell?"

She fought against a desire to wrinkle her nose. "*That* smell." It should be obvious to anyone with a nose.

He sniffed hard and looked around. "I smell cows and horses and pigs, but nothing out of the ordinary." His gaze jerked to her. "Do you object to the farm smells?"

Object! To such an offensive stench? Now, why would the idea cross his mind? But she wasn't so overcome with the odor that she couldn't see that she'd better tread carefully. She swallowed hard and kept her breathing as shallow as possible. "What's to object to?" If this was the worst she'd encounter in this strange environment, then she could handle it. But her insides quaked so hard she feared she would swoon as another thought occurred to her. What if it was only the beginning?

She tucked in her chin hard. She could do this. She was capable and strong...not just a rich, city girl.

But she fought a desire to cling to the strength of his hand as he helped her down. Instead, she pulled away. She would not reveal any weakness to this man. Or anyone.

She reached for the baby Colton held, but he shook his head. "I'll take him." His low words rang with insistence and something else. Desperation? She studied him as he faced the door. Was he afraid to face his own parents?

Heidi clung to Rebecca's hand. "He said they were nice," she whispered.

Her words jolted Colton from his staring. "They are nice. They're my parents, remember? Now, come along." He led them to the door, opened it and hesitated. "You won't be offended if I go first?"

She started to sigh, then stopped, not wanting him to think she'd sniffed. "I'll overlook it this one time."

He chuckled. "I'll bear that in mind." He stepped into the room.

Rebecca caught a glimpse of a table cluttered with dishes, chairs scattered around it, a stove with pots sitting on top and a cupboard equally untidy. She swallowed back a growing alarm that screamed to escape.

Heidi peeked around her. "It's a little messy," she whispered.

She'd never noticed before the child's knack for understatement. Likely because they'd never before faced a disaster area.

"Ma, Pa, I brought company." He stepped to a doorway leading from the kitchen.

Rebecca saw the tension in Colton's back, making the muscles across his shoulders bunch. That couldn't be a good sign.

"Company?" A woman's voice quivered. "How can I deal with company?"

Colton moved out of sight.

"Where did you get a baby?" asked a deeper voice. Colton's pa.

"A baby!" Mrs. Hayes sounded positively alarmed.

"I'll explain everything after you meet the company." Colton sounded guarded.

He returned to the doorway and waved them forward.

Clinging to the rigid lessons in proper deportment that had been drummed into her head all her life, Rebecca stepped forward, her head high, no fear on her face. Heidi clung to her like a burr.

A cot stood against one wall of the room with a woman perched on its side. Seemed she had been resting there until Colton made his surprise announcement. She was thin except for her protruding stomach, with gray hair that needed brushing and green eyes like Colton's. A table stood before the cot, covered with a huge assortment of dishes. From where she stood, Rebecca saw dried food scraps on many of them. Every space not covered with dishes held assorted papers and books, like a hodgepodge of life laid out for display.

She couldn't say what she'd expected, but not this. Not a house littered from wall to wall. Rebecca steeled her expression to reveal none of her distress.

"Ma, Pa, this is Rebecca Sterling and Heidi... Sorry, I don't know your last name." He directed the latter statement at Heidi.

"Strauss," she whispered.

"Heidi, Rebecca, my father, Louis Hayes."

Mr. Hayes sat in a wooden rocker next to the table. He was a big, handsome man with features Colton obviously inherited. Deep lines on his face hinted at the pain Colton had told them about. He tried to get to his feet and the lines deepened.

Colton sprang forward. "Pa, what are you doing?"

"I have to stand to shake hands."

Colton tucked the baby into his left arm and helped his father to his feet.

Mr. Hayes offered his hand to Rebecca. "I'm pleased to meet you."

She shook his hand gingerly, suspecting that every movement increased his pain, and withdrew as quickly as she could and still be polite.

Mr. Hayes turned to Heidi. "Pleased to meet you, too, little lady." He held out his hand.

Heidi brushed her palm to his without lifting her head and Colton helped the man back to his chair. He sat in a way that signaled pain.

Colton waited until he was settled, then indicated his mother. "Mrs. Estelle Hayes."

The woman didn't stand, didn't offer her hand, extended no welcome.

Rebecca smiled. "Pleased to meet you and thank you for your hospitality."

Mrs. Hayes's expression didn't soften. "You're the woman who brought the orphans to town." She shifted her gaze to Colton. "Think you'd better explain about the baby."

Rebecca clung to Heidi as hard as the child clung to her, wondering if Mrs. Hayes disapproved of her on principle or because she was an agent for the Orphan Salvation Society.

Colton told them about finding the baby at the orphanage. "Look at this quilt." He showed it to his parents.

"It's grandmother's design. How did this baby end up with one of her quilts? They aren't given outside the family." Mrs. Hayes sounded more concerned with the quilt than the baby.

But Colton seemed unaware of it. "Which leads me to think this baby is somehow related to us. So I decided to bring him home and look after him."

Mrs. Hayes shook her head. "I don't see how he can be related. I'm unaware of any female relatives in the family way. Besides, no Hayes would abandon her baby. No, I'm certain you're wrong."

Mrs. Hayes turned toward Rebecca. Her gaze burned a path up and down Rebecca's length, but Rebecca would not flinch. She would not allow the woman to intimidate her. She had been taught not to react to such slights. *Hold your head high and never reveal a hint of dismay.* She thanked her mother's voice for enabling her to stand straight and tall.

Colton followed the direction of his mother's stare. "Miss Sterling insisted that, as the supervisor of the orphanage project, she be in charge of the baby, since the basket was left on the orphanage's grounds. Rather than fight about it, we struck an agreement. We'll share responsibility. A hotel is no place for a tiny baby, so I brought them here."

His father nodded. "Rightly so."

"Who is going to look after him?" Mrs. Hayes pointed to her feet. She wore slippers—men's slippers—and Rebecca saw why. Her swollen ankles made any other kind of footwear impossible.

"I intend to care for him," Rebecca said. "I would have preferred to keep him in town so I could tend to my other responsibilities as well, but Colton insisted."

Mr. Hayes chuckled. "He can be quite persuasive. Maybe even argumentative."

"Pa, don't you be spreading gossip about me." The men smiled at each other.

"Babies are a lot of work." Mrs. Hayes's words seemed to warn them all that they would regret this decision.

Rebecca's spine stiffened at the suggestion. "I can handle it."

Again, the older woman studied Rebecca from head to toe. "No doubt you've had a fine education, but I don't suppose it's included learning to care for a baby." Before Rebecca could defend herself, the woman addressed Heidi. "Why are you hiding? Step out so I can see you."

Heidi obeyed with much fear and trembling.

Mrs. Hayes studied her openly. To her credit she did not flinch. "How old are you, child?"

"I'm ten."

"Is that a scar on your face?"

Heidi hung her head and squeezed Rebecca's hand so tightly Rebecca's fingers grew numb.

"Yes," Heidi mumbled.

"What happened?"

Rebecca answered for her. "She was burned in a fire that killed her parents."

"Come here, child," Mr. Hayes said.

Heidi shuddered.

Rebecca glanced at the door. For half a copper coin, she would take Heidi and walk back to town. She slid her gaze toward Colton. He smiled and nodded.

Rebecca took courage from his look and drew Heidi forward.

Mr. Hayes sat on eye level with the child. He flipped her hair away from her face, paying no attention to the way she flinched from his touch. He looked at the scars, revealing no disgust in his expression.

"Heidi, tell me one thing. Does it hurt?"

Heidi jerked her head up and faced him full-on. "No, sir. Not anymore."

Mr. Hayes nodded and smiled. "Then it's of no consequence, is it?"

Heidi studied him a full moment. Then a sigh the size of the great outdoors escaped her lungs. "No, sir." Her voice rang with more confidence than Rebecca had ever heard.

Heidi touched the older man's gnarled hand. "Does it hurt?"

"Only when I think about it, and I try not to."

"I wish it didn't hurt at all."

He rested his hand on Heidi's shoulder. "Me, too."

Tears stung Rebecca's eyes. She dare not look toward Colton, afraid her emotion would spill down her cheeks, but right then and there she vowed she would tolerate Mrs. Hayes for the sole purpose of allowing Heidi to enjoy a place where she found acceptance.

"I can't look after anyone," Mrs. Hayes said. "I certainly hope you can look after yourselves."

"Of course we can." Rebecca didn't feel nearly as certain of that as she sounded. Exactly what did looking after oneself in this environment include?

"She'll do better'n that," Colton added. "She's going to run the house while I take care of supervising building the orphanage."

Rebecca thanked her upbringing for enabling her to smile as if she had every confidence that she could handle the challenge.

But this was beyond anything she had imagined and inside she was screaming, *I don't even know where to start.*

Chapter Six

Colton noticed how Rebecca's gaze slid toward the door after Ma's comments. Ma could be blunt to the point of rudeness and honest to a hurtful degree. But he could have hugged his pa for his words. Of course, he made no move to do so. The old man didn't care for such signs of affection, and even if he did, Colton knew a hug would cause his pa a great deal of pain.

Pa's gentleness with Heidi had erased all regret from Rebecca's face.

And from his own heart.

He sprang into action. "I'll bring in your things and show you to your room." He handed Rebecca the baby and dashed outside to hurriedly untie the trunk, hoisting it to his shoulder.

He'd arranged for someone to ride his horse out to the farm and take the buggy back. The man rode up at that moment and offered to put the horse in the barn. Normally, Colton would have taken care of his mount, but this time he thanked the man and let him do it.

He trotted back with the luggage, admitting to himself that he feared leaving the pair alone with his parents until Ma decided to be charitable.

"I'll take them to the north room." It was the farthest from Ma and Pa's room. The baby would disturb his parents less at that distance.

Ma nodded.

"Come on, girls." He indicated that Rebecca and Heidi should follow him through the mostly unused parlor. The curtains were kept shut, which hid most of the dust. One doorway opened to a short hall. He and his parents had bedrooms there. A second doorway opened to a matching hall with two more bedrooms. He went to the larger of the two. "I hope you'll be comfortable here."

The room held a big brass bed, covered with a quilt his mother had made many years ago. There was a washstand, a highboy dresser and a wardrobe. There was even a tiny table with two chairs that guests could use as a reading and writing desk.

He'd always thought his mother had dolled it up nicely for company, even though they'd had little of that for years. But now he viewed it through Rebecca's eyes and saw its flaws. It wasn't overly large. The furniture suddenly seemed merely adequate, not special, as he'd once believed. "I'm afraid it's the best we have to offer."

"It's fine," Rebecca said.

"Lots better than the hotel room." Heidi slipped away to look out the window, making certain to tip her head so her hair hid her face. The view to the north allowed them to see the rolling fields, the sheltering trees and, if he wasn't mistaken, they should be able to see a patch of wildflowers— bright yellow black-eyed Susans and, early in the morning, blue wild flax. Like Rebecca's eyes.

In her arms little Gabriel started to fuss.

"Feeding time again?" he asked.

"How often does he need to eat?"

He didn't know. "I guess whenever he's hungry."

"If you'd show me the kitchen?"

"I'll get his things first." He dashed outside for the basket. As he returned, Ma spoke.

"Don't you get your heart set on that young lady or that baby. You'll just end up getting hurt." She shook her head. "She's a city girl."

She didn't need to say it so dismissively. "Ma, I'm only doing this because the baby's family. I feel an obligation to take care of him until his parents are found."

"You pause to consider that they might not want to be discovered?"

He nodded. "If that's the case, there must be a reason."

"Let the boy do it," Pa said. "Might be nice to have a little life around this place."

I'm alive. I do everything I can to make your lives happy. But Colton bit back the words. He understood what Pa meant because he shared the feeling. Having a baby, a little girl and a beautiful woman in the house would indeed infuse every activity with new joy and purpose.

Ma sighed heavily. "I'm not up to it. And I guarantee that young woman isn't used to any sort of real work."

"I'll do the work," Colton said. "You won't have to do anything."

"Didn't I understand you to say you meant to see to the building of the orphanage?" Ma's voice sharpened. "Hardly think you can be in two places at once."

He couldn't. Misery curled up his bones and tangled in his head.

Ma's forehead furrowed so deeply he worried it would cut off the blood supply to her brain. "You are far too gullible."

"So Miss Ward said."

That jerked Ma's furrow into a question mark. "Beatrice? Is she still up to her troublemaking ways?"

"Ma, Miss Ward has not grown mellow with the passing

of time, and she takes objection to all the orphans coming to the community."

Ma made a dismissive noise.

Gabriel wailed in the background.

Colton nodded toward the sound. "I gotta take this stuff to Rebecca." He dashed to the bedroom before Ma could raise any more objections.

As soon as he appeared, Heidi dug out a dry diaper and handed it to Rebecca, who gingerly changed the baby. As far as he could tell, she didn't do a bad job for someone who obviously had never done it before. He certainly couldn't do any better.

Colton thought of his ma's misgivings. But he dismissed them as unworthy. Even a city girl knew how to do the simple things required to run a house. After all, it wasn't as if he had high standards. The basics were good enough for him and his parents.

Rebecca wrapped the baby up again and touched his quivering chin. "Now let's get you a bottle." She turned toward Colton, her expression expectant.

"Right. The kitchen."

He led them back to the kitchen. "Help yourself to whatever you need."

She didn't quite manage to hide her distress as she glanced around.

He noticed the dirty dishes, the soup thickening in the pot. He stuck a lid on the pot.

One look at the floor would convince everyone that it hadn't been scrubbed in longer than he could remember. What must Rebecca think of the signs of neglect?

Anxious to cover up the inadequacies of his home, he stirred the embers in the stove, added wood and then set a kettle of water to boil.

He scrubbed the bottle and scalded it with hot water as

Rebecca instructed. Then he filled it with milk and warmed it before handing the bottle to Rebecca. She sat on a chair by the grimy kitchen table and fed the baby.

He watched Gabriel suck contentedly, but he could not ignore the dirty kitchen. "I'll clean up."

"I thought we'd agreed that I would look after the house."

He fought an internal battle. Ma's words filled him with doubt about Rebecca's abilities. But Rebecca's flax-blue eyes challenged him to trust her.

She ducked her head as if concentrating on the baby. "I know everyone thinks a city girl is useless in a farming community, but I could prove you wrong if you gave me a chance."

What choice did he have? "I don't think you're useless. If you're sure about all this—" He vaguely indicated the kitchen that he now realized would take more than a little tidying. A lot more. "Then I'll tend to my horse." And some of the other chores that he'd neglected of late. Seemed that between caring for his folks and the ranch, attending town meetings and a hundred other things, he never quite caught up. Only the essentials got done.

He ducked out the door before Ma or Pa could call him and loped across to the barn. His horse needed brushing. The stalls needed cleaning. The mangers needed to be filled.

Having Rebecca taking care of the household chores might prove to be a real advantage for him.

Heidi hung over Rebecca's shoulder, watching the baby. He finished his bottle and made little noises with his mouth, waving his fists as Rebecca talked to him. She held him as he snuggled contentedly, keeping her attention on the sleeping infant, rather than confronting the room. She'd offered to clean up out of determination to prove herself, not out of any confidence about how to do it.

How did one tackle such a mess?

I can do all things through Christ, who strengthens me.

She repeated the words over and over. Christ might give her strength, but despite her desperate need, He wasn't giving her instructions.

One thing seemed obvious. She couldn't accomplish anything if she sat cradling the baby. "Heidi, would you get Gabriel's basket, please?"

As Heidi ran to do her bidding, Rebecca glanced around the room. She could wash dishes—she knew how to do that. A smile tugged at her mouth. That task would occupy what was left of the morning, so she'd have all that time to figure out what to do next.

Heidi returned and they settled the baby in his basket, covering him with the quilt. It was beautiful. Rebecca wondered briefly if she could learn to sew something like that. She knew how to do fancy stitchwork. Had learned how on a sampler that hung in the nursery in her home back in New York, beside one her mother had made at an early age. But she yearned to create something practical.

In the room beyond, she heard the murmured voices of Colton's parents. His pa's voice rumbled in a way that convinced Rebecca he was trying to calm his wife. Mrs. Hayes's voice carried a sharp edge. Clearly, she did not welcome the intruders. Twice Rebecca overheard the word *useless* and knew they were talking about her.

She wasn't useless.

She straightened and confronted the room. "Looks like we have our job cut out for us."

Heidi jammed her little hands on her hips. "I'd say they should be glad we came along to help."

Rebecca shared the thought, but kept her opinion to herself. She poured the rest of the hot water into a big basin, refilled the kettle from the bucket on the shelf and started on the dishes. She scraped and scrubbed, and Heidi dried and arranged the dishes on a shelf she'd wiped clean.

The water was soon too dirty to continue, but the water bucket was empty. She looked about for a pump and saw nothing but more dirty dishes.

She lifted the lid on a pot on the back of the stove, but found only a thick, gelatinous substance. She choked back a gag and returned the lid. She'd deal with that later.

"Heidi, where do we get more water?"

"Must be a pump outside. Let's go see." She grabbed the bucket and headed for the door, but drew to a halt before she passed the sitting room where Colton's parents sat.

Rebecca grabbed her free hand and they fled outside.

Heidi pointed out the well and pumped the handle up and down until the pail was full of water. A dipper hung nearby and they both drank.

"Ohh, cold." Rebecca grinned. The water at the hotel had been tepid. This was a real treat.

She looked around. The odor she'd objected to lingered, but she forced herself to ignore it. She and Heidi laughed as a little calf frolicked in front of the barn.

Rebecca tipped her head and listened. "Do you hear that?"

Heidi listened, then pressed her fingers to her mouth to hide a giggle.

Rebecca signaled Heidi to follow her and they tiptoed toward the barn.

The calf bolted away to the far corner of the pen to watch them. When Heidi wiggled her fingers, he bounced over to butt at her hand.

Rebecca smiled. She'd never seen a baby calf before.

But it was the voice coming from the barn that held her attention.

"'Wait for the wagon, wait for the wagon.'" Colton belted out the song with gusto.

Oh, to feel so free. So uncaring about what others thought.

"Hey there, mama cat. How're your babies doing?"

She imagined him stooping over to pet a cat, and her throat tightened. Then the singing began again.

Without warning, he appeared in the doorway. Thankfully, he wasn't looking in their direction, but it was only a matter of time before he turned his head.

She grabbed Heidi's hand and dashed back to the pump. She caught up the pail, intending to race back to the house before he noticed them. Before he thought they'd been spying on him. But the bucket weighed more than she expected, and if she hurried, the water slopped over the edge, so she was forced to walk slowly and cautiously.

From behind her came a deep-throated chuckle, then he sang softly, "'Oh, where have you been, Billy Boy, Billy Boy?'" He paused. "Guess I should say, 'Oh, where have you been, Rebecca girl, Rebecca girl?'"

She ground to a halt and turned about to face him. She meant to scold him for mocking her, but his wide grin and the flash of green in his eyes dried up every protest. "Just getting more water," she managed to choke out.

"Yup."

She had a suspicion he knew they'd gone farther than the pump.

He leaned on the fence and continued to grin. "Are you taking the water to the house?"

Of course she was. She swung about, careful not to slop too much water, and hurried as fast as possible back to the house.

Certain he had watched them the whole way, she glanced over her shoulder when she reached the doorway.

He touched the brim of his hat in a goodbye gesture, then sauntered back to the barn, singing loudly and confidently. It would be nice to be so certain one's place in life, she thought.

Not long ago, she had been equally certain, following the route mapped out for her from birth. Oliver was part of that plan.

Pain stabbed her in the breastbone. Tears filled her heart, but she had learned to keep them there. Would she ever get over being so unceremoniously dismissed? In such a public, humiliating way? Without explanation? There had been unkind gossip. But none had more questions, more accusations than she flung at herself. Why wasn't she good enough? Why had he pretended he cared?

Why had she believed him?

She'd learned her lesson. She'd guard her heart with rock-solid fences and learn to be an asset in practical ways. She'd make herself invaluable. This was a very good place to start.

She and Heidi hurried back to the kitchen, heated more water and resumed washing dishes. The songs she'd heard Colton sing ran through her head. It was so much more cheerful than the parlor music she had grown up listening to.

She jerked her head up as Mrs. Hayes limped into the kitchen.

"Don't suppose it occurred to anyone to think of dinner."

Heidi ducked behind Rebecca, and Rebecca froze with her hands in the wash water. Dinner? She hadn't even given it a thought.

The woman shuffled to the stove, groaning with every step. Her swollen feet looked very uncomfortable. She lifted the lid on the pot. "Guess this will have to do." And she claimed one of the clean bowls, without a word of thanks for the fact that it had been washed, and filled it with the mixture. "'Twas a time I made decent meals around here before my heart started acting up and rendered me useless." She scowled at Rebecca. "My mother did her duty in teaching me to be a good housewife." She grabbed the back of a chair for support as she turned toward the sitting room.

Rebecca stared. She'd been about to empty the pot into the slop bucket, but apparently it was dinner.

At that moment, Colton strode into the kitchen. "Ma, let me do that." He tossed his hat at the wall, where it missed the hook and fell to the floor amid a collection of boots and harnesses. He eased the bowl from his mother's hands and guided her back to the other room.

Out of sight, his ma heaved a huge sigh. "If you're going to bring home a girl, least you could do is find one who knows her way around a kitchen."

Colton chuckled. "Ma, she's a fast learner."

"Well, I'm not up to teaching her, and seems to me you have plenty enough to do already."

Heidi nudged Rebecca. "It's okay, Miss Sterling. I'll help you."

Rebecca nodded. Humbling as it was to have to depend on a ten-year-old for instruction, she was grateful for the offer. She leaned over to whisper to Heidi, "What's in that pot?"

Heidi lifted the lid and sniffed. She took a spoon and tasted. "Think it's cream of vegetable soup. Here, have a taste." She held out a spoonful to Rebecca.

She had to pretend she didn't find the mixture off-putting and tasted it. Surprisingly, it was savory, with chunks of potatoes and carrots. "Not bad."

"Not bad!"

Neither of them had heard Colton return. Heidi dropped the lid back on the pot with a crash and hurried to Rebecca's side. Rebecca choked back annoyance and alarm. At the same time, she told herself it was his house and he could come and go as he pleased.

He crossed to the stove, grabbed another bowl and filled it. "I'll have you know I made that soup and I'm not a half-bad cook."

Rebecca couldn't contain her sense of mischief. "We've seen the bad half. Where's the good half?"

From the other room came a snort that she knew was Mr. Hayes trying to stifle his amusement.

Colton leaned close and lowered his voice so it wouldn't be heard in the other room. "You'll soon discover it isn't as easy as you might think." He took the bowl to his father.

"Son, we have company. Shouldn't you offer them dinner, as well?"

Rebecca wondered if they had to go all day without eating, then recalled that the noon meal was called dinner. The evening meal was supper.

Colton returned to the kitchen. "Pa says to join them for dinner. Go ahead. I'll bring the soup." He grabbed three more bowls and began to fill them.

"I'll help." She'd have preferred to sit in the kitchen with only Heidi to share the meal, but there was no gracious way to turn down the invitation.

Colton looked about ready to refuse, then handed her a bowl full of soup and led the way back to the other room.

When she saw the look on Mrs. Hayes's face, Rebecca almost turned back. The invitation issued by Mr. Hayes plainly was not echoed by his wife.

Colton pushed aside a stack of papers and put down bowls for himself and Heidi. He tipped two chairs to dump their contents on the floor, then shoved them toward the table. "Haven't had time to clean lately, but we get by."

Colton looked around the room. It showed signs of being overused and undercared for. He never seemed to have time to do everything. And Ma didn't like him disturbing her things.

Ma's knitting was piled in a basket by the cot. She hadn't

touched it in quite a while. She had a stack of books she kept nearby. Bookmarks stuck out that never seemed to move.

When had a bit and reins made their way to the room?

Pa said grace and they ate the soup. No one made a comment until they finished.

"He does the best he can," Ma said.

He had long ago chosen not to take offense at the way she voiced her praise—more criticism than approval—but he wished she were a little more positive in front of Rebecca. He knew how poor his meal was, but cooking took time.

"We'd starve without him," Pa said.

Ma scowled. "It isn't like I don't know how to cook."

Pa waved his hand in a calming way. "I know that, Estelle. But you aren't well. You need to rest."

"I wish I didn't."

"Wishing is for children," he said.

Ma gave Rebecca a frown-laced look. "Do you know how to cook?"

"I'll learn." She sat with her hands folded on her lap, her expression revealing nothing. But Colton felt the power of her determination. By the set of her shoulders, he suspected she hid anger.

This arrangement seemed destined to fail. Ma was opposed to the idea. Rebecca was clearly uncertain about what to do. Heidi looked ready to run for the hills.

The walls closed in on him and he jerked to his feet. His first thought was to escape to the barn, go for a long, hard ride, dig a well, climb the hill behind the house, plow a field...anything but stay in the house with the air crackling with tension.

A cry shattered the tension, reminding him why he had to make this work. "I'll get him."

"I'll feed him." Rebecca grabbed her bowl and headed for the kitchen with Heidi on her heels.

Ma cleared her throat. "Can't she manage on her own?"

"She certainly can." Colton would not follow them, lest his ma think it proved she couldn't. He gathered up rest of the dirty dishes. He'd take them to the kitchen later.

Then he grabbed the stacks of papers, planning to burn them. The bit and reins he tossed toward the door. He'd take them to the barn next time he went out.

Ma fluttered her hand. "Stop fussing. It makes me tired." She settled back against the pillows with a heavy sigh.

Colton hurried over to help put her feet up. "Look how swollen your legs are," he murmured. "You've had them down far too long."

"Leave me be. I'm too tired to listen." She labored over her breathing.

He pulled a gray knitted blanket over her, one she'd made before her health began to fail.

He heard Rebecca murmuring to the baby in the other room and longed to join them and watch the baby eat.

But Ma and Pa were his life. His responsibility. There was room for nothing more. And if he ever considered otherwise, Ma would soon enough set him straight.

As if reading his mind, she touched his hand. "We won't live forever. Then you'll be free to do as you please. But promise me one thing." She waited for his promise.

"Ma, you're not dying. Neither of you." Though they were more elderly than many parents with sons and daughters his age. Colton had been born late in their lives, a special gift from God, they used to say. How long was it since they'd said that? Did they still feel that way? He shook his head. Of course they loved him. And he loved them. They needed him. It was as simple as that.

"Promise me." Ma's words brought him back to the current situation.

"If it's possible. You know that."

"Promise me you won't marry unwisely." She shot a glance toward the kitchen. "You need a good farm girl as a wife."

"Marriage is the last thing on my mind." He could honestly say that. Marriage had no place in his plans. Not that he hadn't thought of it, but Ma and Pa were a full load. Not one a new bride should have to take on. And even if he found someone who said she would, he wouldn't ask it of her. No, marriage while his parents needed him was out of the question. After all, he owed it to them.

In the kitchen, Rebecca and Heidi laughed. Had the baby done something cute? He wanted to see for himself.

"I'll take the dishes to the kitchen."

"Let that woman wash them," Ma said. "That was your agreement."

He didn't reply. What was the point? Rebecca glanced up as he stepped into the kitchen. Heidi ducked behind her.

"Is he doing okay?" He tipped his head toward the baby.

She considered him briefly before she answered, "He looks fine to me, but I have had no experience with babies."

He guessed from the guarded tone of her voice that she had overhead Ma. Not that Ma made any attempt to hide the fact that she didn't think a city girl belonged here. Nor had he deceived himself into thinking otherwise. Rebecca was only here in his home because he'd given her little choice. Still, he tried to think how to erase the power of Ma's words. What could he say to apologize for them that didn't make it sound as if he actually put some stock in those harsh words? Nothing came to mind.

So instead he dumped out the dirty dishwater and stacked the dishes in the pan.

"What are you doing?" Her soft voice carried a trace of warning.

"Washing dishes?" Somehow he knew that was the wrong answer.

"I believe our agreement was for me to take care of the house in order for you to take care of the orphanage."

"But I can't do anything until the supplies arrive."

"An agreement is an agreement."

"Rebecca, she didn't mean—"

"I am perfectly capable." The brittleness in her eyes stopped any attempt at an explanation.

"Fine. I have fences to fix. I'll be back for supper. There are pork chops in the icebox." He fled the room, taking the reins and bit with him. If she wanted everything to be cut-and-dried, marked with indelible ink, that was the way it would be.

Chapter Seven

The next morning, Rebecca tiptoed into the kitchen, carrying Gabriel in his basket. No one else appeared to be up yet. Good. That gave her a chance to make breakfast.

Gabriel had kept her awake most of the night. She'd fed him. She'd bounced him. Rocked him. Walked him. Patted his tummy. Nothing worked. She obviously failed at caring for a baby. He slept now, but for how long she couldn't guess. While he slept, she meant to fulfill her part of this awkward agreement.

Thankfully, Heidi had slept through the crying and still slept peacefully.

She'd managed a fair supper last night, with Heidi's help. Now she faced the kitchen on her own. Mrs. Hayes's continued disapproval touched a tender nerve. She'd failed at home and now she failed here. But only if she accepted defeat.

And she wasn't about to do that.

She'd had plenty of time during the night to consider what she'd make for breakfast.

The stove was cold. As she'd seen Colton do, she lifted the lid to stir the ashes, but they were stone-cold. Never mind. She'd watched Holly start a fire. She could do it. A few minutes later, she struck a match and set it to the paper and wood she'd placed inside. The flames flared. The wood began to burn. Good. She put the lid on and turned to the ice-box, where she'd seen eggs. Five people. Five eggs. She put them in a pot, covered them with water and set it on the stove.

A twist of smoke came from around the lid. Must be something wrong with the wood. The smoke grew thicker. Coughing and waving a towel, she opened a window, then turned her attention to the loaf of bread. Toast fingers with a bit of honey would complete the meal.

The smoke got even thicker, stinging her eyes. What was wrong? She lifted the lid to check and flames erupted. She flicked the tea towel at them, but that only fanned them higher. She ducked back, shielding her face from the heat.

Flames licked up the towel toward her hand. Stifling a scream, she dropped the towel and jerked her skirts away before they caught on fire. The flames roared, licked toward her. A terrifying beast. She edged away as the beast taunted her.

A chair jabbed her back, stopping her escape. She sucked in air. Was she going to burn the house down around them? Was this how Heidi felt as she escaped a burning building? *Dear God, help me.*

Think. Think. Put the fire out. Water. She needed water and grabbed the bucket. The biggest fire was in the stove and she swung the bucket back to toss the contents on the flames.

But something held the bucket. She jerked. It jerked back. She spun away from the mesmerizing, terrifying flames and came face-to-face with Colton. She released the bucket.

"Are you trying to burn the place down?" He stomped out the flames of the burning towel. "You never throw water on a hot stove. You'd likely crack something." He adjusted something on the top of the stove, then grabbed a rag and stuck the lid in place. The flaming monster disappeared. "You had the damper closed."

He faced her, anger darkening his eyes to the color of deep, still water. "What were you thinking?"

Her mouth too dry to even swallow, her tongue wooden and stiff, she couldn't answer.

He grabbed her shoulders and gave a little shake. "You could have burned us to death in our sleep."

She nodded. Her eyes felt too wide, her cheeks stiff. "I—" The word was a pitiful croak that threatened to turn into a wail. She would not cry. She would not. But a shudder snaked up her spine and rattled loose her self-control. She blinked hard, but the tears won, streaming down her face.

Colton groaned and pulled her to his chest. "Don't cry. I'm not angry. Just scared." He patted her back.

A thousand emotions rose up and threatened her. Jilted. Rejected. Never quite meeting expectations. A complete idiot on a farm. She fought for control, but a sob tore up her throat. She was powerless to contain it. She dare not let her emotions rule. She feared their power if she ever released them. But another sob shook her.

"It's not that bad," Colton soothed. "No real harm was done."

His words and touch eased the power of her emotions. She clung to his shirtfront, her fingers buried in the fabric. When had she ever felt so sheltered, protected?

Suddenly his arms loosened and he dropped them to his sides. "Hi, Ma."

"What is going on?"

After one glance at the woman's harsh expression, Rebecca kept her attention on the remnants of the burned towel on the floor. Would the dark spot wash off or would it remain forever as a mocking reminder of her incompetence?

"Ma, it's nothing. A tea towel caught fire is all."

Mrs. Hayes shuffled around, saw the evidence. "That girl

is going to be the death of us." She glanced at the stove. "Your pa will be up wanting his coffee."

"I'll make it immediately." Colton sprang into action as his mother limped to the sitting room.

Rebecca went to get the broom and dustpan. That was when she saw Heidi hovering by the door, her eyes as wide as twin moons. "Heidi?"

The child blinked, but her gaze never faltered as she stared at the stove.

Had she seen the flames? If so, Rebecca couldn't begin to imagine how terrified she must be. She moved closer and reached for the child, but Heidi wheeled around and raced away through the sitting room.

"She's been spooked by the fire." Mrs. Hayes's tone clearly accused Rebecca of deliberately frightening Heidi.

Rebecca ignored the woman and dashed after Heidi. The girl lay facedown on the bed. Rebecca expected crying, but Heidi lay stiff and motionless.

Rebecca sat beside her, touched her shoulder. "Heidi?"

Heidi shrank away.

"Honey, I was careless with the fire." Her inexperience had almost exacted a terrible price. "But Colton quickly put it to rights." She waited for a reaction from Heidi, but she saw no indication that the child even heard. "I'm sorry it reminded you of something so frightening." Still nothing. Rebecca offered up a silent prayer for help. "I can't imagine how scared you must have been. I was so scared I couldn't think." Even too scared to act. Her hands still shook. Her insides felt like a flock of nervous moths.

Heidi shifted, keeping her back to Rebecca. Slowly she pushed herself up to a sitting position. "I'm okay." She stood, brushed her skirts smooth and headed for the door.

Rebecca watched her. She wasn't okay. And Rebecca was

to blame. Even her good intentions failed to live up to what she wanted to achieve.

She followed Heidi.

Mr. Hayes was in the sitting room. He watched Heidi then turned to Rebecca. "Are you okay? Is she?"

"We're fine." But she wondered if she would ever be fine.

Mrs. Hayes barely waited for her to step out of sight before she spoke. "I don't know how Colton expects us to deal with her incompetence."

Rebecca gritted her teeth. She'd escaped Miss Ward by agreeing to come to the ranch. Seemed she'd jumped from the frying pan into the fire. A hot, scalding fire. One that Colton couldn't put out.

Heidi sat cross-legged on the floor by Gabriel's basket.

Colton stood at the stove and fried some kind of meat. The eggs had been pushed aside. He studied her for a heartbeat. Two. Until she could feel her pulse thrumming in her cheekbones. "She doesn't mean to be unkind."

He meant his mother. Rebecca wondered if that was true, but wasn't about to argue.

"It's hard for her not to be able to do all the things she used to. It makes her feel inadequate."

That was a sentiment Rebecca could identify with and vowed to show the woman more understanding. "Has she seen a doctor?"

"Dr. Simpson says he knows of nothing more to do for her."

"I wonder—" But she went no further. No point in stirring up false hope, but she would write her father, describing the woman's symptoms, and ask if his physician could help.

"You can watch the meat while I fry leftover potatoes."

He handed her a fork and she stared at the pan, wondering why she needed a fork to watch it.

He leaned close to whisper in her ear, "Turn it to keep it from burning."

Startled by his breath against her ear, she gripped the fork and couldn't move.

He gently pried the utensil from her clenched fingers.

His fingers against hers sent her nerves into full alert. She summoned every bit of self-control to keep from jerking back.

He flipped over a couple of strips of meat. "Got it?" He held the fork toward her.

She took it. "I think I can handle the job."

"I'm quite sure you can. If only to prove something. Though I'm not sure what it is you feel you have to prove or who you intend to prove it to."

She gave him what she hoped would be construed as an innocent smile and said nothing. It wasn't any of his concern. He had no idea what her upbringing had been like. Not until recently had she questioned it herself.

A few minutes later they sat at the table and shared breakfast with the others. Heidi sat silent throughout the meal.

As soon as they finished, Colton bolted to his feet. "I haven't done the morning chores." He rushed from the room.

Her heart heavy in her chest, she watched him go. She felt alone with him gone. Nonsense, she told herself. She tucked her chin, gathered up the dirty dishes and escaped to the kitchen. Gabriel started to fuss and she prepared a bottle.

"Heidi, would you pick him up, please?" Maybe the baby could comfort Heidi when nothing else seemed to.

In a few minutes Heidi started talking to the baby, saying how cute and sweet he was. Then her talk shifted. "Did you smell the smoke?"

Gabriel snuffled.

"You're okay," Heidi said, her voice growing stronger. "You're safe. We'll take care of you."

"Do you want to feed him?"

The little girl took the bottle and sat cuddling the baby as he ate.

The baby settled back to sleep as soon as he was finished, and with Heidi's help Rebecca washed dishes, cleaned cupboards, swept and scrubbed the wooden floor. She scrubbed the blackened spot until her knuckles hurt, but the stain wouldn't go away.

She sat back on her heels and studied the dark reminder of her failure. She stared at her hands. Wouldn't her mother be alarmed to see their condition?

With a deep sigh, she came to a firm conclusion.

She did not fit in here. It had been foolish to think she could. Her pride had almost resulted in a disaster. She watched Heidi sitting by the baby basket. Her actions had pulled the scab off Heidi's inner wound.

"Heidi, honey, will you watch the baby while I tend to something in the bedroom?"

She hurried past Mrs. Hayes snoring on the cot and Mr. Hayes with his head back in his rocking chair.

She packed enough things for an overnight stay. She would send for the rest later. For now, she wanted to avoid an argument with Colton.

A few minutes later he drove to the house in the buggy.

She went outside to speak to him. "I'd like to go to town with you today."

His gaze slid past her to the house.

"I know you thought I would remain here and take care of the house and your parents." Though his mother didn't exactly welcome her help. "But there's something I need to take care of."

He leaned back.

She realized that he was waiting for her to explain. "It's

personal." She knew her cheeks were flaring pink at how he might take it.

He coughed. "Of course. How long will it take to get ready?"

"Not long." She returned to the house and announced that she would accompany Colton to town for the day.

Again she murmured something about personal business and even Mrs. Hayes looked uncomfortable and didn't press the matter except to say, "I can't look after the children."

"I plan to take them with me."

The baby slept peacefully. Why couldn't he be that content in the night?

"Colton makes dinner before he leaves us," Mrs. Hayes said. Her message was clear. Rebecca should do it.

"I can make something if you tell me what you want." And how to do it.

"I'll help." Heidi sprang to her side.

She wanted to hug the child, who understood how much assistance Rebecca needed and offered it without judgment.

"Cheese sandwiches will be fine."

Rebecca and Heidi made the sandwiches, making enough for those going to town to have for dinner, as well. "Shall I trim the crusts?"

Mrs. Hayes snorted. "I'm still capable of chewing, thanks all the same."

"We can manage everything else," Mr. Hayes said, his tone soothing.

More and more, Rebecca appreciated the older man's gentleness. Colton was a lot like him. He'd grow even more gentle and kind as he aged.

What did she care what he would be like when he got old? She wouldn't ever see it. She had come west to do a job. Living at the ranch was meant to achieve that purpose, but it simply wasn't working.

She took the baby and her packed bag outside and they were soon on their way to town.

"Did you sleep okay?" Colton asked. "The bed wasn't too hard?"

"It was fine, thank you." She would not complain and give him any more reason to think she was spoiled.

"The baby cried a lot," Heidi said.

Rebecca felt Colton's gaze on her, but she looked straight ahead as if something on the trail demanded her complete attention.

Finally, he spoke. "That would explain the shadows under your eyes."

"I could pretend to be offended, but frankly, I haven't the energy."

"You should have said something. You could have stayed home and rested."

"Don't be offended, but I feel like I need to remind everyone constantly that I can do what I came to do."

"Hmm. Interesting. Why should you need to?"

Why indeed? "Because no one expects me to be able to do anything useful."

They rode on in silence for several minutes until Colton spoke.

"But you want to help and you're willing to learn."

She tried to decide if she should see his words as a compliment or a reinforcement of his perception of her as a rich, city girl. She sighed. "I'm too tired to argue."

He chuckled. "Good, because I didn't intend to start an argument."

They would soon be in town. They'd pass Miss Ward's house. Was it only yesterday that the older woman had rained down her vitriol? It seemed like a lifetime ago.

In fact, Rebecca's previous life of privilege and advantage seemed like the distant past. Something she'd dreamed of. And now? Challenge, change, criticism and Miss Ward.

She'd proven she didn't belong on the ranch. Or even in the community.

But where did she belong?

Chapter Eight

Colton felt the tension from Heidi and Rebecca like a burr under his skin. He scoured his brain to think of a way to ease the situation. But his normally active mind could find no solution and the miles slipped away. They would soon reach town.

"I'm sorry," he murmured. Inadequate words, but they came from his heart.

Rebecca started, as if he'd interrupted her thoughts. "For what?"

Everything. His situation. His parents. "I should have shown you how to start a fire. Explained how the stove worked."

She shrugged. "I should have known." Her expression remained guarded, distant.

"A person isn't born knowing. I remember when Ma first got sick and I had to make meals. I didn't even know how to boil eggs." He grinned at her. "At least you knew that."

Another shrug.

He shifted his attention to Heidi, who was watching the passing scenery. He wondered if she actually saw it. "Heidi, I'm sorry I didn't show Rebecca how to make a fire in the stove. It's my fault it got out of control."

She pressed back against the seat and kept her gaze riveted on the fence line.

Colton sighed. He was failing miserably at changing the atmosphere.

A neighbor rode by on horseback. "How are your parents?"

"They're well enough. Thank you."

"Miss Rebecca." The man tipped his hat and rode on.

By then town was in sight. "Where do you want me to take you?"

"To Holly's, please."

The schoolyard was across from the town square, with the schoolteacher's house on one end of the lot. He stopped there and jumped down to assist her. Heidi skittered away before he could help her.

He headed for the door, with Gabriel asleep in the basket. Hard to believe the baby hadn't slept well during the night.

Rebecca touched his arm. "Wait. We need to talk."

Now? He'd tried to pry a word or two from her all the way to town. But now was better than never. "Sure."

"I'm not going back to the ranch."

His smile slid off his face and landed upside down in his heart. "Ma's unwelcoming, but she'll mellow."

"It's not your ma. It's me. In my ignorance I could have burned down the house. I don't belong on a ranch."

He had no answer for that. He could hardly blame her for thinking she deserved something nicer than he had to offer. She was a city girl, used to fine things. His ranch was little more than a glorified farm. As she'd observed the first moment, it smelled like a farm. And his folks were…well, difficult. "What about Gabriel?"

"I think it's best if I keep him. If you don't want to help at the orphanage, I understand. I'll manage."

He stumbled through his thoughts, trying to sort out

what he wanted. What he wanted was so far out of reach he couldn't even admit it to himself.

"No, I never start a job without finishing it. I'll see if the lumber has arrived in town and get it delivered to the site."

"Thank you. I'll arrange for someone to fetch the rest of my things."

"Never mind. I'll bring them." All the right words came from his mouth. But inside, he protested. He realized he had allowed himself a little dream. It couldn't be permanent. He knew that. But for a few days he thought he could enjoy having a beautiful woman and children in the house.

"Again, thank you," she said. "And I'm sorry that—"

He waited, but she didn't explain. "For what?"

She stared past him. "For everything and nothing and I don't know."

If his insides weren't so painful, he would have laughed. "You have nothing to be sorry for."

He drove away and went directly to the store. Mr. Gavin said the supplies had been off-loaded at the station, so he rented a wagon and brought the piles of lumber to the orphanage site.

Once that was done, he set out to inspect the building.

He stepped inside, where a staircase would lead to the upper floor. He ground to a halt and stared, his mind unable to make sense of what he saw. A dead rat hung through the opening, dangling at eye level. He had seen many a dead animal, but this was a deliberate warning. A threat. He pulled out his pocketknife, cut the rope and took the animal out to bury it in the yard.

But even digging a hole did not ease his anger. It rose in his throat, backed up along his veins until he saw and felt raw and red with every heartbeat. What if Rebecca had been the one to discover the animal? Who would do such a vile thing? How far would they go?

He circled the building, checking for clues, but found nothing. He swung up to the second floor. Apart from some smudged footprints, there were no clues as to who was responsible.

He returned to the ground floor and explored the surrounding area. Finally, he went back to the mercantile. Mr. Gavin looked eager to serve him.

"Got the supplies, did ya?"

"All unloaded at the orphanage site." He studied the display of candy. Maybe Heidi would like something. "You seen any suspicious activity around there?"

Mr. Gavin shook his head. "Still looking for the woman who lost a baby?"

"Have you seen her?" He'd almost forgotten about Gabriel's mother in his worry over whoever had vandalized the orphanage.

"Nope. Haven't seen a soul who didn't belong here."

Colton chose a selection of penny candy to take to Heidi. Except she wasn't going to be living at the ranch anymore.

He left the store and continued his journey around town, asking about strangers or strange behavior. Keeping his eyes open for clues.

But he saw nothing suspicious.

By the time he'd been through the town, one thing was certain: Miss Ward wouldn't have touched a rat, so she wasn't responsible.

Whoever was at the root of this was evil. Who could say what such a person would do next? Perhaps directly attack anyone involved with the orphanage. Which made a second thing certain. Rebecca couldn't stay in town. It wasn't safe. He would not admit he welcomed the excuse to ask her back.

But how could he convince her? If he told her the real

reason—the rat—she'd be frightened. And the more compelling reason—that he wanted her to return—would frighten her even more.

Rebecca sat across the table from Holly. Before each of them were pretty china teacups. Outside, Liam and Heidi played. When Heidi's laugh carried through the open window, Rebecca sighed in relief. "I was afraid I had done her irreparable damage."

Holly tipped her head to consider Rebecca. "That sounds like a story."

"A tale of woe, you could say." She told her friend about starting the fire.

By the time she finished, Holly was laughing merrily. "You should write a book."

"I fail to see any humor in the situation."

"The Misadventures of the Rich and Famous." Holly's grin persisted despite Rebecca's lack of response.

"I'm neither rich nor famous. In fact, I could well be the death of certain people."

Holly sobered instantly. "You're plotting murder?"

"Of course not." She explained Mrs. Hayes's comment and her lack of welcome. "I'm not going back to the farm. There's no room for a city girl there."

"And Mr. Hayes shared his wife's opinion?"

"Oh, not at all." She told Holly what he'd said about Heidi's scars.

"It sounds like a good place for Heidi."

"Maybe it was until I undid all that good by reminding her of the fire that took her parents."

Holly sipped some tea before she answered, "I doubt you are responsible for Heidi's memories." She ran her finger along the rim of her pretty china cup. "I remember how you stood so strong after Mr. Arlington was shot and killed. Then how you kept everyone in control after the school fire. Nothing put you off-kilter. How often did you say, 'I can do all things through Christ, who gives me strength?'" She fixed a demanding look at Rebecca. "Why are you letting this situation defeat you?"

"I—I—" She stammered. "I'm not defeated. Just inadequate."

Holly laughed. When she saw that Rebecca didn't join her, she sobered. "You're serious, aren't you?"

Rebecca nodded.

"My friend, you aren't inadequate. You're inexperienced. At least at farm living. Only one way to fix that."

"Get back to New York as soon as possible."

"Is that what you want?"

Rebecca took her time answering. "That's always been the plan."

"Yours or someone else's?"

She tried to think. Had she ever had a choice in the plans laid out for her? "I don't know."

Holly's look was both challenging and sympathetic. "Don't you think it's something you *should* know? Are you pursuing the life you want or one that's expected of you? They might be the same, but if they're not, then I warn you, you won't be happy unless you listen to your heart."

"But I don't even know what that means."

"Then perhaps you need to take the time to learn. Care for more tea?"

Rebecca shook her head. Last time she'd listened to her heart, it had been broken by Oliver. Hadn't it? But had she truly been following her heart? Her father had approved of Oliver. Said he'd be a fine son-in-law. Did he still think that? Did he blame her for Oliver's decision not to marry her? It was so complicated.

She went to the window to check on Heidi, who was playing on the swings with Liam. Liam appeared to do all the talking. "Why isn't Liam with Mason today?"

"Mason gave him some chores to do. He said he'd return later and Liam could go with him if he had his chores done."

"I hope we aren't keeping you from work."

"Not at all."

At that moment, Gabriel awakened for his feeding.

A little later, Mason returned and took Liam with him.

Heidi wandered into the house and flopped onto the sofa. "When is Colton coming back?"

"He's not."

Heidi sat upright. "Why not?"

Rebecca wished Holly would explain, but her friend gave her an it's-your-responsibility look. Very well. "Honey, I've decided not to go back there."

Heidi's face blanched, making her red scars stand out in sharp contrast. "It's because of me, isn't it? His ma and pa said we couldn't stay there." She bolted to her feet.

Rebecca caught the girl before she could race out the door. "No, honey. No one asked us to leave. I thought it was best. I'm not very good at farm living."

"What difference does living on a farm make?"

How did she explain her ineptitude?

Heidi rushed on. "I like it there. Mr. Hayes is nice. 'Sides, there's no one else around."

Rebecca struggled for a reply. She'd thought Heidi would welcome the news that they wouldn't be returning to the place where Rebecca had scared her so badly. She felt Holly's study of her. Was she right? Was it inexperience alone that made her not fit in?

Holly edged closer. "I have a book that will help you learn everything you need to know about running a farmhouse."

"I doubt there's a book big enough to accomplish that."

Heidi grabbed her hand. "Please, Miss Sterling. Pleeeease.

I'll be oh, so good. And I'll help you. I'll even stay up and look after Gabriel at night."

She couldn't ignore the child's pleas, but could she face the challenges of farm life again? "Let me think about it."

"Okay, but I know you'll change your mind." Heidi confidently returned outside.

Rebecca wished she could be as certain of what to do.

Holly grabbed a book off the shelf and handed it to Rebecca. *Practical Information for the Farm Wife.*

Rebecca turned several pages. Receipts. Advice on everything from laundry to pickling. Even something on how to tell which mushrooms were safe to eat. "I'm only a visitor, not a wife."

"I'd say you are a temporary housewife." Holly's eyes sparkled. "Unless you decide you like it enough to make it permanent."

Rebecca's laughter contained regret. But that didn't make any sense. She'd only agreed to go to the ranch until the orphanage was built and the orphans were safely housed. After that? Well, she'd like to see both Heidi and Gabriel in real homes with loving families before she left. But was that possible? Would she have to accept defeat in this area and leave them in the orphanage? Why did it hurt so much to think the answer was yes?

Her father would be expecting her to return home and resume her duties as a New York socialite—social events, charitable work, hostess of her father's house. It was what she'd been raised to do.

Holly's words echoed in her thoughts. What did *she* want?

"What does your heart say?" Holly asked.

"My heart says I don't fit in with the Hayeses. I'm going to be a problem to everyone there." She turned the book over in her hands. "But…"

"Exactly. You could learn. Prove you're an asset."

"Rather than a liability?" Still, she liked the idea. "I'll do it. For Heidi."

"And for yourself."

Rebecca laughed. "And for myself. I'll have to find Colton and let him know I've changed my mind." Doubts clawed at her mind. "Maybe he will withdraw his invitation."

Holly laughed.

"But before I go, I have to write a letter." She'd ask her father to speak to his doctor about Mrs. Hayes. And she'd tell him she meant to extend her stay until she had completed her tasks. "Can I borrow pen and paper?"

Holly chuckled. "You're going to use posting the letter as an excuse to find Colton and speak to him. My, my, aren't you a schemer?"

A little later she left the children with Holly and crossed the town square to the post office. She couldn't see the orphanage from there, but as the person responsible for the project, she had every right to check on the progress. She headed down Victory Street. Before she reached the corner, she saw lumber piled in the yard. *Thank You, God.* Perhaps this was a sign that things were going to be better from here on.

She turned the corner. When she saw Colton bent over a stack of lumber, her footsteps slowed. He'd seen how incompetent she was. Would he still be willing to put up with her simply to keep Gabriel close? *Lord God*— But she didn't even know what to pray for. For courage to approach Colton? Maybe God was telling her it was time to go back home to the life she'd been raised to live.

She tucked in her chin. She would pray for God to show her where she belonged and she would forge onward.

Colton straightened, a board in his hand. He turned, saw her and set the board down. He headed toward her and said, "I need to talk to you."

That sounded ominous. She almost changed her mind.

"I've had time to think about this situation and I'm afraid I can't agree with your staying in town. I want you to come back to the ranch." He added, as an afterthought, "Please."

She realized her mouth had fallen open and shut it. Then she started to laugh.

He clamped his lips tight. His eyes shuttered. "No need to mock me."

"I'm not."

"A simple refusal would suffice." He turned back to the pile of wood.

"Colton, wait." She grabbed his arm, surprised at the strength and power of his muscles as they rippled beneath her fingers. She brought her focus back to her mission. "The reason I laughed was because I came here, full of fear and trepidation, to say I've changed my mind and want to go back to the ranch." She lowered her gaze a moment. "If you're willing to put up with my inexperience." Oh, that word felt so much better than *inadequacy*.

He touched her shoulder and she jerked her gaze back to him. Had she put that glow in his green eyes? All she'd done was agree to return to the ranch.

"I am glad to live with your inexperience."

His gaze seemed to promise a world of opportunity and joy. He dropped his hand from her shoulder. "Let's get the children and take them home."

They were soon on their way back to the ranch, Heidi sucking on a candy. Colton kept darting glances at Rebecca and grinning. For the first time in ages, she felt welcomed.

He let her off at the doorway. "I'll take care of the horse."

Rebecca carried Gabriel in his basket, and Heidi followed close on her heels. The little girl might want to stay at the ranch, but she hadn't lost her sense of caution.

They went inside and Rebecca glanced into the sitting room. Mr. Hayes sat in the rocking chair, his head tipped back as he snored loudly. Mrs. Hayes wasn't in the room. She must have gone to her bedroom to nap. Rebecca headed to the kitchen, a smile in her heart.

He had asked her to return. Said he didn't mind her inexperience. She hugged the joy of that thought close. Then she stepped farther into the kitchen and gasped.

Beyond the table, Mrs. Hayes sat unmoving on the floor, a bowl of sugar spilled around her. She stared at Rebecca with wide eyes.

Chapter Nine

Rebecca handed the basket to Heidi. "Watch Gabriel." She eased down to Mrs. Hayes's side, wondering if the woman would welcome her help.

"What happened?"

Mrs. Hayes blinked hard. "I needed sugar for the coffee." Two full cups sat on the table. "I couldn't breathe. I guess I fell."

Rebecca squatted before the older woman. "Are you hurt?"

Mrs. Hayes moved her feet, looked at her arms. "I don't think so. But I can't seem to get up."

"Let me help you." She'd watched the nurse tending her mother and knew to reach under Mrs. Hayes's arms and guide her to her feet. The woman struggled as if her legs didn't want to work, but she managed to stand, Rebecca holding her close.

"Are you okay?"

"None too steady."

Rebecca could feel her trembling. "Let's get you back to your cot." She held the woman as they shuffled past the table, past Heidi, who watched wide-eyed. They crossed the sitting room and Rebecca eased the woman to the cot, then lifted her feet. She didn't mention how badly swollen Mrs. Hayes's lower limbs were. "Do you still want coffee?"

"If you don't mind."

Rebecca hurried back to the kitchen, swept up the spilled sugar, dumped out the cold coffee and poured a fresh cup.

Mr. Hayes jerked awake as she put cups before each of them. "You're back," he murmured. "Good to see you."

Mrs. Hayes caught Rebecca's arm and pulled her close. "Don't tell them about my fall. They already worry enough. Colton would never leave us alone if he heard." She sank back. "I am such a burden to him."

Rebecca plumped the pillows behind the older woman so she could drink her coffee and pulled the blanket over her legs, as much to hide their swelling as to provide warmth. "I won't say anything, but I know Colton doesn't consider you a burden."

Mrs. Hayes sighed. "You don't know the whole story."

"I don't suppose I do." And she never would unless Colton chose to tell her. But why would he? She was only a temporary necessity.

Yet when she tucked the blanket into place and Mrs. Hayes gave her a weak smile—the first smile she'd gotten from the woman—she thought that she might have finally proven herself useful. And there was satisfaction enough in that.

Colton whistled as he did the chores. Rebecca had come back. Had planned to return even without him begging. It was only temporary. He knew that. Knew it was all he could expect. She was high society; he was working class. She was big city; he was country. She came from privilege and opportunity. He had a small ranch and a set of parents who needed his constant attention. But he meant to enjoy her presence while he could.

It took him almost an hour to feed the animals, gather the eggs and do the hundred things that needed doing every day.

With nothing planned for supper, they might have to settle for eggs. He'd always considered such meals adequate, until now.

His chores finished, he headed for the house. Never mind what they ate: sharing it with Rebecca and Heidi, and watching little Gabriel eat, was pleasure enough.

He stepped into the house. The table was set. The smell of food filled the room. Rebecca stood before the stove, smiling with satisfaction.

He stared at her and in that moment something he thought he'd put to death and buried was resurrected. The dream of a home and family of his own. Rebecca fit perfectly into the dream.

Her smiled faded. Her eyes clouded with uncertainty. "I thought I would go ahead and make the meal."

"I'm glad you did." More glad than a meal already prepared warranted.

She grinned. "I told you. I'm a fast learner. Wash up and sit down. Everything is ready."

He did. Boiled potatoes, fried steak, green beans and—he sniffed—was that chocolate pudding? "How did you do this?"

Pa grinned. "She planned it in town."

"She bought the things at the store." Heidi enjoyed Rebecca's success as if it were her own.

Rebecca looked pleased. "I asked Holly for a cookbook and some help."

"It's delicious."

"I didn't try gravy." She ducked her head, but not before he caught the flash of a smile. "I wasn't sure I could manage that."

He laughed. "Gravy or not, this is the best meal I've had in a long time." To have her in the kitchen, preparing a meal, greeting him with a smile every day—

He jammed a cork in the thoughts pouring forth.

Ma pushed her potatoes around on her plate. "You and Pa really liked your potatoes riced. Remember that?"

"I'd forgotten. No reason we can't do it again." He couldn't stop himself from smiling at Rebecca, at the same time hoping she hadn't noticed that he said *we*. "Ma, where is that ricer?"

"Can't say as I recall." Ma gave him a look full of what he could only describe as warning.

Not that he'd forgotten her words. He wasn't going to get too fond of a rich, city girl. Not if he knew what was good for him.

But when Rebecca served them each a bowl of luscious chocolate pudding, topped with spoon-thick cream, he couldn't help wondering what was wrong with a rich, city girl if she could cook like this.

"Son, get my Bible," Pa said.

At first, Colton didn't move. Pa hadn't asked for the Bible, nor offered to read to them, for a long time.

"I think the occasion and these guests call for us to live like our family has always done."

Pa didn't need to explain his request. Colton was happy to see the return of old rituals. He got the Bible and listened as Pa read a passage and then prayed a blessing on them all. This was how he remembered his family. How it used to be. Before Pa got hurt.

He pushed from the table. He was to blame for Pa's accident. And he'd care for him until he died.

There was no room in his life for dreams.

But he couldn't escape the stirrings of those long-denied hopes and wishes as he helped Rebecca and Heidi wash the dishes and clean the kitchen. They were chores he'd done on his own for a number of years, but sharing them with his guests made them a joy rather than a job.

Most likely, it was unusual and perhaps unwelcome work

for Rebecca. The least he could do was show her one of the wonders of the ranch. He pretended that was the only reason for what he wanted to do and denied a longing to share his pleasure and his time with her.

He hung the damp tea towel on the rack behind the stove. "Rebecca, the baby is sleeping. Heidi can watch him. Would you like to go for a walk to see more of the place?"

Her eyes lit up with eagerness, then she turned to Heidi. "Would you be okay with that?"

Heidi nodded. "I don't mind."

"I'll show you around later," Colton promised the girl. "We won't be long. If you need us, there's a triangle outside the door." He showed her. "You bang it with this rod and I'll come running."

She giggled. "You'd run?"

"Every step of the way."

She considered him with a steady brown gaze, her eyes trusting him.

His heartbeat felt sluggish. He wanted to promise Heidi he would always come running if she needed him. But it wasn't possible. He reiterated the reasons and reminded himself of all he owed Ma and Pa.

He stepped out the door, Rebecca at his side, and directed their footsteps to a path that led away from the house and the outbuildings. "Pa came out here twenty years ago. One of the earliest settlers. I was eight years old. I loved the place from the first day."

They reached a knoll. "I stood on this very spot and stared out across rolling fields, wondering if they went on forever."

He let her take in the view.

She turned brilliant eyes toward him. "Do they?"

"Almost."

She grinned. "It reminds me of the ocean. The way the grass bends and sways is like rolling waves."

"I've never seen the ocean."

"It's big." She laughed.

"Kind of figured that out on my own. It ain't like I'm stupid just 'cause I'm a farmer." He did his best to sound dull.

She rolled her head back and forth. "Are you purposely taking offense at an innocent statement?"

"Maybe." Maybe he just wanted to remind himself of the differences between them.

She turned to consider the scenery again. "Are those wildflowers over there?"

He nodded. "Want to see them?"

"I'd love to." She picked up her skirts and trotted across the grass.

He followed more slowly, enjoying the scenery—every bit of it—but especially the blond-haired girl running toward the flowers.

She reached them and fell to her knees, cupping her hands about the blossoms. "What are they called?"

He named them—black-eyed Susans, coneflowers, pink asters. "Wild flax blooms in the morning. It's a very pretty blue."

She parted the grass and studied the pink asters. "So beautiful yet untended."

"God's a good gardener."

She let out a deep sigh. "He is, isn't He?" She lifted her face to the sky and closed her eyes. Was she praying? He kept quiet, just in case.

She opened her eyes, saw him watching and smiled. "I was asking God to help me with my responsibilities. I need to see the orphanage built before the children arrive and I want Heidi to have a home. But I'm running out of time." She rose and stared out at the landscape. "I've already been told to return to New York. I begged for an extension, but I don't know how long I will be allowed to remain here."

His heart leaped a little when she said she'd asked to stay…
but it was just for an extension, not forever. Sooner or later,
she planned to return to New York. Not that he didn't know
that, but he'd tried to forget it. "What will happen to Heidi?"
The words ached in his throat.

"She will stay here in the new orphanage."

His fists clenched at his sides. Life could be so unfair.
"Can you stop it?" Shock deepened his voice.

Her eyes narrowed. Her nostrils flared. "I've tried to place
her in a home." She looked away and swallowed hard. "I'm
still hoping to find a family to take her in. I've considered
asking my father to give her a place in the household."

Shouldn't she sound a bit more enthusiastic? "That would
be good. She should be part of a family."

Her expression clouded. "She'd likely be a kitchen maid."
She must have noticed his confusion. "The cook would be
good to her."

"She'd be a servant?" He tried to picture what she meant.
How many servants did they have? "What's your home like?"

"It's—" She shot him a look he could only describe as
uncertain. Then she shrugged. "I don't know how to describe it."

He narrowed his eyes. "You're afraid to tell me about it.
Why?"

"I'm not afraid," she huffed. "I'm proud of my home.
But—" She gave a great deal of attention to brushing a fleck
of dirt from her dress.

He studied her downturned head, the golden halo of her
hair. "I realize you're from a well-to-do family. So I expect
you live in a fine, big house. I only wanted to picture it."

She flashed him a smile so innocently charming that his
heart crashed against his rib cage.

"Very well. It was built seventy-five years ago by my
great-grandfather Patton Sterling as a testament to his success

in wheat farming and milling operations—" she lowered her voice "—among other things, some of which are never mentioned. It is a three-story Greek Revival–style home with a freestanding spiral staircase from the parlors on the ground floor to the bedrooms above." She sounded as if she were reading from a script.

Colton realized he was staring at her gape-mouthed and jerked his mouth shut. Greek Revival? Parlor?

Her eyes twinkled like sunshine. "Did you want the official tour speech or something less formal?"

"I think less formal."

"What I remember best is the nursery. It was filled with toys and books. My favorite spot was a window seat overlooking the orchard."

A nursery? An orchard? Each word humbled him more and more. He must look like a real country hick to brag about the wildflowers and the rolling hills.

She continued, "I used to curl up on the padded seat and read. Often I would get so lost in my imagination that the nurse would have to tap me on the shoulder to get my attention."

"You had a nurse? Were you sick?"

She chuckled. "No, the nurse took care of me while my mother tended to her duties."

He swallowed twice to think she'd been raised by a hired servant.

"How big is this house?"

"Thirty rooms," she mumbled.

"Did you say thirty? But I thought you were an only child."

"I am."

"I can see why your mother was so busy she didn't have time to care for you. All those rooms to clean."

"The servants cleaned the house." She shifted her gaze to something beyond his shoulder.

"Exactly what did your mother do?"

Rebecca wiped a finger along her chin. "It's complicated. She planned dinner parties for my father. She made afternoon visits to women of like mind."

He noticed how she stumbled to find words to describe her mother's activities. To him they sounded useless and silly, but he wouldn't voice the thought. Thirty rooms? Servants? A child raised by a servant? He floundered to make sense of it, let alone picture her or Heidi in that situation. "Didn't you get lost in a house that size?"

She laughed. "I did once, when I was very young. Usually my nurse took me where I had to go, but I had slipped away from her and couldn't remember which way to turn. I had everyone searching for me for hours because, when I couldn't find the room I wanted, I simply curled up on the carpet and fell asleep."

He understood she found the story amusing, but he could only stare.

That was what Heidi would go to? A huge house. Servants but not family. It didn't seem ideal to him, even though Rebecca seemed to think it was normal. There had to be something else for the child. A thousand solutions sprang to his mind...all of them stamped with impossibility. He knew of no one he felt would take Heidi. He couldn't keep her. Single men simply weren't allowed to adopt children.

What if he married?

But who would marry a man with needy parents who also wanted to adopt a little girl?

He wanted to punch something, kick something, shake his fist at the sky.

At God?

No. He would follow Rebecca's example. He lifted his face and closed his eyes. *God in heaven, there's a little girl who needs a home. A baby who needs parents. You can make a field of flowers bloom. I expect finding homes for these two dear children couldn't be any harder.*

Peace replaced anger. Faith replaced frustration. He didn't know what the solution was for these children, but he would trust God to provide an answer.

"Would you care to see more?" He almost reached for her hand, then reminded himself it would be inappropriate and likely most unwelcome.

They returned to the house in a roundabout way until they reached the barn. He pointed out various things about the farm. "I prefer to call it a ranch." He chuckled at the way he thought one word preferable to another. "I like the cows and horses. Don't care much for farming, even though I know it's necessary if only to raise feed for the animals."

"I know nothing about either farming or ranching. What kind of animals are those?" She pointed toward the pasture.

He laughed. "You really are a city girl, aren't you?"

She pressed her hand to her chest and gave him a pleading look. "You mustn't mock me because I'm uninformed about such things."

"That—" he pointed toward the herd "—my dear girl, is part of our very fine herd of cows."

"Thank you, kind sir, for informing me. I may not always get it right, so I hope you'll be patient with me." She looked up at him, her eyes wide and full of innocence.

Way too much innocence.

Suspicion narrowed his eyes. "You aren't really that ignorant, are you?"

She widened her eyes. "But, sir, I know not what you mean."

He groaned. "You can stop playing the dumb, city girl."

Her eyes flashed with mischief and she pressed her lips together to hold back her laughter.

He shook his head. "You tricked me."

She laughed merrily, a sweet tinkling sound.

He chuckled, pleased to hear her laugh, more pleased that she cared enough to play a joke on him.

She stopped laughing—almost—and wiped her eyes. "I think I got even with you for that nonsense about us girls sharing a room with your mother and your being forced to sleep on the floor."

"Now I'm supposed to believe anything you say?"

"You simply have to remember not to judge me as a spoiled, city girl."

"I'll do my best to keep that in mind." He smiled at her dancing expression.

The tabby barn cat came out at that moment and meowed for attention. He scratched her ears and stroked her back. "And how are your babies today?" He talked to the cat out of habit. Would Rebecca think him foolish? He straightened slowly, keeping his gaze focused on the barn.

"She has babies?"

"Four kittens."

"Can I see them?"

He eyed her gunmetal-gray dress, her fine leather shoes. "They're in the loft."

She waited. When he didn't say anything more, she sighed. "I get it. City girls don't go to lofts."

"I don't know what city girls do or don't do. But I can't see you climbing to the loft in that pretty dress and those fancy shoes."

She planted her fists on her hips and looked him up and down, her mouth pursed. "I don't know anything about farm boys, but somehow I can't see them caring for ailing parents and doing household chores." A beat of silence. "And yet you do." Her gaze challenged his opinion of her.

Her observation, and unspoken approval of what he did, made his heart beat a little stronger. "Very well. If you insist,

I'll take you to the kittens." He escorted her through the barn doors, into the stall and pointed to the opening in the roof.

She eyed the opening and the ladder on the wall then lifted her skirts and stepped to the first rung. On each rung she had to fight her skirts, but she climbed upward.

He stood at the bottom, lest she fall. She made it to the top and grinned down at him. "You afraid to climb the ladder?"

"Ha. Ha."

"Just checking. This is all new to me. For all I know, farm boys are afraid of lofts."

He headed up the ladder.

"Or maybe," she called, her voice full of mock fear, "the ladder isn't strong enough for a man of your size."

His limbs refused to work. Not because he wondered about the stability of the rungs beneath his feet, but because of her comment about his size. Did she admire it or find him big and clumsy? He forced himself upward until his feet were planted on the floor of the loft and he smiled at her. "I built the ladder to hold me."

She nodded, suggesting approval.

His thoughts tangled. Approval of the sturdy ladder? Or his skill in building it? When she spoke about her home, he got the sense that the folks in her family hired people to do all the hands-on work. Did she admire him for making things himself?

From the way she suddenly lowered her eyes and clasped her hands to stop their fluttering, he allowed himself to hope she appreciated his abilities.

Then Ma's warning and his own good sense reminded him that it didn't matter what she thought of him.

He stepped away and went to the corner where Mrs. Cat had her kittens. Rebecca knelt at his side.

"Oh, how sweet. Can I touch them?"

"Of course." He handed each of them to her. "Their eyes opened a few days ago."

Two of the kittens were black, one was white with black spots and the fourth was a calico who would turn into a very pretty mother cat.

Rebecca rubbed her cheek against the fur of each kitten. He enjoyed watching her far more than he had any right to.

"Have you named them?" she asked.

"Nope."

"Would you show them to Heidi and let her name them?"

"That's a great idea."

Mrs. Cat meowed and Rebecca put the kittens back in the box, then patted the mother cat. "You're doing a very good job," she told the cat, then pushed herself to her feet. "I should get back to my responsibilities."

"Me, too. I'll go down first."

"You think I might fall?"

"Of course not. But just in case, I'll be there to catch you."

Her head jerked up and she stared at him. The dust motes disappeared. The musty smell of old hay vanished. All that remained was the shimmering tension between them. Awareness. Caution. Regret. Useless wishes. All on his part. He didn't know what she felt about this moment or about him.

One thing he knew for certain. None of what he felt could be acted on. He understood the impossible distance separating them. Even without that, his future meant caring for his parents, which effectively excluded anything else.

He swung down the ladder and waited for her to follow, then headed back to the house. "I'll go to town tomorrow and oversee the construction." He rattled on about the things he'd do.

She stopped walking and stared at him. "And where will I be?"

"Home. Here. Taking care of Gabriel and Heidi."

"That's your idea of working together? I agreed to help with your house and parents in exchange for your help. But I still need to supervise the orphanage. There are hundreds of little decisions I must make. Did you think you'd get me out here and then take over?"

"Yes. No. Maybe."

She drew herself up tall, pushed her shoulders back and tucked in her chin. "Mr. Hayes, what do I have to do to convince you that I will not relinquish my responsibilities?" She whirled about and headed toward the house in a fine fury.

Her anger wasn't unexpected, yet it brought answering annoyance from him. Why did she have to be so stubborn and prideful? He closed the distance between them and caught her arm. "What do you propose to do with Gabriel?"

"I'll take him and Heidi with me."

He grunted. By the way she raised her eyebrows, he knew that she considered it an inadequate way of communicating. But he didn't care. He was through trying to get her to see reason. She'd find out for herself how difficult it would be to supervise the building, *and* watch Gabriel and Heidi, *and* take care of all the household chores.

She jerked away and continued her return to the house.

He followed on her heels. But two steps later, he slowed. He'd known she'd object to him taking control of the job they'd agreed to work together on. Yet he'd done so anyway.

As if he invited her anger.

Perhaps he did. Because it reminded him of their differences and enabled him to insulate his feelings behind those differences. So why did he feel as if he had swallowed scalding-hot water? If this was what he wanted, why did he have to restrain himself from rushing forward to apologize and beg her forgiveness?

How would he survive the war of reality and dreams that raged in his heart?

Chapter Ten

Rebecca slipped into the house. She didn't have to supervise the construction at this stage. And she understood he thought their agreement meant she would stay at the ranch. But she couldn't stay here all the time. Pretending she knew how to run a household. Looking out the window, seeing that patch of wildflowers and recalling that tender moment when they stood side by side. When she'd wished he'd take her hand and say something sweet. Every minute spent here increased a longing in her heart to belong, to be part of something real.

How silly. Her life in New York was real. What would her mother say to her in this situation? But she couldn't hear her mother's voice.

Gabriel started to cry.

She prepared a bottle while Heidi changed the baby and bounced him. She fed the baby as usual, but he did not settle. She rocked him, but he cried all the louder.

"Can he still be hungry?" she asked. She offered him more, but he refused the bottle and screamed louder.

She jostled him, then walked about trying to calm him. All she knew to do was feed him again, but he refused the bottle.

"Want me to try?" Heidi asked.

Shouldn't she be the one to calm Gabriel? But Rebecca

sucked in her cheeks and shifted the baby to the young girl. Heidi walked and bounced and talked, but Gabriel kept crying, and after a few minutes Heidi handed him back to Rebecca.

Rebecca's frustration mounted as Gabriel screamed. What was she doing wrong? Was she totally incompetent at everything but presiding over formal dinners?

Would Mrs. Hayes know? She went to the sitting room. "Mrs. Hayes, what am I doing wrong?"

The woman sighed, but Rebecca thought she detected a flicker of interest. "Babies usually have a fussy period. I guess this is his."

A fussy period? That didn't sound so bad. But as the baby continued to cry, Rebecca admitted it felt terrible. "What do I do?"

Mrs. Hayes held out her arms. "Give him to me. I'll see if I can help."

Rebecca handed her the baby. The woman placed his tummy on her round stomach and patted his back.

Gabriel stopped crying, but still fussed.

"My padding is useful for something," Mrs. Hayes said.

Rebecca chuckled. "I think it's more than that."

"Estelle always had a way with babies," Mr. Hayes said, his voice filled with admiration and affection.

Mrs. Hayes waved at him dismissively. "Oh, Louis, that was a long time ago." But she smiled at her husband.

It was only the second time Rebecca had seen the woman smile, and it made her smile, too.

At that moment, Colton returned to the house, saw his mother with Gabriel perched on her stomach and grinned. "Now, Ma, don't you be getting too fond of that little one. I'm set on finding his real parents."

His mother waved away his comment.

A few minutes later, Mr. Hayes yawned. "I think I'll head

for bed." He pushed to his feet, but before he could hobble out of the room, Colton was beside him, letting the man lean heavily on him.

Mrs. Hayes watched them depart. "Poor Louis has never recovered from his accident. He needs Colton's help to do everything."

Rebecca nodded.

"We're very dependent on him. What with my old ticker not working the way it should and Louis all crippled up, we couldn't get along without him." Her words were brisk and her look full of warning.

Rebecca sat back. Was Mrs. Hayes suggesting that Rebecca might want to change things? That couldn't be further from her goals. "I'm expected back in New York soon. I only want to see the orphanage built and the children safe before I go."

She gave Mrs. Hayes a steady, unblinking look, hoping the woman understood she had no designs on her son.

A little later the baby fell asleep.

"You can take him." Rebecca did so and the woman lumbered to her feet. "Think you can manage now?"

"I'll manage just fine. Thanks for the help."

The woman shuffled away.

Heidi yawned.

"Let's go to bed," Rebecca said. She prepared a bottle for the night and Heidi lifted the basket. They were about to leave the room when Colton returned.

"Are you going to bed, too?"

At his disappointment, she almost changed her mind, but his mother's warning words still rang in her ears. Not that she needed such warning. Her own conscience had not been silent. *Do your job and go back to your real life in the city.* "It's been a long day."

"I guess it has." He moved closer to touch the baby's cheek.

A thousand butterflies fluttered up Rebecca's veins and gathered in her heart. She could almost imagine him touching her cheek in the same gentle way.

She stepped out of his reach and, with a hurried goodnight, went to the bedroom.

But she had barely fallen asleep when Gabriel started to cry. She rocked him. She fed him. She changed his diaper. She walked him. *Oh, please, little baby, stop crying.*

He finally slept—about the time dawn creaked over the horizon. She'd get only an hour of shut-eye before she had to get up.

Just before she fell asleep, she decided to stay at the ranch for the day. She might be able to nap while the baby slept. And watch that Mrs. Hayes didn't fall again.

Colton tiptoed from his room. He'd heard Gabriel crying off and on throughout the night. Had Rebecca gotten any sleep? Maybe she'd be tired enough to stay home today.

Her insistence that she would supervise the construction scraped along his nerves. Did she think he needed her oversight?

He'd wanted her to stay home and take care of his parents and the children.

And greet him on his return, as she had yesterday, with a hot meal and a smile.

He groaned. He was building impossible dreams.

He stepped outside into a pink dawn and took in a deep breath. A beautiful day. He stretched, then headed to the barn to do his chores.

An hour later he returned to the house. Again the table was set and food was ready. Rebecca was definitely a fast learner. She glanced up at his entrance. Weariness etched her face. Dark shadows pooled under her eyes. She smiled, but her smile seemed rather weak, as if she lacked the energy to lift the corners of her mouth.

Ma and Pa sat at the table, waiting for him to join them. Heidi perched on her chair, her head tipped down to hide her face. Someday he'd like to see her hold her head high with pride and self-assurance. Recalling Rebecca's words that the child would live in the orphanage or perhaps go back to New York, he wondered if he'd have the opportunity to be part of her healing.

"I heard Gabriel in the night," he said.

Ma sighed heavily. "I heard him, too."

Rebecca looked as if she'd been accused of deliberately disturbing them. "I did my best to keep him quiet."

Colton reached out, wanting to touch her shoulder, pull her close, offer her comfort and assurance. Knowing he didn't have the right, he dropped his hand to his side. "It's not your fault that he cries."

Ma grunted and Rebecca ducked her head.

He slanted his ma a scolding look, but she stared at Rebecca, her eyes tight with judgment.

"Son, sit down so we can eat," Pa said.

Colton sat and bowed his head as Pa said grace.

No one spoke much as they ate. Colton's thoughts churned with things he wanted to say but didn't dare to or didn't know how to. As much because he couldn't figure out what he wanted as that he knew he couldn't have what he wanted.

"I'll clean up," Rebecca said and carried the dishes to the kitchen.

He followed.

"I've decided not to go to town today after all," she said as soon as they were alone.

She wouldn't have surprised him more if she'd slapped him with a wet hand. He'd thought this was what he wanted, but now he already missed her. He'd go to town alone. Wouldn't see her or the children until he returned. But what could he say?

She looked confused by his lack of approval. "I thought that's what you wanted."

"I guess so." He tried to convince himself it was. Seeing the water bucket empty, he grabbed it. "I'll fill this." And he dashed outside.

He jerked to a halt and stared at the pump. Something hung from the handle and he knew what it was without closing the distance. He looked around, but saw no one. Of course the culprit would be long gone or well hidden. Nevertheless, he scoured every inch of the ground around the pump and searched through the buildings and trees. He found nothing.

He veered to the barn, grabbed a shovel and stalked to the pump. He cut the dead rat from the handle and took it to the corner of the field to bury. All the while, his insides churned. Someone meant this as a warning. A threat. And it had something to do with the orphanage. And Rebecca. What would this person do next? She wasn't safe here alone. He had to take her to town where he could keep an eye on her. Ensure her safety.

But how could he convince her?

She could be as stubborn as a mule. He grinned. But a lot prettier.

He would not take no for an answer. To prove it to himself, he hitched the horse to the buggy and drove to the house. His jaw set with determination, he strode into the house.

Rebecca sat by the table feeding Gabriel. It was hard to believe this sweet, content baby had been so fussy during the night. He studied the pair a moment, unable to stifle the longing that rushed up his throat. Heidi sat on the floor, fingering the bit of flannel blanket that covered the baby when he slept. What he wouldn't do to be able to keep and shelter and protect this trio.

It was beyond his ability to do so permanently, but he could make sure that they were safe for today.

"I've decided you need to come to town with me."

She jerked her head toward him and stared. "You've decided? Who gave you the right?" She was all royally righteous indignation. Miss Sterling of New York City didn't take orders from anyone.

"That came out wrong," he explained, backtracking. "I didn't mean to order you around. But as you said, there will be decisions to make. If you were nearby to consult, the work wouldn't have to be interrupted should we need your advice."

Blue eyes full of skepticism considered him. No doubt she wondered why he'd changed his mind, but he would not tell her. No need for her to be alarmed as long as he was around to protect her. His arms ached to pull her and the children close.

She finally released him from her gaze. "I suppose I could go."

His breath whooshed out. He wouldn't have to argue.

A little later they headed out. As they drove to town, he kept his eyes open for any sign of trouble. But they arrived at Evans Grove without seeing anything that gave him cause for concern—a fact that did not ease his mind. Danger lurked out there somewhere, and he'd just as soon confront it as be constantly looking for it.

Both Rebecca and Heidi had been quiet on the trip and Gabriel had slept. He turned to Rebecca now. Her head bobbed. Poor woman was exhausted from being up all night. Maybe she could get a rest if she went where the baby could be watched. "Where can I leave you?"

She jerked up. "I'd like to see Charlotte."

He helped her and Heidi down in front of Charlotte's

house. "I'll be back if I need you." Need, not want, he warned himself. "Otherwise, I'll be back at the end of the day."

"Thank you."

"Goodbye, Heidi." The child flashed him a tentative smile as she murmured goodbye.

He waved to Charlotte and Sasha. They must be anxious for Wyatt to return. His return would mean the arrival of the rescued orphans. As Rebecca often said, the children needed a welcoming place when they reached Evans Grove. He meant to do what he could to see they had that.

He arrived at the orphanage. The sound of hammers and saws filled the air. He counted four men at work. Ted Lang, an experienced carpenter, seemed to be in charge.

"Good to see you." He included all the men in his greeting.

"No excuse for not getting this done now that we have the supplies," Ted said.

According to the list of volunteers, there should have been ten men working, but Colton wasn't about to complain. He understood there were many people who went out of their way to avoid dealing with Miss Ward. He immediately set to work. His insides smoothed as he nailed boards in place. The work was getting done and he had a hand in it.

Suddenly all hammering stopped and he straightened to see if something was wrong. The men all looked toward the street. He followed their gaze.

Rebecca watched them, her arms empty.

He glanced past her as she crossed until she stood staring at the wooden walls.

"I left Heidi and Gabriel with Charlotte."

It was on the tip of his tongue to say she might have stayed there, too. There wasn't a lot she could do right now, but he knew if he said so she would get all fiery. Besides, he didn't mind her company.

"It's nice to see the work going ahead." Her eyes glowed

with approval. She thanked the men and they returned to their tasks.

Colton wondered if she included him in that approval.

She studied the piles of lumber and the men nailing boards to the walls. Slowly, almost reluctantly, her gaze came to him. "I'm grateful for all the help."

"You don't sound very certain of that."

"Please don't misunderstand." Her mouth twisted. "But it makes me feel incompetent that I can't manage to supervise the building on my own."

"Rebecca, everyone needs help. That's what family and community are all about. Working together. Balancing each other's strengths and weaknesses. Learning and growing together."

"I like the sound of that." She smiled, filling his mind with a vision of her bent over the wildflowers. Her gaze slid past him. "We've got visitors," she murmured.

He turned. Miss Ward steamed toward them, Pauline Evans and Curtis Brooks in her wake. Pauline, a regal woman in her late forties with thick auburn hair, had been acting as mayor since her husband died this past spring. Curtis, a man slightly older than the mayor, dressed and acted like the banker he was. He'd come from Newfield to oversee the loan his bank had given the town to enable the residents and businesses to rebuild after the flood. His choice to stay was a bone of contention with Pauline, who didn't think they needed supervision. Colton had heard, though, that the pair worked well together on the selection committee to place Rebecca's orphans with families.

Miss Ward reached them first and churned past to watch the men working. "Just as I said. Shoddy workmanship. A building hastily constructed will soon be a public disgrace."

Rebecca stiffened and opened her mouth to argue.

Colton touched her arm. "Don't add fuel to the fire," he

murmured. "She's fought this from the start, but she has little support. The majority of the town is behind the orphanage."

Rebecca nodded and held her tongue, though her eyes were ablaze.

Curtis scanned the site. "It's good to see that the supplies have finally arrived. Do you mind if I look around?"

No one raised an objection and he walked the perimeter of the building, went into the framed shell and paced out each room. Then he returned.

Pauline crossed her arms and studied the man. "What was that all about? This building is not part of the bank loan."

"I know. I was only curious. Nothing more. No need to be alarmed."

Colton thought the man could have easily substituted the word *suspicious* for *alarmed*.

"I'd say everything is going as well as can be expected." Pauline gave a dismissive nod and headed away, Curtis at her side.

Miss Ward hurried after them. "You saw for yourself my concerns, didn't you?" She addressed Curtis.

Colton couldn't hear his response.

Rebecca waited until they were out of earshot, then grabbed Colton's arms. "Miss Ward is trying to stop construction of the building. We have to get as much done as we can before she succeeds." She picked up a hammer. "Show me what to do."

He knew better than to laugh, though it tickled his insides to see her waving the hammer about. "Have you ever built anything?"

She shook her head, her eyes narrowed.

"You ever hammered a nail?"

"No, but I can learn."

Would there be any point in trying to dissuade her? Every attempt so far had been futile. Besides, this might be fun.

"Very well. Grab the end of that board." He indicated one he had sawed that was ready to nail into place.

She pinched it with two fingertips.

"Help me carry it to the wall." He managed to hide his amusement as he lifted his end, knowing full well that she couldn't pick up her end without using both hands. She lifted the board a few inches before it fell. He glanced at her over his shoulder then hoisted the board and carried it to the wall.

She trotted after him. "You didn't give me a chance."

He held the board in place with his knee. "Nail that end in place."

She took a nail from the sack, watched as he drove one into the board. Then she attempted to do the same.

First blow, the nail ricocheted away.

He handed her another nail.

She smiled sweetly, though the smile went no farther than her lips. "I can do this."

He held up his hands in a gesture of defeat. "Never said you couldn't."

Second blow, the nail fell to the ground.

"Don't you say a word."

"No, ma'am." But he made no attempt to keep the amusement out of his eyes as he handed her another nail.

Third blow, the nail tiptoed into the lumber.

"See," she crowed.

"It actually needs to go through the board and into the stud to do any good."

"I know that." She tapped at the nail, missing it as often as she hit it. It ended up twisted and bent.

He handed her another nail.

"Do. Not. Say. Anything." She ground out the words.

"My lips are sealed." He knew the men were watching. Saw them exchange smiles. "Besides, I know you can do this."

She tapped the nail into place, took the hammer with two hands and finally got the nail most of the way in. "There. I did it."

The men nodded and grinned.

"What next?" she asked.

"Every board needs two nails at the studs—the uprights. And we keep going until the wall is finished."

"Right." She grabbed another nail and managed to hammer it into place.

If Miss Ward saw this, she would have a fit. Shoddy workmanship.

Rebecca moved on to another upright, obviously determined to continue helping.

He could have done the work twice as fast on his own, but remembering how she said she felt incompetent, he kept letting her drive in nails.

Ted Lang moved closer to Colton. "She's got spunk. That's for sure."

Colton watched her driving in nails. "At least she tries."

"She does better than try. Never expected to see a woman in fine clothes helping out."

The other men nodded.

Colton had to agree. She was okay.

They paused to share the dinner they'd brought. He thought she might decide to leave. There were the children and a hundred other reasons to quit. He noticed her arms shook as she lifted a dipper of water to her mouth, but she tucked in her chin and followed him back to the orphanage.

A little later he glanced at the sky to judge the time. "Rebecca and I need to take the children home and take care of chores. Ted." He leaned close to whisper to the man. "Could you pound in a nail or two?" He tipped his head to indicate the places where Rebecca had worked.

"Will do."

He informed Rebecca that they needed to leave. She seemed eager to do so.

"Your arms are going to be sore," he warned her.

"I'll be okay." She walked beside him. "Thank you for letting me help. Even though I didn't do much, at least I contributed something."

"You did your best and then some. No one can say you didn't."

"Thank you."

She went to get the children ready to go home. He'd left the horse and buggy at the livery barn, but he detoured out of his way to go to the sheriff's office to speak again to Mason. "Did you find out anything?" He'd told Mason about Gabriel, but the man had already heard the story from Holly.

"I've asked around discreetly, but the mother must have been someone passing through. After all, it's a small town. If a woman was in the family way, someone would know."

"How would a stranger get my grandmother's quilt?"

"I can't explain that."

"You must have overlooked something."

"I'll keep poking around."

"There's something else." He told the sheriff about the deliberate damage at the orphanage and about the rats. "Someone is sending a very strong warning. I've looked around for clues, but I haven't seen anything I could use."

Mason planted both feet on the floor with a thud. "I heard about the delays and damage, and thought Beatrice Ward might be guilty, but this is beyond her. I'll see what I can uncover."

Colton thanked the sheriff, got the buggy and went to pick up Rebecca and the children.

She had little to say on the ride home, but Heidi more than made up for it, telling them about playing with Sasha and Liam.

Gabriel fussed as they reached the ranch. Colton pulled up to the house and helped Rebecca down.

As he tended to his work, he knew a sense of contentment. He and Rebecca had worked as a team. He liked the feeling.

He turned from feeding the horse and saw the shovel in the corner of the barn where he'd put it only this morning after burying the rat.

A knot of anger replaced any pleasant feeling he'd been savoring. He would not be able to rest until the culprit was found. Until then, he would guard Rebecca and the children. No harm must come to them.

Chapter Eleven

That evening Colton faced Rebecca. "I'll keep the baby tonight."

Rebecca shook her head. "I can do it." In truth, she ached from head to toe and hammers pounded inside her head, but she meant to prove she was capable.

"We're sharing the work, remember? That means I take a turn."

She wanted to argue, wanted to prove she could do this, but the thought of being up most of the night held no appeal. "Fine, we'll take turns. And thank you."

He chuckled. "Don't thank me for doing what I'm supposed to."

Later, as she curled up in bed, she thought of his words as they had worked at the orphanage. Community. Working together. The concepts felt comforting.

The next morning, Mr. and Mrs. Hayes came from their room as Rebecca and Heidi stepped from theirs. The older couple shuffled toward the kitchen. They stopped a few steps into the room.

Rebecca and Heidi followed and stopped, too, staring at the same thing—

Colton was stretched out on the cot, asleep and breathing

deeply, baby Gabriel asleep on his stomach. Colton's arms were crossed over the baby, his fingers interlocked, holding the baby safe and sound.

The sight of the big man cradling the baby filled Rebecca with a thousand sweet thoughts, like butterflies around a cluster of pink flowers. He'd spoken of community—doing things for the sake of others. He exemplified community and family in Rebecca's mind.

Mr. Hayes chuckled. "Now, there's a sight to cheer a man. Mother, you'll have to sit elsewhere for now." He took his wife's arm and led her to his rocker, pulled out a kitchen chair and sat beside her.

"I'll make coffee and start breakfast," Rebecca said, only she didn't move as Colton stirred.

It took him several seconds to surface from his sleep, then he jerked upright, the baby in his arms, and rubbed his eyes. "I thought the little guy would cry all night. I didn't want to disturb you—" he addressed his parents "—so I brought him out here."

He lowered the sleeping infant to his basket. "Ma, how long does this crying at night go on?"

She chuckled.

Rebecca stared. The woman had a soft side.

"You cried at night until you were a year old. Then one day Pa said I was to go visit Grandmother and he would keep the baby." She smiled at her husband. "I never asked what you did to break him of it. Guess I was afraid I might not approve."

Mr. Hayes touched her arm gently. "I simply sat by his bed and patted his back, all the while telling him he wasn't getting up. Our smart little boy finally figured out I meant it and went to sleep."

Colton chuckled. "I don't remember, but I do know that all my life I knew Pa couldn't be wrong."

The three of them shared a laugh.

Colton turned to Rebecca, his eyes alight with joy.

She drowned in his look.

"Sure glad it's your turn to keep the baby tonight."

She surfaced, forced her gaze away and scurried into the kitchen to start the meal.

Later that morning, they returned to town. Rebecca again left the children with Charlotte and went to the orphanage to help. She picked up a hammer, stifling a groan at the pain in her arms. "I'm ready."

Colton smiled so approvingly she thought her heart would burst from her chest. "Let's do it, then."

She held boards for him as he sawed. She drove in nails. At least today she managed to hit the nail more often than she missed it, but oh, how her muscles protested.

Ted Lang sidled up to her. "Ma'am, you're doing just fine."

His simple praise filled her with satisfaction.

Colton waited until he moved away. "He's right, you know."

She waited for him to explain.

"You're doing just fine."

His smile filled her with warmth to the center of her soul. She turned and pounded in another nail, keeping her face averted lest he see her reaction.

By the end of the day, they had made significant progress on the building. And her arms hurt so badly they felt as if they would fall off.

She gratefully accepted Colton's help into the buggy and let him lift Gabriel to her, hoping he would see it as as a form of cooperation, not a response to pain.

Back at the ranch Colton helped them down. "I might have time to show a little girl some kittens before I do chores."

Heidi jumped up and down. "How big are they?"

"Why don't you find out for yourself?" The pair headed for the barn.

Rebecca buried her physical pain, stepped into the house and smiled at Colton's parents.

"How was your day?" Mr. Hayes asked.

She told him about all the men who were helping. "It's so nice to know people are willing and ready to assist."

Mr. Hayes sighed. "'Twas a time I'd have been there, too. But at least Colton can help."

Mrs. Hayes shook her finger at her husband. "Louis, you have done your share in the past. Besides, what would I do if you went to town, too? The day is long enough."

The older man chuckled. "I know you get bored of my company. But for now we have Rebecca and the children to relieve our boredom."

Rebecca decided then and there she would do more to make the days enjoyable for them. Gabriel started to fuss. "Mrs. Hayes, would you like to feed him while I make supper?"

At first the woman looked as if she would refuse, then she reached for him. "As long as you prepare the bottle."

Rebecca put the baby into her arms and got the bottle ready.

Mrs. Hayes rocked Gabriel and murmured to him.

Mr. Hayes caught Rebecca's hand. "Thank you," he murmured, tipping his head toward his wife.

Rebecca smiled. Sometimes all it took was thinking about the needs of others. Like community. She pushed herself through meal preparations, grateful that nothing she did hurt the way driving in nails did.

Heidi rushed into the room. "I brought a kitten for you." She went to Mr. Hayes's side, holding the calico kitten. "Colton let me name them all. I called the two black ones Midnight and Storm. The black-and-white one I called Cloud. But this is my favorite." She lifted it to her cheek.

Heidi had forgotten to hide her scars. She was so happy here, with this family who accepted her for who she was. Rebecca contemplated the older couple. They'd benefit from a child like Heidi to help them and it would give the child a safe and loving home.

Why did it hurt to think of this arrangement? A pain that made the ache in her arms insignificant by comparison. It would be best for Heidi. Better than taking her back to New York. Far better than leaving her in the orphanage.

Her heart beat sluggishly and her limbs were wooden stumps. She didn't want to leave Heidi with anyone.

She wasn't even sure she wanted to go back to New York.

She'd found something here she'd never known before, and it was more than community. But her father and her life were in New York. It was where she belonged. Her whole life she'd been groomed for her role in society. It left her unsuited for life in Evans Grove.

Heidi gave the kitten to Mr. Hayes. "I need help naming her."

Mr. Hayes had a good look at the kitten. "She's a good one. I can tell by the way she watches me. Have a look, Mother."

Rebecca put the sleeping Gabriel into his basket so Mrs. Hayes could take the kitten.

Mrs. Hayes stroked the soft fur. "She's purring. I always wanted a house cat, but you didn't approve." The look she gave her husband silently pleaded.

"Maybe it's time."

Mrs. Hayes smiled and lowered her face to the kitten's fur. "She'll make a good pet."

"But what will we call her?" Heidi asked.

"What do you think when you look at her?" Colton's ma asked.

Heidi pulled a footstool to the woman's knees and studied the kitten. "I think how happy I am."

"Then why don't you call her Happy?"

"Oh, yes. That's perfect."

Rebecca watched the interaction and thought about how perfect the whole picture seemed. Home. Family. Heidi. A baby. Everything she wanted. But she didn't belong in this family or this town. She was just a rich, city girl. She never forgot that, and even if she did, she could well imagine what her father would say to the idea of her staying here.

Colton entered the house.

She couldn't face him. Not until she had her warring emotions carefully hidden. She swallowed hard and hoped no one could hear the rapid beating of her heart. Then she pasted a smile on her face. "Supper will be ready in a few minutes."

Colton regarded her with an amused expression. His gaze slid to Heidi and his parents and back to her. Did he have the same thought as she did? That Heidi seemed to belong here?

Sooner or later she would have to confront that possibility.

But for now she shoved it aside.

Colton wondered at the coolness in Rebecca's gaze. It was as if she didn't want to let him see her feelings. Or maybe she simply hurt all over. He knew her muscles must be protesting at the work she'd done, even though she hid the pain admirably.

He shifted his attention back to Heidi. She'd been bubbly and excited since he'd shown her the kittens. Her enthusiasm had grown by leaps and bounds when Pa said Happy could be a house cat as soon as she was big enough to leave the mama cat.

That temporarily robbed Heidi of her joy. "She has to be an orphan?"

Mr. Hayes squeezed the child's shoulder. "No, honey, not

an orphan. She can see her mama whenever she wants. But the mama cat won't want to be a house cat. She's used to the barn."

Heidi seemed satisfied with that explanation. "How long before Happy can come to the house?"

"Colton?"

He wished he could say immediately, but the kitten had to be able to eat on its own. "A few days yet."

Heidi slumped into a ball of disappointment.

"But you can go visit her in the barn."

"Okay."

"You can take her back to her mama now."

Colton watched out the window. He'd checked the barn and surroundings when they got home and seen nothing to alarm him, nothing to indicate that anyone lurked nearby with another dead-rat warning. Nevertheless, he kept his eyes on Heidi as she inched her way across the yard. "Might take her a week to make it there."

Pa laughed. "It's nice to see her opening up. She's a sweet thing."

"Louis—" Ma sounded angry "—I know what you're thinking, but we're too old."

Colton realized what Pa wanted—to take Heidi into their home. He shifted his gaze to Rebecca. In her eyes he saw the same acknowledgment but something else, too. Pain she tried to mask. He wondered if her arms were the only source of the hurt.

Did she regret that his parents were too old to take in a child?

If only he could give her a home. Heidi and Rebecca— and Gabriel, too.

He shook his head. At some point, between town and home, he seemed to have lost his mind. He wheeled around to look out the window again.

Heidi trotted toward the house.

A little later, they shared another meal prepared by Rebecca. Pa read from the Bible and prayed. He and Rebecca and Heidi cleaned up. When he saw Ma pull out her knitting, he could only stare. She hadn't touched the craft since— Well, a long time ago. And if he wasn't mistaken, this was a completely new project. "What are you making?"

"Just a little something." She shot Colton a warning look. So it was a surprise. For whom? He studied the knitting. Red-and-white stripes. An afghan? For—

He shifted his gaze to Heidi. His parents enjoyed the child's presence. He understood how they felt. For him, having Rebecca in the house made him resent every minute he had to be outside doing chores.

He studied his parents. Both of them smiled at Heidi as she sat at Pa's knees chattering about the kittens.

The child had brought new life into the home.

He considered the idea at length, but his thoughts went round and round in useless circles. What would be the best thing for Heidi? For his parents?

For him?

He wheeled around to stare out the window, but he barely noted the lowering sun. Ma had warned him to guard his heart. He'd tried.

And failed.

He knew one way to get his thoughts sorted out. He thought how his foolish behavior had resulted in Pa's injuries. His resolve restored, he turned back to the others.

Before long, Pa pushed to his feet. "I think I'll turn in." He almost reached the door before Colton jolted into action.

"I'm coming, Pa." Every day since the accident, he'd helped his father get ready for bed.

Ma trundled after them.

A few minutes later, Colton returned to find Rebecca preparing to leave the room. He knew her arms hurt and offered to keep Gabriel a second night, but she refused. "It's my turn. I do my share."

"And then some."

She shot him a disbelieving look before she took the baby.

He had to let her go, though he longed for her to stay. His longing had nothing to do with helping to care for Gabriel.

He waited until she left the room to thump himself on the forehead. Maybe if he left right now and retraced his journey from town, he could get his mind back on track before his thoughts went even further awry. He simply had to remember that he and Rebecca were from different worlds. And even if they weren't, he wasn't free to think of anything but his parents.

They worked together in town for two more days.

"I never realized how much work it took to construct a building," Rebecca said as she studied the progress.

Colton refrained from saying it would go faster if all the men who agreed to work would show up, but the help had trickled down to Ted Lang and his sidekick. He'd seen Beatrice Ward talking to the other men, overheard her dire comments and predictions at the store, and guessed she had convinced the others not to help. Or perhaps they were simply consumed with rebuilding their own lives after the flood.

"We made good progress," Ted said as Rebecca and the men prepared to leave later in the afternoon.

She thanked the men again and let Colton help her into the buggy. "I'll have to see to getting bedding and curtains made and ordering dishes and kitchen equipment." She rattled on as Colton stepped into the buggy and sat beside her. She continued to talk nonstop as they went to pick up the children. She kept up her chatter until Heidi sat behind her and began to tell them about her day.

As she turned to smile at the child, she glanced at Colton's face. He was grinning. She didn't pull away, allowing him to swim in her blue gaze.

"You seem wound a little too tight," he murmured.

"I am not." She jerked about to face forward. "Just excited."

Was her excitement over the progress on the orphanage? Was she so anxious to go back to New York? His heart thudded to his boots. Why did it bother him so much that she meant to leave as soon as possible?

The next day was Sunday. They prepared to attend church as a family. Ma and Pa insisted on sitting in the back of the buggy. Heidi sat between Colton and Rebecca, baby Gabriel cradled in Rebecca's arms.

Colton led his little family into church and positioned himself at Rebecca's side. In case Gabriel needed attention, he told himself. But he could not control an impossible wish that this could be his life forever.

The service began. They sang several hymns. Colton could barely get the words past the tightness in his throat as Rebecca stood at his side, her clear, sweet voice weaving around him.

Then Reverend James Turner spoke. He used the verse "I can do all things through Christ, who strengthens me." He went on to say that when God sent something into a person's life, He provided that person with the strength and wisdom and grace to handle it.

The words went straight to Colton's heart. He would neither shirk his responsibilities nor resent them. God would enable him to stand strong in spite of the longings of his heart.

The sermon had ignited dreams and wishes in Rebecca's heart. Had she proven herself capable? She had done a number of hard things—caring for the orphan children on her own, supervising their placement, learning to run the ranch home, even helping construct the orphanage. *Thank You, God, for giving me the strength and the ability to learn.* But was it enough?

They arrived home. Gabriel fussed to be fed and she tended him. She noted Mr. Hayes's interest. "Would you like to hold the baby?"

"I'd love to." He beamed with pleasure.

"Pa." Colton sprang forward. "Your arms. Your back." He shot Rebecca a scolding look. "He can barely hold a cup of coffee."

Pa shook his head. "I'm okay. I can hold the baby. Rest him in the crook of my arm. The arm of the chair will support him."

Rebecca hesitated a moment, but she couldn't resist the longing in Mr. Hayes's eyes, and before Colton could intervene, Rebecca positioned the baby on the older man's lap. She stood nearby in case he needed help. She had never imagined that a tiny baby could spread so much joy. She'd once thought that she and Oliver would have children. But she'd thought of them in the nursery, dressed in spotless white garments, paraded by the nurse. She'd never known the joy of holding a tiny baby and satisfying his basic needs.

She'd missed a lot in her upbringing.

Mr. Hayes rocked Gabriel gently, a smile driving away the pain lines in his face.

"There's something special about a baby, isn't there?" Rebecca asked. Not that she needed to point it out. Mr. Hayes couldn't stop looking at Gabriel.

He sighed. "Indeed, there is. It's been a long time since I've held a baby, hasn't it, Mother?"

Rebecca couldn't make sense of the older woman's expression. Half disinterest, half smile. Then she scowled. "We're too old for babies now."

"Speak for yourself, woman. I'm looking forward to the day Colton here gives us grandchildren." He studied Colton, then shifted his gaze toward Rebecca.

Ma grunted. "How's he ever going to get married when he has us to look after?" She effectively stole the delight from the moment.

"Pa, you're getting tired." Colton took the baby. "You, little man, are certainly wide-awake."

The baby smacked his lips.

Colton laughed. "Does that mean all you care about is your next meal?"

Mr. Hayes chuckled. "You betcha it does."

Heidi leaned close. "He's trying to figure out where his ma and pa are. Why would anyone abandon a little baby?"

Rebecca's heart beat heavily at the sorrow in her voice. "I suspect there is a very good reason."

"Mine died. That's a good reason, I guess."

Rebecca pulled the child to her lap. "It's a terrible reason, but remember what I've said."

Heidi nodded. "They would want me to be brave and cheerful." She tried to smile, but it faltered.

Rebecca closed her arms about the little girl and pressed her cheek to Heidi's head. "And you are. You're like a little ray of sunshine."

"A pretty bird," Mr. Hayes said.

"A sweet rose," Colton added.

Mrs. Hayes said nothing, but silence was better than stealing the moment from this innocent little girl who giggled at their comments.

Rebecca pulled the child close. "Heidi, sweet child, I believe God has a special plan for you. We just haven't discovered it yet."

Heidi brightened. "Does He really? And for Jakob, too?"

"Certainly." Rebecca felt Colton's warning gaze, but refused to acknowledge it. Yes, she was promising hope, even though she'd encountered nothing but dead ends in finding a home for this child. And there was still no word on her brother, Jakob. *Please, God, don't disappoint this child.*

After the dishes were done, Colton said, "Would you like to go for a walk? It's a beautiful day."

Although she knew it was and longed to share it with him, she feared she wouldn't be able to contain her feelings. But Gabriel slept with Heidi nearby. She could find no reason to say no. "A little walk would be nice." But she would not let her emotions control her actions or words.

They went toward the barn. The mother cat sat in front of the doors, contentedly watching her four kittens tumbling about in play.

Colton paused to observe them. "Happy will soon be big enough to move into the house."

"Heidi can hardly wait."

He slowly turned to confront her. "How can you promise her a happy home?"

"I have to believe something will work out for her. If I can't trust God to provide, then what's the point in any of this?" She waved her hand around.

"You can walk away without any concern for her future."

"That's unfair. I'll see that she is well cared for before I go." Every word burned a hole through her heart, but she was bound by the rules of the Orphan Salvation Society and those of New York society. No matter what she wanted, she had to go home and do the job she'd been trained for. "My father expects me home." Besides, she couldn't stay here and keep hiding the truth that filled her heart. "I have duties at home."

"Duties? Like ordering servants around?"

"That's part of it." She wouldn't let the way he said the words make her feel as if she'd done something wrong. "I've been raised to run the Sterling mansion, to serve as hostess for my father. I love the mansion and my father and want to honor him by fulfilling my duty." An honor, yes. Duty, too, and something more...or was it less? She felt as if the house, her position, her duty owned her.

He shifted and focused on the cows in the distant pasture, preventing her from gauging his reaction.

She turned toward the western sky and tried to concentrate on the scene before her. The sun was lowering, pastel-colored ribbons heralding the approaching sunset. A breeze tickled through the pasture, bringing the scent of grass and earth. Blackbirds danced above a hackberry tree.

"Why did you come west?"

His question surprised her. Made her forget all the wonderful things she'd been taking note of.

"Why, to help with the placement of the orphans."

"But what about your duties back in New York? Aren't you neglecting them?"

The cats joined them and he scooped up one of the black kittens and stroked its fur in slow, gentle movements that riveted her attention to his large hand. A hand that knew how to hold a baby. And how to run a ranch.

"I guess my father thought I was neglecting them already, so he suggested this trip might be just the thing to snap me out of my black mood, as he called it."

"What caused your mood?"

She continued to stare at his hand stroking the kitten. Each movement eased a tightness in her heart. Suddenly she wanted to tell him about Oliver. "I was about to be married."

His hand stilled. "You are?"

"Not any longer. Oliver, my former fiancé—" she'd never described him as that before and found the word freeing "—ran off with a seamstress five days before our wedding." She gave a laugh that lacked any sound of mirth.

His big, gentle hand left the kitten. She followed its path as it moved toward her cheek. She sighed as he cupped her jaw gently and lifted her face upward.

Her gaze caught his—green, steady, full of sympathy and promise. She swallowed once. Promise of what? She wished she knew the answer.

He returned the kitten to the others, then straightened and faced her, only inches separating them. He caught her hands and brought them to his chest. "This Oliver does not sound like much of a bargain."

She tried to nod. Tried to laugh. But although she found the truth of his words soothing, she could not get past the pain and humiliation of Oliver's rejection.

He pulled her close, pressed her to his chest, his big, warm hands on her back. "He had no right to hurt you like that."

She wanted to deny that she'd been hurt. Pretend it didn't matter. But she couldn't. Instead, she clung to him, shamelessly wrapping her arms about him. A steady, solid man. He eased her back enough to claim her mouth with his own.

She breathed in the scent of him. Wood and fire. Animals and flowers. Her surprise quickly gave way to awareness of his size. His strength. His gentleness in the way he offered a kiss but demanded nothing more.

Her pulse stuttered once, then jolted into a gallop.

She returned his kiss.

Oh, my. She understood that he only offered sympathy and understanding, but her heart took a whole lot more.

He was a man who knew what it meant to be faithful.

Not like Oliver.

He broke from their embrace, took her hand and led her back to the house.

Not until she crawled under the covers of her bed did she force her thoughts back to reality. He'd offered nothing more than the kiss. He'd only been swept up in concern about the pain Oliver had inflicted. She wasn't foolish enough to think otherwise.

Chapter Twelve

Colton couldn't help himself. He repeated the excuse over and over again as they prepared to go to town the next morning. He'd been so moved by the misery in her expression that he simply couldn't resist pulling her into his arms and kissing her. He wasn't surprised at his actions. He'd considered doing so more than once. What surprised him was that she hadn't slapped him and demanded he take her to town immediately.

She'd darted little glances at him over breakfast. He was at a loss to know if she was annoyed, angry or simply as confused as he was.

He knew they were worlds apart. A thirty-room mansion said it as clearly as anything. He didn't need his ma's reminder again this morning.

They said little as they drove to town. No need to with Heidi chattering away about her kitten.

He left them at Charlotte's, fully expecting Rebecca to show up at the orphanage within an hour. When she didn't, he told himself he was to blame.

He heard footsteps behind him and relief surged through him. Barely able to contain the grin curving his lips, he turned about.

Pauline and Curtis stood before him.

And at that moment, Rebecca joined them.

"We've called an emergency meeting tonight to discuss the orphanage," Pauline said, sounding put out.

"What is left to discuss?" Rebecca asked, keeping her voice equally expressionless.

Colton wondered how much effort it required for her to speak so calmly and disguise her emotions so completely.

"Miss Ward has some concerns, some suggestions. She's asked to present them to the town. I can't refuse a legitimate request. I'm sorry."

Neither Colton nor Rebecca uttered a word as the pair marched away.

Only when they were out of sight did he turn around. He saw nothing but determination in Rebecca's gaze and swallowed his disappointment. What did he expect? That she would mention his kiss and say she'd enjoyed it? He needed to loosen his hat if he thought that would happen.

"What can Miss Ward do?" she said, sounding worried.

"I suspect that she can only make a lot of noise."

His words did nothing to calm her. "I need to talk to Holly about this." She hustled away.

He didn't see her again until he picked her up to return home.

After supper, he announced, "Ma, Pa, there's a meeting in town about the orphanage. I'm going back to it. Rebecca needs to be there. We'll take the children."

Heidi sighed.

Pa looked at the girl. "Why not leave Heidi here? She's a handy little thing."

Heidi perked up. "Can I stay? I'll bring them coffee or water or whatever they need."

"Sounds like a good idea." He'd feel better knowing she was here. "Rebecca, what do you think?"

"She's very good at being helpful."

"I am." Heidi bounced to her feet and began to gather up the dishes.

Rebecca followed suit.

"Now, wait a minute." Colton held up a hand, stopping the frantic activity. "Heidi, you can help me, but, Rebecca, you made the meal. So I'll do the dishes." He felt Ma frowning at him, but he ignored her.

And Rebecca ignored him. "Nonsense. You were doing chores. We'll clean up."

"Miss Rebecca Sterling, I have never encountered anyone so determined to argue with everything as you."

Pa chuckled. "You should have seen your ma when she was young and fiery."

"I never was."

"Oh, yes, you were. Remember the time I wanted to give you a ride home from the church social? You said you'd walk, thank you very much, and marched on ahead. I followed in the buggy all the way and you wouldn't change your mind."

Ma fluttered her hand. "You were a brash cowboy, too full of yourself for your own good."

"And you were a spunky young thing, too proud to admit you liked me." The way he looked at Ma, Colton knew he'd forgotten the rest of them. "I soon changed your mind."

"I let you think so."

Pa laughed. "Still got the spunk."

Colton turned his attention to washing dishes. Spunk. Ted had said Rebecca had spunk. Not that Colton needed the man to point it out. But Ma and Pa's circumstances were different. They had both grown up in a rural community and both were free to follow their hearts.

He, Colton Hayes, was not free, even if everything else about his and Rebecca's situation was favorable.

"You trying to scrub off the pattern?" Rebecca took a plate from his hand and dried it.

"Just getting it clean," he murmured. Just trying to keep his thoughts straight when all he could think of was the woman standing next to him.

When they finished the dishes, Rebecca prepared Gabriel for the trip and then they returned to town.

Rebecca was very quiet. He could feel her tension.

"I'm sure wisdom will prevail," he said.

"I'm praying it will."

"Me, too." He uttered another silent prayer.

The meeting was at the town hall. As they stepped inside, he saw a large crowd already there and cradled Rebecca's elbow to guide her to a seat, with Gabriel in her arms.

She leaned over to whisper in his ear, "I hope some of these people support the orphanage—otherwise, we'll have a huge fight on our hands."

Her breath tickled his cheek and distracted him until he couldn't think.

"Are you worried?" she asked when he didn't respond.

He jerked his attention back to the crowd and looked around, then whispered to her, "I know what a lot of them think, but there's a goodly number I can't speak for."

She jerked around, her eyes wide and dark in the low lamplight. "Do you suppose Miss Ward has been recruiting supporters?"

"It's possible."

Pauline stood at the front. "The meeting will come to order." Curtis and Beatrice sat at the head table with her. Colton thought Beatrice looked vengeful and victorious at the same time, and his spine tightened.

Pauline explained that there were concerns about the building currently being constructed for use as an orphanage. "I'll let Beatrice explain what she has in mind."

Miss Ward rose. She cleared her throat and smiled around the room.

Colton noticed that when her gaze reached Rebecca, the smile turned malicious. He squeezed his fists as his heart burned with a desire to protect the woman at his side.

"Ladies and gentlemen," Beatrice began, "we suffered a dreadful disaster when the dam broke and flooded our town months ago. But I think we've overlooked the opportunity this disaster has presented."

There came a rumble of protests from those whose businesses and homes had been destroyed.

"I'm not making light of the damage done. My own home was also damaged, as you all know. But now we can take stock and decide what we want our town to be. Do we want it to be a shack town, with buildings hastily constructed, or do we want to turn this disaster into something good? This is our chance to bring in rules about construction. Rules stating that public buildings have to have character. Houses close to the town center have to meet certain standards. People, this is our chance to make our town noteworthy." She went on to describe columns on buildings that spoke of power and majesty. Decorative trim on windows and rooflines. Buildings of brick and mortar that stood the test of time.

Colton wondered if she'd ever finish.

"In conclusion," she said, "I beg you to consider making the most of this opportunity. Thank you." She sat down, as smug as a queen on her throne.

Colton stared around the room. The woman had given a speech that sounded so reasonable, so right, that many nodded.

Rebecca grabbed his hand and hung on. He turned his palm to hers and squeezed encouragement.

She leaned over to whisper, "She makes this sound like it's about making Evans Grove a better place, but really, it's about stopping construction on the orphanage."

He nodded. "Let's wait to see what people say."

Mr. Murdo, who had rebuilt his feed store since the flood, stood. "Ma'am?"

Pauline signaled for him to speak.

"I can't afford to make my business fancy. I had to take out a loan to get it back into production as it was. I'm sure there are those in similar circumstances."

Pauline nodded. "Duly noted."

Several others spoke, some in agreement, others not seeing how Miss Ward's concerns were practical.

"May I speak again?" Beatrice rose when Pauline recognized her. "I would suggest a compromise. Those who already had construction completed would be exempt from any changes, but any new construction must meet whatever requirements we decide upon." She looked at Rebecca, her eyes narrow and mean.

At that point Colton knew for certain her plan was simply to stop the orphanage. Still, he held his peace, waiting for others to speak.

Ted Lang rose. "What you are suggesting is to stop construction on the orphanage. Is that correct?"

Colton squeezed Rebecca's hand to signal his appreciation of Ted's directness.

Pauline turned to Beatrice. "I think you should answer that."

Colton thought Pauline sounded weary of this discussion. He knew her opinion. She favored the orphanage. Her only concern was in discovering who had supplied the funds.

This time Beatrice did not stand. "As it is now, the orphanage will not be an asset to our town. It will not add anything in the way of beauty or stature."

An uproar ensued and Pauline banged her gavel to regain order.

Holly rose. "Miss Ward has been against the orphanage and the orphans from the beginning. This is nothing more than another attempt to exclude them from our community. I object to that. I doubt any of you are going to follow a plan for new construction should the town have one. How many are prepared to spend massive amounts on fancy buildings?"

A murmur of agreement rippled through the crowd.

The discussion raged until Curtis leaned over, gently touched the back of Pauline's hand and spoke to her.

Colton took note of the touch, the way their gazes held each other. Humph. He was only seeing everyone through his own confused emotions. Pauline and Curtis had been at odds since the beginning.

Curtis rose. "I've asked permission to speak. Miss Ward—" he tipped his head toward the woman "—you make some valid points. Certainly buildings should be up to a certain standard. Not ramshackle or firetraps."

Miss Ward fairly preened.

"However—" he turned back to the audience "—it is not fine, impressive buildings that make a town noteworthy. In my opinion, it is a welcoming attitude. A community of people caring about the good of all. If you don't have that, beautiful buildings aren't going to make the town appealing. But if you do, even simple buildings will be regarded with fondness if they're solidly constructed and well maintained. From what I've seen of Evans Grove, you have a community spirit to be proud of. Don't lose sight of that."

He sat down, and Pauline gave him a look of approval.

Colton wondered if there was more to the look than appreciation for his words about the town.

Pauline turned to the audience. "I think we've heard from every point of view. It's time to vote. Those in favor of continuing with the orphanage and putting aside creating rules for new construction, raise your hands."

Rebecca squeezed Colton's hand so hard his fingers would be numb when she released him.

Almost all those in attendance raised their hands.

"Opposed?"

Miss Ward shot her hand into the air. Colton counted only five others who sided with her,

"Majority rules," Pauline said. "Continued construction on the orphanage is approved." She sighed. "If anyone wishes to pursue some kind of building standard for the future, you're welcome to present a formal plan to the town. Meeting adjourned." She banged the gavel and rose.

Curtis took Pauline's arm and escorted her out of the building.

Rebecca sighed so deeply that Colton knew she'd held her breath for a long time. She grinned at Colton. "She didn't stop us."

"She's only one person."

He took the baby, tucked Rebecca's arm through his and they began their exit from the room. It took them a long time to reach the door, as person after person stopped them to say they were in favor of the orphanage. Why, then, hadn't more of them shown up to help with the construction? Again, he wondered if they'd been put off by Beatrice's campaign or were simply consumed with their own concerns.

Rebecca's face glowed by the time they made it to the buggy. "I never knew people could be so supportive."

"Like Curtis said, it's what gives a community strength. People caring about the good of others as much as they care about themselves."

He helped her into the buggy and handed her Gabriel. The little guy squirmed and snuffled. He'd soon need to be fed again.

As they drove home, he thought of how he'd described *community*. The same words could also describe *family*. Taking care of others, thinking of their needs. In his case, that meant taking care of his parents.

He would never regret his responsibilities, even if they left no room for anything else.

The next day was Saturday. The morning dawned clear and bright. Rebecca stretched and sighed. Her arms no longer hurt enough to make her teeth ache. And she quickly discovered she could feel quite normal while missing most of every second night's sleep to care for Gabriel.

She had Colton to thank for that, though she could do without him pointing out at every opportunity that they'd agreed to share duties. She had grown to hate that word. *Duty.* A cold, unfeeling word. Why not say they were working together for the good of others, like a community? Or out of—

The right word stalled in her mind. She could not think it. Could not dream it. *Love.* Love had no place in their relationship, though two nights ago, as he had kissed her, she had allowed herself for one moment to think it was possible. He hadn't even mentioned it. That was how important it had been to him.

She'd received a letter from her father, saying she should get on the train and return to New York and her duties there. *Duty.* There was that word again. But New York was where she belonged.

She knew it. Accepted it. But her heart ached with an unknown pain. What was it she wanted?

Against her wishes, her gaze darted to Colton as he drove the buggy into town. They belonged in different worlds. He knew it. She knew it. His mother made it clear every chance she got, warning her that Colton had his hands full caring for them. It was his duty. And, lest Rebecca not consider that enough reason, his mother never let Rebecca forget that she was a rich, city girl who would never fit into the rural community.

A deep sorrow filled her from beginning to end. Despite

it, she managed to smile at something Heidi said as they took the children to stay with Charlotte.

In their brief visit, she noticed that Charlotte laughed for no reason.

"You seem all excited. What's going on?"

Charlotte ducked her head. "I'm in love with life."

Rebecca shook her head and tried to look shocked, but her friend did have a new husband and daughter. "I'm glad for you."

Once the children were settled, she let Colton hand her back into the buggy. He did it often, and each time she informed herself that the gesture was simple courtesy. Nothing more. Her heart refused to listen and skittered against her ribs each time his strong, warm hand touched hers. She tried and failed to convince herself that he didn't hold her grasp a second or two longer than good manners required. She gave him a smile and murmured her thanks. The way his eyes lingered jolted through her.

She settled herself and forced her foolishness into submission.

Then the orphanage came into view and she forgot her own concerns. Wagons filled the street. Ladders had been positioned against the walls and men stood on each one.

"It's a beehive of activity." Her words were filled with awe.

Half a dozen men rushed forward to greet them.

"We're having a work bee," Ted Lang said. "Time to get this place closed in."

"There are so many people here." She couldn't believe it.

"Time the community got behind the work." Ted moved away, speaking to the men, pointing one place and another, organizing the tasks.

Rebecca reached for a hammer.

Colton opened his mouth. She knew from the look on

his face that he meant to tell her to put it down and join the women gathered in clusters under the trees.

She spoke first. "It's my responsibility."

"You aren't going up on a ladder." The walls had reached a point that required their use. He sounded ready to do battle right here before the whole community.

He was only being stubborn, but she rather enjoyed the idea that he might want to protect her. So she smiled. "I'm sure I can do something from the ground."

"Very well."

She followed him to the bottom of a ladder. "Can I hand things up to you?"

He considered her until her cheeks warmed. Then he sighed. "You could get me some nails." He handed her a leather pouch.

She trotted over and filled it. As she handed it to him, her heart again reacted to the brush of his fingers and she stepped back so quickly she jostled Ted.

He steadied her. "Careful there."

She laughed and hoped no one else thought it high-pitched. "Thank you."

Colton had scrambled up the ladder and now nailed in place his end of a board.

"How can I help?" she asked Ted.

He looked around. "You could gather up the bits and pieces of wood before someone falls on them, and stack them over there."

She hurried to follow his bidding even before he finished speaking.

The stack of scraps grew as the morning passed.

Men stopped to speak to her as she scurried about, assuring her that they were behind this project. More and more she felt she was part of the venture, not simply in charge of the anonymous funds. She paused a second to consider why the money had been sent to her. Was it simply because it seemed a natural extension of her role as the agent for the orphans? But who would have chosen her?

She dropped a handful of scraps and pivoted right into a very broad chest. "Umph." She knew that chest. Just as she knew the scent of this man. She jerked back, but only a few inches, as Colton's hands caught her shoulders.

"Slow down, Rebecca. It makes me tired just watching you hustle about so."

She tried to believe he meant to scold her, but his husky words felt like a blessing, and she couldn't keep herself from smiling widely as she looked up at him. "I'm enjoying myself too much to slow down."

"What exactly are you enjoying?" He slid his hands off her arms and stepped back, leaving her alone and cold.

She considered her answer. Suddenly she knew exactly what she felt—apart from foolish awareness of this big, handsome cowboy. "Community. I've never seen this kind of thing before." She waved to indicate the men working on the building. "I thought I had to prove I could do this on my own. It was a scary thought. But having the community work with me is a wonderful feeling."

"Like you belong?" He spoke softly, the words grave.

Belong? Was it possible? She knew it wasn't. "I belong back in New York. My father is expecting me." He would not approve of her abandoning the life for which he and Mother had groomed her.

Colton's eyes turned hard. His jaw clenched and he wheeled about and climbed a ladder without so much as a backward glance in her direction.

She returned to her task. What did he expect her to say?

Women from town began to gather. Long trestle tables were erected. Charlotte came with the children.

Heidi hung back, her head lowered so her hair hid her face.

Rebecca's throat tightened. This was such a marked contrast to the happy, confident child she saw at the ranch. She turned to Colton. He looked sad and thoughtful.

Charlotte hurried to Rebecca's side. "If you take Gabriel, I'll help set out the meal."

Colton jogged to her side. "Let's show him around. Maybe someone will say something that gives us a clue as to who his mother is."

They strolled over to the growing crowd. Dishes of food covered a table, filling the air with the smells of fried chicken, apple pie and beans. Rebecca's mouth flooded with saliva. Would she ever learn to cook something like this—something she'd be proud to bring to a community dinner?

"It looks like everyone is here," she murmured, though, thankfully, she had not seen Miss Ward yet. Children raced about laughing as they played tag. No one seemed to mind the noise.

"Who would want to miss a community picnic?"

They reached the first cluster of women.

"So this is the baby someone left on the doorstep," one woman said as she peered at Gabriel.

"He's very sweet."

Another said, "Tsk, I can't imagine what sort of woman would abandon her baby."

Others said the mother must have had a good reason.

Rebecca and Colton moved through the group, but no one seemed to know of a woman who might be Gabriel's mother.

Pauline and Curtis approached, the latter carrying a steaming pot. Before they reached the others, he said something to Pauline that made the woman smile and give him a look Rebecca could only describe as adoring. She studied the pair as they approached. Was there something romantic going on between them?

Charlotte and Sasha joined Rebecca and Colton. Heidi

took Sasha's hand and led her away. The children sat by themselves under a tree and played.

Charlotte watched. "Heidi is so good with younger children. It's a shame adults can't see past her scars."

Rebecca nodded. "I wish Heidi could forget she had them. Any word from Wyatt?"

"He wired Sheriff Mason to say he'd located some children at a mine in Colorado and was arranging for their release."

"That's good news. Any reports on Jakob?" He was always so protective of Heidi. Rebecca and several others assumed that when Jakob ran away, it was because he wanted to find his sister. Wyatt had even reported seeing a boy who matched Jakob's description in Greenville, asking about the orphans. The lad had bolted before Wyatt could find out his name. If it *had* been Jakob, then he must have learned that Heidi was in Evans Grove. Rebecca hoped he would show up soon.

"Nothing certain." She squeezed Rebecca's arm. "I'm sorry. I know you're anxious to locate him."

The doctor strode over. Rebecca had met him earlier. A man in his forties with jet-black hair and snapping black eyes. Ezra Simpson struck her as a no-nonsense man. "Colton, can we talk a moment?"

"What is it?"

"How is your mother?"

Rebecca listened shamelessly.

"She's often short of breath and her legs swell badly. She doesn't have a lot of energy."

"I'd like to visit her. I've learned of something that might ease her symptoms."

"I'm sure Ma would welcome a visit."

"Fine." Dr. Simpson stepped past Colton and lifted the corner of the quilt to look at Gabriel. "He looks happy and healthy."

Rebecca nodded. "He is, though he cries at night."

The doctor chuckled. "Typical behavior. No word on his mother?"

"Nothing."

"I hope she's all right."

Rebecca nodded agreement.

Dr. Simpson patted the baby. "How fortunate that he is with people like you and the Hayeses. I couldn't hope for a better home for him." He nodded and moved on to another group.

Rebecca considered his words. He thought they provided a good home for the baby. And he'd included her. Did he not realize this was temporary? If they didn't locate the baby's parents, what would become of Gabriel? It was all she could do not to clutch the baby too tightly.

Reverend Turner stood on a bench. She hadn't noticed him in the crowd before. "People, if you quiet down I'll ask the blessing on this bounty. I know if the smells are making you as hungry as they are making me, you're ready to eat."

Mothers drew their children to their sides as the crowd quieted and men snatched off their hats. The preacher asked the blessing, then everyone lined up to file past the food tables.

Rebecca wondered how she would fill her plate while holding Gabriel, but she didn't have to wonder for long.

Colton picked up two plates. "I'll do this. Trust me. It's for your own good. I know who makes the best food. For instance, these are Pauline's beans and they are wonderful. Those—" he indicated another pot of beans "—are best not sampled." The sorrowful look he gave her tickled her funny bone and she giggled.

"I take it you speak from experience."

He nodded. "Sad and bitter experience."

She laughed again as he drew his mouth back in a grimace. As they continued down the table, she grew alarmed at how much food he was piling on her plate. "I can't possibly eat all that," she said, though the crispy fried chicken looked good enough to entice her to seconds.

"I thought you could share with Heidi." The child clung to Rebecca's side, an empty plate dangling from her hand.

At the sound of her name, she jerked her head up to stare at Colton. Her eyes were wide with distress.

He shot a questioning look at Rebecca, but she shook her head. She didn't know the particulars of what had upset Heidi, though she'd witnessed that look many times and it always twisted her insides.

They reached the end of the food table and Colton led them to a dining table. He sat at the end and put Heidi between himself and Rebecca, then leaned over to speak to her.

"Heidi, what's wrong?"

She hung her head. "Nothin'."

Colton's quick look at Rebecca revealed that the child's unhappiness hurt him as much as it did her. She wrapped an arm about the child's shoulders. So did Colton. His arm pressed hers. Her heart thumped hard against her chest and she sucked in a deep breath to calm it. This was about Heidi—not Rebecca's foolish thoughts, her hopes and dreams and useless wishes.

Colton bent again. "I know something is wrong because you're hiding again and I've gotten used to seeing your lovely smile."

Heidi shook her head. "I don't have a nice smile. I'm ugly."

Colton's jaw tightened so much Rebecca feared for his teeth. "Really? Who says you're ugly?"

"A boy." Her words were barely a whisper.

Colton stared around the crowd. Rebecca did, too. Who was the guilty party? She glanced at Colton. The look in his eyes was hot enough to fry bacon.

She tried to smile, hoping to calm him. But failed. Most

likely, her eyes revealed the same emotion. This child did not deserve to be the target of such meanness.

Colton turned back to Heidi. "Honey, remember what I said about ugly. People who are unkind are ugly on the inside and outside. You aren't." He tipped her chin upward and smiled at her then kissed the tip of her nose. "You are beautiful and sweet."

Rebecca's throat clogged at the tenderness. This was the kind of love Heidi deserved. She deserved to have parents who loved her as Colton and Rebecca did. She deserved to have Colton and Rebecca themselves as her parents.

She jerked her attention away from the Colton and Heidi.

She knew her father would find the idea utterly unacceptable. He had specifically sent Rebecca on this trip so she would get over her moping and return to resume her place in New York society.

"Miss Sterling."

She turned toward Reverend Turner.

"The community wants to thank you for cooperating with us in placing the orphans here. Those who have taken a child are pleased with the way things are going."

Several couples nodded.

"It is I who should thank you."

"Everyone needs to hear it." He helped her to her feet. "Ladies and gentlemen, Miss Sterling has something she'd like to say."

Every pair of eyes turned her way. She looked around the crowd. These were good people who worked together, who took care of each other and helped those in need. "I want to thank you all for being so welcoming—both toward the children I brought from New York, and toward the children I hope will arrive soon, the children this orphanage is being built to serve. Charlotte tells me Wyatt has located some of the children that were put out to work." She didn't say *as slaves,* though that was what had happened. "They will soon be here. It will be good if the home is finished by the time they arrive. That wouldn't be possible without all of your help."

Ted held up a hand. "We'll do our best, Miss."

"I know you will." The man had proven to be a diligent worker.

The preacher addressed her again. "Miss Sterling, have you given any thought to who will run the orphanage when you leave?"

Every pair of adult eyes studied her, awaiting her answer.

Her veins burned with the shock. They all expected her to leave. It was a foregone conclusion. She forced an answer from her tight throat. "I'm sure Pauline and the placement committee will take care of that."

And she sat down before her legs buckled beneath her.

The food smelled heavy and greasy. Too much fried chicken. The clang of cutlery as the women gathered up the dirty dishes rang like a hammer against the inside of her head.

She was not part of this community.

Colton touched her shoulder. "It's time to get back to work."

"You go ahead. I'll tend to Gabriel."

"Rebecca, are you okay?"

She straightened her spine, grateful for the many lessons she'd had in disguising her emotions. "Of course. But Gabriel needs feeding."

The men moved away. Hammers and saws provided a background noise to the women washing the dishes.

Rebecca and a few other women tended babies. She welcomed the warmth and comfort of Gabriel's small body in her arms. But her insides were as icy as a November storm.

Beside her, Pauline sat down. "Do you mind if I join you?"

"Of course not." She sensed this was more than a social visit and waited for the older woman to speak.

"You haven't had any more correspondence or contact with our donor, have you?"

Rebecca managed a regretful smile. "No. I'm sorry." The woman seemed determined to discover the source of the money.

"I see. Now, don't you worry about finding someone to oversee the orphanage. The committee will arrange that."

"I expected as much." Good training be thanked for her calm words.

"However, we need to discuss what will happen to this baby when you leave."

Rebecca thought her throat would bleed from holding back a groan. Were they so anxious for her to leave that they conspired to remind her at every opportunity? She had to snap out of this self-pitying state and consider what was best for Gabriel and Heidi. With far more calmness than she felt, she answered, "I'd suggest a foster home for Gabriel." She studied the cluster of women. "Maybe Charlotte. She's always wanted many children. If she took Heidi, too, she'd have help with the baby and Sasha."

How could she turn the children and the orphanage over to someone else and walk away? But what was wrong with her to even question the decision? That had been the plan from the beginning. She set out with a job thrust upon her by her father. She had vowed to prove she could do something useful—and she had succeeded. Now she could return to New York with her head held high.

Only, the thought of returning now felt as unappealing as this trip had in the beginning.

She studied the orphanage. Found what she sought. Colton. Their gazes met across the distance. Her heart beat out a plea.

He smiled—a slow, sweet, powerful smile that deepened

her sadness and emptied her heart. The hollowness echoed with two words.

She tried not to hear the words, but they rattled against her ears.

If only... If only... If only...

The afternoon passed in slow, painful minutes. Only one thing eased her distress and that was seeing the walls nearing completion.

The women served a hurried afternoon tea.

Ted didn't even bother to sit down to drink his. "Everyone wants to finish up before supper so they can take their little ones home and prepare for Sunday." He thanked the ladies for the cookies and tea and strode back to the building. The men followed him.

Colton paused only long enough to ask Rebecca if Heidi was okay.

"She's playing with Sasha." Rebecca had watched her closely all afternoon to make sure no one else teased her.

Two hours later the men gathered up their tools and took their families home.

In a few minutes, only Colton, Rebecca, Mason, Holly and the children remained. The adults studied the orphanage, its shell now completed.

"Many hands make light work," Holly said.

"It looks lovely." Rebecca knew her voice lacked enthusiasm and Colton picked up on it immediately.

"But what?"

"I'm wondering how long it will take to finish the inside."

Colton turned to Mason. "How long until the children arrive?"

Mason's face reflected his worries. "Wyatt has met with some challenges. The mine owner insists he has an ironclad agreement. He's asked a judge to verify his claim."

Rebecca grabbed Colton's arm without thinking, and once

she realized what she'd done, she could not let go. "You mean the children are still forced into labor?"

"Wyatt says he's badly outnumbered or he'd kidnap the lot of them."

"I trust there won't be a very long delay," Rebecca said. "I will pray to that end. But we need to be ready when they arrive."

Colton cupped his hand over hers as it clutched his arm. "If today is any indication, we can count on the community to help."

She set aside every other emotion and allowed herself nothing but gratitude. "They really pulled together. I am amazed at how much they accomplished in one day."

"There is definitely strength in numbers," Holly said, then turned to Mason. "We need to get Liam home and scrub off the dirt."

They departed and Colton went to get the buggy for Rebecca and the children.

She stared at the orphanage. It would soon be finished. It was time to set aside her private, foolish desires.

She had accomplished what she had set out to do. Even Heidi's future would be secure if Charlotte and Wyatt agreed to take her. She was pleased with her success.

She could not allow her inner pain to interfere with doing her duty.

Chapter Thirteen

The next morning, Colton rose with his heart alive with anticipation and anxiety. He felt that he and Rebecca had drawn closer during the work bee, shared a common concern for Heidi's future. He hoped it might be enough to convince her to stay. Maybe they could work something out. But everything he considered ran into a dead end. Too many things conspired to keep them apart.

Both Heidi and Rebecca emerged from their room with swollen eyes. Rebecca refused to meet his gaze and Heidi kept her head down.

Ma and Pa exchanged troubled looks.

"Heidi, my dear," Pa said, "what's troubling you?"

Heidi's shoulders rose and fell. "Can I bring Happy in?"

"We have to leave for church soon," Pa answered. "But yes, you'll have time to visit for a few minutes."

Pa waited until Heidi left to ask Rebecca, "What's happened to our little ray of sunshine?"

"She cried out for Jakob in the night. She misses her brother."

"Poor child," Ma murmured. "She has every right to feel sorry for herself, and yet, for the most part, she seems to love to help others."

Everyone was quiet and watchful as Heidi returned.

Pa pulled the stool close to his rocker and Heidi sat there, quiet as she clutched the kitten to her face. The kitten licked her cheek and Heidi laughed, though she sounded close to tears.

Colton looked at Rebecca, certain he saw the same sorrow and regret he felt. This child deserved a loving home. As did Gabriel.

He planned to see that they both got that.

"Time to take the kitten back to its mama." Pa spoke gently, as if he hated to end the peaceful moment.

They left for church soon afterward. Folks were in a joyous mood after a successful Saturday. Everyone except Heidi, who clung to Rebecca.

Reverend Turner's text came from James, Chapter 1, Verse 27. "True religion is this—'to visit the fatherless and widows in their affliction.'"

Miss Ward, in her customary spot in the second pew, could be heard to sniff all the way to the back of the church, but Reverend Turner paid her no mind and continued, exhorting the congregation to apply the words of scripture at every opportunity. "Sheriff Mason tells me Wyatt Reed will soon be returning with orphans. We need to have the building ready. Agreed?"

A murmur of consent rippled across the congregation.

"Let us dedicate ourselves to the work." The reverend gave the benediction and closed the service.

It took a few minutes for them to leave the sanctuary as so many wanted to talk to Rebecca and thank her for the work she'd done. Others stopped Ma and Pa to ask after their health.

Dr. Simpson approached Ma. "Mrs. Hayes, I'd like to pay you a visit, if I may. I think I might be able to help you."

Colton half expected her to refuse. More than once she'd

said she didn't want to try any more dubious remedies. But Dr. Simpson waited, his gaze unblinking.

Ma finally agreed, "You'll find us home anytime."

In the buggy she said, "That man can be very persuasive without uttering a word."

Pa chuckled. "But if he has something that helps you, you'll be happy you agreed."

She took his hand. "I would be for sure."

Colton silently prayed Dr. Simpson could offer Ma relief. She'd suffered so many years...since his birth. And her suffering grew worse with the passing of time.

They returned home and had a dinner of sandwiches and milk. He wondered why everyone was so quiet. It made his nerves itch, as if he were waiting for a storm to burst.

Normally Ma and Pa rested after dinner. "Can I help you to bed?" he asked his father.

Pa shook his head. "Why don't you take Rebecca for a walk and leave Heidi with us for a few hours?"

He stared at one parent and the other, then at Rebecca, who shrugged to indicate that she had no idea why they'd made this request.

Ma nodded. "We have something special planned for her."

Heidi perked up. "For me? What is it?"

"Guess you'll have to wait and see."

Heidi shot Colton a look that hinted he should hurry up and leave. He laughed. He couldn't think of anything he'd like more than to take Rebecca out for a walk. Just the two of them. "What about Gabriel?"

Ma looked unconcerned. "He'll sleep for a bit. If he awakens, we can manage."

"Mother has done this before," Pa reminded him.

Colton laughed again. "Twenty-eight years ago."

"Some things you never forget." Ma hadn't been so confident about doing anything for such a long time that he could barely imagine her suggesting this.

"You're sure you can manage?"

Ma flapped her hands in a shooing motion.

Pa said, "Take Rebecca and go."

"Hurry up," Heidi added.

Colton wanted to cheer to the heavens. "We're going. Come on, Rebecca." He held the door open and bowed for her to exit.

"Where are we going?" She looked about eagerly.

Did it matter where they went or what they did? Not to him. "Would you like to walk?"

She tipped her head to the sky and breathed deeply. "A walk sounds lovely."

He took her hand, hoping she would think he needed to guide her. In reality, the path was level. He only wanted to hold her close. Cherish this moment. He led her to his favorite spot, the one he'd shown her the very first time they'd walked together. He knew of a natural bench on the hillside and they sat down side by side, their shoulders brushing, their fingers entwined. He let her drink her fill of the scenery while he drank in her nearness, the warmth of her shoulder against his, the feel of her fingers braided with his. They were long and shapely, the fingers of a refined woman.

He faltered. Was he foolish to think she could belong in his world? She felt as duty-bound to please her father as he felt to care for his. But in her case, he wasn't sure how far that duty went or exactly what it meant.

"It's so calm and peaceful here," she murmured. "Nobody rushing by or calling out."

"You mean it's noisy in New York?"

"It's busy."

Another blast of doubt attacked his confidence. But his idea made perfect sense. They could make this work.

"I hate to see Heidi so upset. She and Gabriel belong here."

She didn't answer, so he rushed on.

"Gabriel is somehow connected to the family and needs a real home. So does Heidi."

She nodded. "Pauline and I discussed asking Charlotte to take them. We'd have to wait for Wyatt to return so they can discuss it."

He jolted so hard that she mistook it for withdrawal and pulled her hand to her lap.

"It makes perfect sense." She rushed on as if she had to convince him of the wisdom of the idea. "Charlotte has always wanted a large family and Heidi is very good with babies. She'll be a great help."

Stunned, he fought to find an argument or rather to shepherd the many he had into something convincing. "That's an awful lot to ask of newlyweds, isn't it? Sasha, Gabriel and Heidi."

She faced him, her expression determined. "But wouldn't it be ideal?"

"No." He sprang to his feet. "No."

The enthusiasm fled from her face. She pressed her lips into a tight line, then forced her mouth open. "Then what do you suggest?"

"You could stay at Evans Grove and keep them." It wasn't what he'd wanted to say, but the persuasive words refused to come.

"It seems that if I stayed it would make sense for me to oversee the orphanage."

No. Not that. Why couldn't he say what he felt? "Do you want to stay?"

She looked into the distance, her mouth tense, her fists curled in her lap. Finally, with a little sigh, she shook her head. "My father would not allow it."

"And you must do what your father says?" His voice sounded harsh, critical, even to himself.

She rose and faced him, a good six feet between them. "I thought you'd understand. Don't you live by the fifth commandment, to honor your father and mother? Can I do any less?"

He couldn't face her. Or was it his guilt he couldn't face? "It's different for me. I owe it to them to care for them as long as they need." His voice fell to a rumble. "It's my fault Pa's crippled."

"Your fault? What do you mean?"

He stepped away a half a dozen strides and stared at the distant horizon, then spun about on his heel and returned to watch her face as he told his story.

She held his gaze steadily, revealing neither shock nor disbelief. For the first time, he was grateful that she could so expertly hide her feelings.

"I knew better. I let my emotions affect my behavior. Make me stupid." And he was about to risk doing it again. "When I said you should stay, I didn't mean in town or at the orphanage."

Her eyebrows rose. "Then what did you mean?"

"I meant stay here. At the ranch. We could care for the children together."

She stared, her mouth a little O.

He'd expected a little more enthusiasm for what he considered an excellent idea.

"Rebecca, say something."

"Why would you want that?"

He thought he'd already explained his reasons. "Isn't it working well?"

She took two steps backward and shifted her gaze to something behind him. "I can't stay. My father needs me. It's my duty." She turned and fled.

It was a good thing he hadn't asked her to marry him. It was what he'd wanted to do from the beginning, but he was too cowardly to ask. And now he could see that asking her would have been a waste of breath. She had no intention of staying.

He strode after her as she burst into the kitchen. The door would have slammed in his face except he caught it before it could. "Is everyone okay?" Her breathless words indicated that she'd beaten a hasty retreat.

Ma held Gabriel, feeding him. Heidi sat on the stool at Pa's knees. For a moment he thought she held another baby then realized it was a doll wrapped in a tiny blanket.

"Your mama gave me a doll," Heidi told Colton, her eyes gleaming with pleasure. "And this nice blanket she knitted." She pressed the red-and-white blanket to her cheek, then turned her attention back to the doll.

"It was mine when I was a girl," Ma said. "I'd hoped to give it to a daughter, but seeing as I never had one, I want Heidi to have it."

"It's like a real baby." Heidi placed the doll on the table and unwrapped it, pulled off a white flannel nightgown to reveal a body made of white muslin. The head, made of the same material, had features embroidered on it and hair of black yarn.

"Mrs. Hayes, it looks like a very special doll," Rebecca said, a note of surprise in her voice.

"My mother made it for me. And now I want Heidi to have it. A special doll for a special girl."

Heidi re-dressed the doll, wrapped it in the little blanket and clutched it to her chest.

Colton looked at Rebecca. She looked everywhere but at him. He waited. Finally, she jerked her gaze to him. He regarded her with unblinking intensity, tipping his head toward the happy child. *Do you see her?* He silently demanded. *She's so open and free here. She trusts Ma and Pa, and they're so fond of her.*

Why would you rob her of this?

Rebecca's granite expression slid by him without softening.

Rebecca could not think of Colton's suggestion that she should stay and take care of the children. Most of all she could not abide the accusation in his eyes at her refusal. He seemed to be saying that she was being selfish and hardhearted.

She turned to his mother. "Do you want me to finish feeding Gabriel?" Her heart filled with gratitude when the woman allowed her to take the baby. If she hadn't, Rebecca would have rushed from the room. Hidden in the bedroom.

She settled on the cot beside Mrs. Hayes and watched little Gabriel drink his milk. The little guy focused on her, his eyes full of innocent wisdom. As if he knew he was in safe hands.

The baby deserved a home.

But she couldn't stay simply to provide security for Heidi and Gabriel. She glanced from one child to the other. Not that she didn't see the benefits. Not even that she didn't want to.

She rocked Gabriel, the motion an attempt to ease her inner turmoil.

What did she want?

She couldn't allow herself to answer the question. Instead she asked a more important one.

What did God want of her?

Honor her father. That was one of the commandments. Not an option. Her duty.

She couldn't remain in Nebraska, even if her heart cried out to belong here, to be part of the community. Besides her father's disapproval, the community clearly did not see her as a one of them.

Her heart cracked open to reveal the truth she'd tried so hard to deny.

What she really wanted was to belong in this home. In Colton's heart. Not as a caregiver for the children, but as the recipient of his love.

He had not offered that.

She wiped tears from Gabriel's cheeks and realized the tears were her own. She secretly swabbed at her eyes and forced the tears to stop.

The minutes dragged by. She was saved from deep depression only by Heidi's joy over the doll.

Finally, Colton, who had been reading the weekly news, folded the paper. "I'd better see to the chores. Anyone want to come see the kittens?"

Heidi bounced to her feet. "I do." She took the doll to Mrs. Hayes. "Would you hold Dolly for me?"

Mrs. Hayes took the toy. "Dolly? Is that what you named her?"

Heidi stood before the woman, a worried look on her face. "Before the fire—" she touched her cheek to indicate the fire she meant "—I had a doll my mama gave me. I named her Dolly." She rocked back and forth. "I hope you don't mind if I use the same name."

Mrs. Hayes patted Heidi's shoulder. "I don't mind at all."

Heidi's face cleared and she beamed. "Good." She went to Rebecca and whispered, "I didn't know if it's okay to remember my mama and papa."

Rebecca hugged the little girl. "Of course it's okay." Her heart cracked deeper. She loved this child who showed everyone the true meaning of courage and joy.

Heidi trotted over to join Colton, took his hand and they left the house.

* * *

Rebecca escaped the kitchen as soon as she could that night, pleading tiredness. The excuse was true. Her limbs were so heavy she could barely carry the baby. Her heart ached clear to her toes. She was too tired to even write her father. And he expected to hear from her on a regular basis.

The next morning, fatigue hung over her like a shawl as she faced the new day. Before she left the room, she knelt by the bed. *Please, God, give me the strength to do what I must.* And self-control that would let her work at Colton's side without revealing anything of her errant emotions. *And please, God, help us get the building done in time for the children who are coming.*

The ride to town was full of silent disappointment that what she wanted was so far from what was offered. But as they drove toward the orphanage after leaving the children with Charlotte, she sat up straight, her distress forgotten. Two wagons and half a dozen horses stood in front of the orphanage. Ted saw them approaching and waved a greeting.

"Looks like another work bee," Colton said. "Not a community-size one, though." He stopped the wagon and helped her down.

At his touch, awareness swirled through her heart. She sucked in a deep breath to still the jolt of longing and held her inhalation until he released her. As soon as he did, she hurried to the building, hoping he would think she was anxious to view the work when she really wanted to outrun her feelings.

He followed so closely on her heels that she couldn't still her inner turmoil.

Ted joined them. "We have several men with us today who are experienced carpenters." He introduced them. "And Mort and his sons can plaster so fast it will make you dizzy. Miss, we'll have this place ready in record time. Won't we, men?"

Everyone called out a loud "Yes."

"Thank you all." Rebecca's heart grew still. She looked around the building. She'd come to Evans Grove as an OSS agent. She'd placed all the children save Heidi. She'd also been instrumental in seeing a home constructed for the Greenville orphans who would soon arrive. She'd accomplished something after all and had made her mark on this town, even if she couldn't stay.

She pushed up her sleeves. "What can I do?"

They allowed her to help. Other than stopping for dinner, they worked steadily throughout the day.

"We made good progress," Ted said as Rebecca and the men prepared to leave later in the afternoon.

She thanked the men again and let Colton help her into the buggy. "I can hardly believe how quickly it's going when a bunch of men work together." She rattled on about the final details as Colton stepped into the buggy and sat beside her. She continued to talk fast as they went to pick up the children. It kept her from being so aware of him at her side that she couldn't think straight. She must. Her heart, full of useless longings, could not be allowed to overrule her head. Her chatter continued until Heidi sat behind her and began to talk about her day.

When Colton asked Rebecca to go for a walk after supper, she almost refused, certain he would try to change her mind about his suggestion from the day before.

But she agreed to the walk, knowing that even if he tried, he wouldn't be able to alter her decision. Nothing could change the facts. No matter what she wanted or what he offered, she had to go home and do the job she'd been trained for. *You will be the hostess for your father. You will be a light in the social circles, organizing fund-raisers and taking over my many responsibilities.* Her mother's voice rang loud and clear in her mind.

He led the way out to the grassy place that seemed to be his favorite spot. "You see how happy Heidi is here."

Rebecca could be, too. But only if she was offered love. And she hadn't been. "My father expects me home." She couldn't stay here hiding the truth that filled her heart.

He shifted to hide his expression. "I understand your desire to do what your father wants. But I've been thinking about it. Is duty the same thing as honoring?"

His question surprised her. Did he mean to accuse her of wrongheaded motives? "Are you asking or telling?"

"Just wondering." He spoke softly, without a hint of accusation or harshness. Had she heard either one, she would have felt the need to defend herself. But his quiet demeanor left her floundering for answers.

She cleared her throat and brought the words to her mouth. "It's one way of honoring."

"One way? What are some others?"

"Well, certainly caring for them when they need it. As you do with your parents. Obeying them."

"When does obeying end?"

"Does it ever?"

He plucked a black-eyed Susan and offered it to her.

She took it absentmindedly.

"I don't know much about obeying." He sounded preoccupied. "My parents let me make my own decisions from a young age. They guided me with suggestions, but mostly I did what I thought was best, based on what I'd been taught or learned from experience."

She compared his sort of upbringing to the strict rules of conduct that had been drilled into her. "It's different out here. People are more accepting. More tolerant of differences."

"Maybe they are more willing to change. Try new things. They learn, as I did, to assess a situation and think for themselves."

She flicked the petals of the flower as she sorted out her reaction to his words. His voice remained low, but now carried a hint of challenge or criticism. Of her? For honoring her father? Doing her duty? She stared at him. "Are you suggesting that I am using my father as an excuse to avoid something? What?"

He shrugged, but his it-doesn't-matter gesture did not go with the glittering hardness in his eyes. "I don't know. Maybe it's easier to let someone else make the decisions. That way, if they don't work out, the person can lay the blame on the person who made that choice."

"Stop talking about some nonexistent person." He had no idea how difficult it often was to please her father, to live up to his expectations. "You're saying I let my father make my choices so I don't have to take responsibility for them."

She thought the warning note in her voice might be enough to stop him from going further, but he pretended not to notice.

"Let's take Oliver, for example. Your father's choice?"

She would not answer.

"Yes? Your trip out here? That was your father's decision."

Her eyes burned at the unfairness of this accusation. "My father arranged the trip, but I decided to embrace the task. I vowed I would see each child placed. And when the other orphans needed rescuing, I let the Society know and asked permission to remain in Evans Grove and see them settled."

"You did a fine job. So tell me this. Did you need your father's approval to take on the extra work? Did you consult him when you chose to come out to the ranch? I'm not trying to upset you, Rebecca. I only want you to decide your future based on what you want, what you need to do. What God is directing you to do. Something special that you alone can do. It wouldn't be dishonoring your father. In fact, I think it would mean becoming all that he and God know you can be."

He caught her hands and stopped their nervous fluttering.

"You have so much to offer this family, the community and especially Gabriel and Heidi. Your staying would make such a big difference to their lives. Think about it, won't you?"

Think about it? She couldn't stop picturing herself in the community. But could she belong here and not belong in his heart?

Chapter Fourteen

Over the next few days, Colton watched Rebecca closely, trying to assess her reaction to his comments. He'd worried she'd be angry. Accuse him of suggesting she break the fifth commandment.

Even more, he feared she'd simply say that leaving when the time came was her choice because she wanted to go. As the construction on the orphanage progressed, he feared the announcement of her departure more each day. He wanted to stop her, but he had no idea how. He had nothing on his side. He wanted to keep the children, but he had no claim to them except a desire to protect them and a growing love for them both. As he cared for Gabriel in the dark night hours, a bond was forged between his heart and the baby's. But he couldn't care for them on his own. Nor could his parents provide care, especially for the baby.

No, the best thing would be for Rebecca to stay.

Not just for the children's sake. For his, too, even if he had nothing to offer a rich, city girl.

As he considered her time with him, he realized that her life had revolved around work, either at the orphanage or at the ranch. How could he expect her to jump at his offer?

She was probably used to all sorts of outings and fine entertainment.

He had to show her the lighter side of life in rural Nebraska, and he knew just the thing.

But as the hours passed, she kept awfully busy and didn't give him a chance to bring up the subject. Either she was with one of the men working at the new building or sitting by Ma or discussing something with Pa.

But he wasn't about to give up.

Each morning they left the children with Charlotte. For a few minutes as they journeyed to the orphanage, they were alone.

Today, Thursday morning, he meant to ask Rebecca to accompany him on a special outing.

He barely waited until they left Holly's before he asked, "Do you like listening to music?"

"For the most part I do."

"Do you like opera?"

"It's not my favorite. I prefer classical or popular music." She shifted to consider him. "Why do you ask?"

A perfect opening. "There's a musical variety show in Newfield this Saturday. The program will present some of the best of New York and Chicago music. Performed by Miriam Strong, Michael Moorehead and company." He'd memorized the advertisement and hoped he got it right, giving his words just enough enthusiasm that she would interpret an interest on his part. Not that he didn't like music, but normally he wouldn't have considered going to Newfield to listen to someone sing.

"Miriam Strong? I heard good reviews of her work back in New York."

His chest lifted with pride. "Guess we aren't quite so backwoods as one might think."

She chuckled. "You've heard that term applied to your town?"

He realized that he hadn't. He only thought city people, especially rich, city people, might think so. "Did you think that when you came here?"

"Honestly? When I first got here, I was scrambling to make sense of life. The agent I was helping had been killed in a botched robbery. The children were frightened. I was suddenly in charge and not sure I could handle the responsibility. But I was comforted by strangers, the children were fed and settled, and I saw how everyone pulled together. I saw community at work. After that I never considered anything else."

Her evaluation made his chest swell. "There's nothing like people working together, helping each other."

They were almost at the orphanage and already Rebecca's attention had shifted to the place.

He pulled back on the reins until the buggy barely moved. "Would you like to hear the musical program in Newfield?"

She brought her gaze back to him. "I don't understand."

"Rebecca, would you do me the honor of letting me escort you to hear the musical program?"

Blue sky seemed to fill her eyes. "I'd love to hear the singers. Yes, I'll go with you."

It wasn't quite the answer he'd hoped for. She made it sound as if it was the singers who won her agreement. But he wouldn't let doubts deter him. Perhaps after the evening, when he'd had a chance to show her what fine company he could be, she'd forget the music and remember her escort.

The buggy jostled along the road to Newfield. Rebecca wore a pretty pink dress, a pink bonnet on her head, bringing out the color in her cheeks and filling him with sweet memories of summer days and summer skies. Golden curls caressed her cheeks. Every time she shifted to look at something, Colton savored the smell of rosewater.

"You're sure Charlotte didn't mind keeping the children for the evening?" she asked. "After all, we leave them there every day of the week. She might like some time without them."

"She was pleased to be asked. She told me the days were long without Wyatt." He didn't tell her what else Charlotte had said. That it was about time he did something special for Rebecca.

Charlotte had stood before him with Gabriel in her arms. "Rebecca has been a real trouper since the first day she came here. She deserves a little fun. You see that she gets it."

"Yes, ma'am."

He had rehearsed what to say to Rebecca on the journey—scintillating conversation to convince her that he was more than a cowboy, but now he couldn't remember one word, even though his mind overflowed with questions. He wanted to know more about her, but his wooden tongue refused to utter a word. He sat mute as the miles passed. A crow cawed mockingly, snapping him out of his inertia.

"I'm still trying to picture a house with thirty rooms. I thought Pa was extravagant building a house with seven rooms. And we don't use all of them." It was nothing like what he'd planned to say, but he couldn't help thinking that nothing anyone in Nebraska offered could hold a stick to a mansion in New York. "Must make our countryside look awfully primitive."

Her eyes flashed blue lightning. "Are you suggesting that I couldn't fit in anywhere but in a mansion in New York?"

He heard the warning note in her voice, but couldn't understand what it meant. "I don't know."

Her stubborn eyes met his confused ones. "I don't know who you are," he managed to squeak out.

She drew herself up tall, her shoulders square, her expression regal. "I'm the young woman who has been in your home for almost two weeks. The same one who arrived in town two months ago and saw to the placement of the remaining children. I've cared for Heidi and Gabriel. Indeed, I am the person who has worked side by side with you and the other men at the orphanage. I have hammered nails, sawed lumber, fetched and carried. I have made meals, washed diapers and a hundred other things. But now I'm a stranger?" Her voice trembled and she stared to the side.

"Rebecca." He reached for her hand. "I didn't mean it like that. I'm just overwhelmed at how different the life you're used to is from mine."

She didn't answer, and her hand lay lifeless in his.

"I planned this day to show you that Nebraska has culture and suitable entertainment to offer you and now I feel foolish."

Slowly, she brought her gaze to him. "Colton Hayes, you are a snob."

"I beg your pardon?"

"You are judging me by the size of a house miles away that you've never even seen. It's a house, Colton. Rooms with walls and windows and doors. And rooms that are often empty and lonely. Can you imagine wandering through a house and seeing no one but a maid in a uniform who won't even meet your eyes? Yet you think of me as privileged." She sighed.

"Are you saying you prefer the Hayes household, where you are never alone for more than a moment and people crowd into a modest sitting room?"

"Would you believe me if I said I did?" She shook her head. "Everyone has been clear since the beginning that I don't belong here, although I've tried my best to fit in. After the work bee, people were anxious to know when I was leaving. I thought—" She shrugged. "Never mind."

He pulled her hand into his. "You do fit in. You've worked hard and succeeded in everything you've tried. You are efficient and capable. I don't think there is anything you couldn't do if you put your mind to it. I have no right to change my judgment of you simply because your house has thirty rooms." He shifted his voice to teasing. "And a spiral staircase and goodness knows what else. Likely Grecian statues, famous paintings and golden doorknobs." He sighed. "I can't even imagine."

She chuckled. "No gold doorknobs." Her fingers curled into his.

"Am I forgiven for being a snob?"

"Am I really efficient and capable?" Her whisper echoed with longing.

At that moment he glimpsed her need to believe in herself. "You are an indomitable force to be reckoned with."

A rush of emotions filled her blue eyes. Joy and wild hope combined with raw gratitude. "You are forgiven." Her voice grew husky.

They reached Newfield. He reluctantly released her hand and she straightened her glove.

He would do everything in his power to help her have fun and feel at home in his world. She might live in a house with thirty rooms, but at least there were no gold doorknobs.

He grinned as he helped her to the ground. "Now let's go enjoy ourselves," he said as joy mingled with excitement and anticipation.

In her mind Rebecca kept repeating Colton's words. *Efficient and capable. A force to be reckoned with.* She let the words settle deep in her heart. Let them bubble from one side to the other with little jolts of joy. No one had ever praised her efforts before, and it made her feel ten feet tall. She stifled a giggle as Colton helped her from the buggy. Good thing she wasn't that tall. She'd be banging her head on everything.

Joy accompanied every step she took at Colton's side. He tucked her hand into the crook of his arm and held her close as the crowd jostled them.

"We're early," he said. "I think we have time to look around."

The town was much larger than Evans Grove and many of the buildings were more stately—something she had not noted before, but now she compared it to Evans Grove. They paused before the Prairie Trust Bank of Nebraska.

She gazed at the impressive building. Red bricks, white columns on either side of the entryway. White cornices formed a charming contrast to the bricks. They moved on. The town hall was equally impressive. "Miss Ward should move here. She'd approve of the buildings."

Colton laughed. "Why don't you suggest it? I'm sure she'd be happier here." He lowered his voice to a teasing whisper. "Others might appreciate it, too."

She joined in his laughter. "I know she gets on your nerves. Mine, too. But she is very efficient at organizing things. I'll never forget how she got the ladies' society to serve us a meal after the robbery. I surely did appreciate it."

"No hard feelings because she doesn't want the orphans placed in Evans Grove?"

"I think the children will prove their value."

"Is it fair to expect children to have to prove their worth? Shouldn't they simply be accepted and loved and treated kindly for their own sake?"

She contemplated his question as they turned down the main street and passed a mercantile, a newspaper office and several other businesses. "It sounds really nice, but life isn't that simple. For the most part, people take in these children for what they can do—help care for little ones, work on the farm or in a mill or whatever, clean house or care for sick folk." Wasn't that what she hoped Colton and his parents would see that Heidi could do for them? She had tried very hard to convince herself that she wanted Colton's parents to see Heidi as an asset. Barring that, she hoped Charlotte and Wyatt would take her because she was capable of caring for Gabriel. Surely it would be best if Heidi could find a home with someone who appreciated her abilities, but deep in her heart Rebecca knew that wasn't what she wanted for the little girl.

She wanted to keep Heidi with her. She could give the child a decent home back in New York. But she'd never convince her father to adopt Heidi. She could hear his arguments. He was too old. Rebecca knew nothing about raising a child. A deep dissatisfaction burned in the pit of her stomach. It wasn't ideal.

"Holly and Mason, Charlotte and Wyatt, and—" He named some of the others who had taken in the children she had brought with her to town. "They certainly don't view their children that way. Not that they don't expect them to work and help out. All children should be given useful things to do. It makes them feel important. But those families love the children, too."

She didn't know when they had stopped walking and simply stood before a store window. Only peripherally did she see the pretty blue parasol and a very fetching bonnet in the display.

Children should feel useful and important? She never had. Often she'd wondered if her parents had forgotten she existed. Certainly that had changed as she grew older and her mother groomed her for her "position in society." Then later, after Mother's death, Father had shifted more duties to her.

"Are you longing for a new bonnet?" Colton asked.

"Not at all. I think I've found what I want and it isn't in the store window."

He took her arm and drew her along the sidewalk, their boots echoing on the wooden boards. "So what have you found?"

She wished she hadn't blurted out the words and tried to think how to explain them. They reached a bench tucked in between two buildings and sheltered by a bur-oak tree.

He indicated that they should sit, and she did.

"Is this discovery something you don't care to discuss?"

She heard the gentle pleading in his voice and knew she must be honest with him. "It's something you gave me." She kept her attention on the scene across the street as a harried mother tried to shepherd her four children in the same direction at the same time.

"Me? Seems as if all I've ever given you is work."

She brought her gaze to him, kept her eyes wide and honest despite her many lessons on hiding her emotions. She let him see her growing confidence and fragile hope. "Didn't you just say giving someone something to do makes them feel useful? Valuable even."

He nodded, his gaze riveted to hers as he waited for her to explain.

"You said I was capable. A force to be reckoned with." Her voice had fallen to an uncertain whisper. Perhaps she had misunderstood his intent.

"But surely you already knew that?"

She lowered her head, studied her fingers clutched tightly in her lap. "I've always worried that I would fail. Not live up to people's expectations."

"But now you know differently."

It wasn't a question but a statement of fact, and she flashed him a smile she feared revealed not only how much she appreciated his comments but the man himself.

Nearby, a clock chimed the hour. Colton listened and counted aloud. "It's time to make our way to the opera house. Now, don't think it's an opera house like ones you would be familiar with. It's just a fancy name for a wooden hall with balconies." He tucked her hand in the crook of his arm.

"Colton, don't you think it's about time you stopped apologizing for Nebraska?"

He half missed a step. "Is that what I'm doing? I guess I am. I'm sorry."

"I should think so. I suspect that you're actually proud of your town. I know you're proud of your ranch. Or at least you were until I told you about the Sterling house."

They turned the corner.

"There's the opera house."

It was an impressively large building with a balcony surrounding the entire second story. The balcony's overhang was the roof for a wide veranda on the ground floor. Already people were walking through the doors. They hurried to join them. Colton quickly paid their admission and led her about halfway down the carpeted aisle to theater seats upholstered in burgundy velvet.

"This is very nice," she murmured as they sat side by side.

"Really?"

She sighed. "Will you stop that?"

"I'm trying."

A man came onto the stage and called for attention. She sat back and prepared to enjoy herself.

The first song was one she'd never heard before. Michael Moorehead sang "My Western Home."

"'Oh, give me a home where the buffalo roam. Where the deer and the antelope play. Where seldom is heard a discouraging word.'"

The lyrics tugged at her heart and filled her with an echoing response. She wanted to belong here. In Nebraska. The ache of the words settled deep. She wiped a tear from her eyes and hoped Colton didn't notice. Then a second man played Beethoven's "Ode to Joy" on the piano and her heart threatened to break into a hundred weeping pieces.

Her hand lay on the armrest between them and he rested his hand over it. His touch deepened her distress.

Where did she belong? Where was her home? Her place of joy?

It was all she could do not to turn her palm to his and cling to him with all her might.

Colton kept his hand firmly on Rebecca's and resisted the urge to squeeze tight as she wiped her eyes. He couldn't help wondering if hearing the songs and music made her homesick.

Then the main male singer stood and sang "Silver Threads among the Gold." About a person growing old, getting silver in his hair and still in love with his wife, seeing her as he'd seen her when she was young. The words tightened his throat. Would he ever find someone to share his life? He shook away the thought. Not as long as he had parents to care for. That was where his first loyalty lay.

Surely he could enjoy a good musical program without the words twisting his thoughts out of control.

Later, as they headed home, he talked to keep himself from thinking. And perhaps doing something foolish like pulling her into his arms and kissing her soundly.

"I never told you that I was sick for a couple of years when I was a kid."

"No, you didn't. What was wrong?"

"Rheumatic fever. I had to rest day and night. I was seven years old and used to being active. If Ma and Pa hadn't devoted themselves to entertaining me, I doubt I would have obeyed the doctor's orders." The extra work had been especially hard on his ma. She'd never fully recovered her strength after his birth.

"I wonder…" She didn't finish.

"What?"

"It's nothing."

"It's something or you wouldn't have started to say it. Tell me." He nudged her shoulder and kept his voice teasing.

She favored him with a sky-blue look. "Your ma said I didn't know the whole story. Maybe that's what she meant."

"I owe them for so much. They were older when I was born. They've given me everything I need. A loving home. Care when I was sick. Approval."

"And you feel you owe them. I understand that."

He tried to convince himself that he appreciated her understanding. But he didn't. He wanted her to indicate she didn't like it. Wished things could be different. Even suggest a compromise or a willingness to accept his situation and still fit into his life.

He knew it was impossible.

She was city. She had duty. He was country. He had parents he was responsible for.

And yet…

His heart would not accept that there was no solution.

Chapter Fifteen

Rebecca understood that there existed an impossible distance between herself and Colton, between her wishes and her reality.

Nothing had changed. Nothing could.

In the days that followed, they continued their work on the orphanage.

"The rooms are taking shape and need to be furnished. I expect the children any day." Rebecca went through the building, checking her lists. She'd ordered the furniture and supplies from Mr. Gavin and hoped they'd arrive in good time.

"Miss Sterling."

She half jolted out of her shoes at the imperious tone. *Please, Lord, patience.* Slowly, she turned to face Miss Ward. "Good morning. What can I do for you?" The woman showed up at the orphanage at unexpected times to fuss about some detail.

"These doors don't look square to me. Have you had a real carpenter check them?"

Today it was doors. Two days ago, the windows. Before that, the chimney. "Mr. Lang personally inspected them. I believe he is a carpenter of some repute."

"Yes, yes. That's all well and good. But look here." She bent over the door frame and eyed it. "Isn't that a splinter?" She picked off a speck. "Shoddy work." She stomped from the room, glancing over her shoulder. "Are you coming?"

For two wooden nails Rebecca would have refused, but she'd learned that the best way to deal with the woman was to humor her.

Miss Ward saw a pile of sawdust where up to a moment ago the men had been working on a closet. Now they were all strangely absent. No doubt they'd seen Miss Ward coming and abandoned Rebecca to deal with the situation on her own. Miss Ward pointed at the sawdust. "Shameful. That constitutes a fire hazard." She spun about to confront Rebecca face-to-face. "You should be more cautious. After all, that little girl you have was scarred in a fire."

Miss Ward plowed on without giving Rebecca a chance to reply.

She completed her inspection and sniffed. "I suggest you get that cleaned up before I report you to the sheriff. Humph." She stormed out.

Rebecca stared.

"I heard that," Colton said from behind her. "Don't pay her any mind."

Rebecca shook her head. "I simply can't believe how vitriolic she is."

He squeezed her shoulders. "You've won a battle to continue construction of the orphanage, and she doesn't want to admit that she's lost."

"Apart from her, this community will provide the kind of support these children will need."

"Then pay her no mind."

"Easier said than done when she pops in all the time. It seems as if she always sneaks up on me and catches me unprepared."

"I wouldn't expect that is any accident."

A noise turned their attention to the doorway, and Rebecca was surprised to see Amelia Hicks. She'd gotten to know the woman a little—Amelia had been very kind to the orphans when they first arrived. But it had been difficult to get to know her well. Amelia's husband, Vern Hicks, was a domineering man, and it seemed that the only thing he enjoyed more than drinking at the saloon was bossing and berating his timid wife.

"Amelia?" Colton said. "I thought you were visiting your sister."

"Is she gone? Miss Ward, is she gone?"

"Yes." Colton rushed to his cousin's side. "Are you okay? You look awfully pale." The only place for her to sit was on a bench one of the men used as he worked, and Colton led Amelia to it.

Rebecca knelt by the woman's side and rubbed her hands. She glanced at Colton, her eyes filled with worry.

Colton knew that Amelia's husband drank too much, too frequently and then tended to use his fists on Amelia. He'd suggested a few times that she leave him, but she said he would only track her down and then things would be worse. Had the man injured Amelia this time?

He curled and uncurled his fists. He had the same raging reaction every time he thought of this tiny woman facing her angry husband. So defenseless. So vulnerable.

He fought his anger, and when he had it under control, he knelt by Amelia's side.

She lifted big green eyes to his. They silently pleaded.

"Amelia, what's wrong?"

"I've been very, very wicked."

He strained to hear her whisper. "Vern?" he asked. "Did you—" Had she been driven to hurt him?

"I don't know where Vern is. I haven't seen him since—" Her throat worked hard. "For three weeks. He thinks I'm in Kansas visiting my sister, Amanda."

"When did you come back?"

"This morning."

What had brought Amelia to the orphanage? "Are you afraid to go home?"

She nodded, her eyes bleak. "I did something awful."

"Amelia, what is it?"

"It's too awful to talk about."

He chuckled. "Then why are you here aching to tell me?"

"You'll hate me, but no more than I hate myself."

He hugged her. "I could never hate you. We're family—and you're like a sister to me."

Rebecca settled back, watching and waiting, her expression guarded. He understood that she had far less reason to know Amelia could not harm anyone than he did. He'd known Amelia all his life. They'd often been playmates.

"I think you'd better tell me what you did that you consider so awful," Colton said.

Her eyes clung to his, bored into his soul, demanded understanding.

He took her hands. "Amelia, it can't be that bad."

She swallowed audibly. "I had a baby."

"Congratulations." Did she mean she'd delivered a baby while in Kansas? But if so, where was the child? "A boy or a girl? When can I meet the little one?"

"It's a boy. You can't meet him." She rocked her head back and forth.

Horror as dark as a storm filled his thoughts. The same reaction filled Rebecca's eyes. "The baby died?"

Tears filled Amelia's eyes and she shook her head. "I don't know where he is."

Colton sat back on his heels and tried to make sense of

her words. "You lost him?" A worse thought tore at his gut. "Vern took him?"

Amelia rocked her head back and forth and moaned. "I abandoned him. I don't know if Gabriel is even alive." Her moans intensified.

Colton jolted to his feet. "Where did you leave him? When? I'll find him."

Rebecca touched his arm. "She said *Gabriel*."

Of course. It made perfect sense. He'd given up finding Gabriel's mother, assuming it had been a woman in desperate straits, someone passing through Evans Grove. He squatted before Amelia. "Tell me everything."

She nodded. "Vern didn't want children and I didn't, either. How would I defend a child? So I let him think I was only putting on weight." She snorted. "Wasn't hard to convince him of it because I've steadily done so since we got married."

Colton nodded. Some might think Amelia's weight reflected a well-kept woman. In her case, it showed a troubled woman.

"But I feared what he would do if he ever learned the truth. So I had the baby in secret and left him on this doorstep." With a tortured wail, she pointed to the spot where Colton had found the baby.

He grabbed Amelia's hands and shook her gently to gain her attention. "I have Gabriel. Rebecca and I. He's fine. He's safe. We've been caring for him out at the ranch."

Amelia fell back. If not for the wall behind her, she would have tumbled from the bench. Her hand splayed over her chest. "He's safe? Praise God. Praise God." She murmured the words over and over again.

Colton grinned at Rebecca. He thought her answering smile seemed a bit strained, but before he could consider the idea, she knelt before Amelia.

"The baby is doing very well. He's beautiful and strong."

"Can I go to the ranch and see him?"

"What about Vern?" Colton didn't trust the man. Never had. He'd tried to talk Amelia out of marrying him, but Vern could be charming when he wanted to be and when he was sober. He'd persuaded Amelia that he would reform if she married him. Amelia had soon learned the emptiness of promises from a drinking man.

The joy fled from Amelia's face, replaced by fear. "If he learns about the baby—" She clutched at her throat.

"Then he must not know the baby is yours," Rebecca said.

Colton turned to her. "What do you have in mind?"

"No one needs to know she's Gabriel mother. No one even needs to know she's back in town. She could come with us to the ranch and look after the children. It would certainly be easier for everyone than bringing them to town every day. Plus, if Amelia is at the ranch, someone would be with your parents."

"Excellent idea. What do you think, Amelia?"

"I'll do anything to be with my baby. Anything."

"It's agreed, then. In the meantime, you need to stay out of sight until we can get you to the ranch. Let Vern continue to think you are in Kansas." He had no desire to deal with the man, who would surely be angry, demanding that his wife return to her home to care for him.

It was several hours before they would normally head back to the ranch and he tried to think of a way to keep Amelia hidden until that time. He went to the nearest window and looked out. Miss Ward stood before the orphanage staring at it. He thought she'd left long ago, but she couldn't stop looking for something wrong. Never mind the interfering woman.

She saw him and marched away, her head high, her nose tipped toward the sky.

He turned back to consider the two women. "Amelia, do you have a shawl?"

"In my bag." She pointed to the overstuffed container at the doorway.

"Put it on and cover your head with it."

She did so. "Now go out the side door. Keep your head down and your face hidden as much as possible. Go out of town to the south." Fewer people would see her than if she went through the center of town. "Once you're away from town, make your way around to that little hill where you found that pretty silver rock. You remember the place?"

"I remember."

"Wait there and we'll get you on the way home."

She pulled the shawl tight to her neck and slipped away.

Rebecca joined Colton and they watched her until she was out of sight.

"I would have never guessed," he said.

"Poor woman. I hope she'll be safe."

Rebecca found it difficult to keep her mind from continually returning to Amelia's announcement. She was Gabriel's mother. That changed things. There was no need for two women at the ranch to care for the children or take care of the cooking and cleaning. She was no longer needed.

As she went from room to room in the orphanage and answered questions from the workers, she pondered her problem.

Rebecca didn't need to stay at the ranch. But where did Heidi belong? Until the orphanage was finished and staffed, Heidi was still her responsibility and needed to stay in her care. Perhaps she would put off any change until she'd had more time to evaluate the situation.

She and Colton worked until late afternoon, picked up the children and left town. They paused at the appointed place.

"Why are we stopping?" Heidi asked.

Rebecca let Colton answer. "To pick up Gabriel's mother."

"Why is she here?"

Rebecca and Colton had discussed how much to tell Heidi and he gave their agreed-upon answer. "She has to hide with us at the ranch. Otherwise, someone might try to hurt her or the baby."

Heidi's eyes widened and she spoke to Colton. "But you will take care of her."

"She'll be safe at the ranch as long as no one mentions she's here or says anything about her being Gabriel's mama."

"I won't. I promise." She crossed her heart.

Amelia reached the buggy and Colton jumped down to help her into the backseat.

"My baby?" She was breathless.

Gabriel slept in his basket and Rebecca handed him to his mother. Amelia pressed him to her cheek as her tears flowed unchecked.

"Do you remember me? I'm Heidi," the child said. "Sometimes I help with the baby."

Amelia didn't answer. Rebecca realized that the woman was too overcome with emotion.

At the ranch, Amelia was welcomed with open arms by her aunt and uncle.

"Colton said the baby belonged in the family," Mrs. Hayes said. "Even without the quilt, I should have seen the resemblance."

Heidi hung back, watching.

Rebecca watched, too, wondering if a baby who belonged in the family and a prodigal niece who'd returned would replace Heidi in the Hayeses' affections.

But Colton pulled the girl to his lap, and Heidi melted against his chest. His pa smiled at Heidi.

"So what do you think of Gabriel getting a mama?" Colton asked the girl.

"I think he is very, very, very happy."

They all laughed at her exuberance.

"I thank you for caring for Gabriel and now sheltering me." Amelia looked about. "But I don't need looking after." She handed the baby to Mrs. Hayes and set to work in a kitchen that was obviously familiar to her. "Aunt Estelle, I remember when you taught Amanda and me to make the best chocolate cake. I still use your recipe. Anyone care for cake later?"

Rebecca joined in the chorus of approval.

Amelia bustled. There was no other word for it. She whipped up a cake, put it in the oven. She gave Heidi the bowl to lick, then had the child scrub potatoes. She gave Rebecca a turnip to peel while she filled the bottle for Gabriel. "I'll feed him."

Rebecca heard the longing in her voice. She'd missed the baby's early days and now she'd likely be reluctant to share any of the feedings for quite some time.

The baby finished his bottle.

Rebecca saw the glisten of tears in Amelia's eyes before she turned to Heidi. "Would you like to hold the baby while I make gravy?"

When Heidi danced over to the cot and settled down, Amelia placed the baby in her arms.

"I've held him lots already," Heidi said. "He likes me holding him."

The baby looked into Heidi's face, his mouth puckered into a sweet bow.

"I can see that he does."

At bedtime, Amelia went to the room across the hall with Gabriel, leaving Heidi and Rebecca alone in the room they'd shared since their arrival at the ranch.

"I don't have to go to town tomorrow?" Heidi asked.

"There's no need with Amelia here."

"Good. Mr. Hayes said I should spend more time with Happy."

"That's a great idea."

Twice in the night, Rebecca jerked awake at Gabriel's cry, then remembered that someone else was responsible for him and quickly fell asleep again.

It was strange to be alone with Colton the next morning as they headed to town. One thing worried Rebecca above all else. "How long do you think it will be before Amelia's husband learns that she's at the ranch with a baby?"

"I hope he never hears."

"Is that possible?"

"He sure won't hear it from me."

"Or me. But sooner or later he's going to expect his wife to return and then what? Won't he find out that she's not in Kansas and start looking for her?"

Colton rocked his head back and forth. "Let's cross that bridge when we come to it."

She wished she could so easily dismiss the problem, but she wasn't confident that Vern Hicks wouldn't cause trouble in one way or another. This concerned her more and more over the next few days as her admiration for Amelia grew. She was efficient, organized and kind to one and all. It was awful to think that the poor woman was so frightened of her husband that she'd felt driven to abandon the baby she obviously loved dearly. Surely there must be a way she and Gabriel could be protected from Vern. But no matter how much time Rebecca spent pondering the problem, she couldn't come up with a solution.

On Saturday, Amelia announced, "I wish I could go to church tomorrow. I've missed it."

Colton jumped right out of his chair. "You can't let Vern know where you are."

She got a stubborn look on her face that reminded Rebecca so much of Colton that she had to suppress a smile.

"I can't hide forever. I'm proud of my little man." She stroked Gabriel's cheek. "I want to show him off."

"You can't go to church." Colton revealed every bit of his stubborn nature in his words. "You'd be putting yourself and Gabriel in danger."

Amelia nodded. "I guess you're right."

Rebecca knew it was only a matter of time before this argument came up again.

Later in the day, as they enjoyed a leisurely walk without having to keep in mind Gabriel's feeding time, Colton spoke about the matter. "My cousin will not be put off much longer. I guess she can't hide forever, either."

"I wouldn't expect her to. Why not talk to her and decide how to deal with this situation?"

"You don't know Vern the way I do."

She'd seen enough of the man to understand that he was most unpleasant when he'd been drinking. Having never seen him in any other state, she couldn't judge if he had any redeeming qualities. "There must be something we can do to help Amelia."

"He's a vindictive man."

Rebecca's breath lodged in her throat. "Would he come to the ranch and hurt people here?"

Colton's eyes were dark with concern. "I can't say with certainty that he wouldn't. We have to be sure he doesn't find out she's here."

Rebecca rubbed her breastbone. "Every day we've left them here unguarded. Now I'm worried."

He squeezed her shoulder. "No need to worry as long as Vern doesn't know."

She leaned into his touch. Longed for more. But he hadn't offered more.

"Someone's coming."

Her heart thundered against her ribs. "Vern?" She could barely squeeze the word from her throat.

Colton shaded his eyes and studied the swirl of dust that signaled approaching visitors. "Looks like a horse and buggy. I've never seen Vern on anything but an old piebald gelding." He grabbed her hand. "We'd better hurry back."

She felt his urgency matching her own and trotted at his side back to the house, arriving as the buggy pulled to a halt at the house.

Colton's lungs emptied in a whoosh. "It's Doc Simpson. He said he wanted to visit Ma."

"He'll see Amelia." She urged him to hurry onward.

They dashed for the door, but Doc Simpson had already knocked.

They reached his side. "Doc," Colton said, his voice revealing only a slight note of strain, "what brings you out on a Sunday afternoon?"

"Promised your mother a week ago I'd visit. I have something I'd like her to try for her heart. Something a doctor from New York sent me." He slanted a look at Rebecca. "I think you might know something about that."

Behind the door came the sound of scurrying. Rebecca guessed that Amelia was dashing into her room.

"I asked my father to speak to our doctor," Rebecca explained. "If he knows of something that will help, it would be wonderful."

Colton stood with his hand on the doorknob. "She'll be glad if it does." He cleared his throat, gave a little cough, then opened the door slowly.

Rebecca saw him relax and guessed that Amelia had disappeared. The gentlemen both stepped aside and allowed Rebecca to enter.

Heidi sat at Mrs. Hayes's side, her eyes wide. Mrs. Hayes held the baby and smiled, but Rebecca saw the worry in her expression. Only Mr. Hayes appeared completely at ease. The man had a knack for pretense.

"How do, Doc?" Mr. Hayes said. "Come sit a spell."

"I'll make tea," Rebecca said and hurried to the stove. She served slices of Amelia's cake, as well.

The room vibrated with tension. She wondered how the doctor didn't feel it, but he drank his tea and ate a slice of cake with no sign of discomfort. "Good cake. Thank you." Done, he shoved aside his dish. "Mrs. Hayes, thanks to Miss Sterling's request, a doctor in New York sent me a new medicine I believe will ease your symptoms." He went on to tell Mrs. Hayes the benefits and how to take it.

"I'll give it a try," she promised, taking the powders he handed her.

Heidi watched with keen interest, but her gaze darted often to the door through which Amelia had gone.

"Now let's have a look at the little one."

Mrs. Hayes handed him over, somewhat reluctantly, Rebecca thought.

"No one has come forward to claim this little man?" Doc listened to the baby's chest, flexed his legs and examined his ears as he talked.

No one answered.

Mr. Hayes cleared his throat. "Doc, have you heard of anyone who might be the mother?"

Dr. Simpson bundled the baby up in his blanket and handed him back to Mrs. Hayes. "No, and it's a shame. He's such a sturdy baby."

"He's mine."

Everyone turned to stare at Amelia standing in the doorway, her eyes flashing determination.

Chapter Sixteen

Colton's throat was as dry and dusty as the road the doctor had recently traveled. He didn't know if he wanted to muzzle Amelia or shove her into the other room and close the door. From the silence in the room, he knew he wasn't the only one who couldn't decide what to say or do.

Dr. Simpson found his tongue first. "Amelia, how are you? I see you've lost some weight." His voice carried a note of humor.

Amelia crossed the room and sat at the table. She looked at each one of them. "I know you want me to hide, but I can't."

Colton's fear and anger boiled over. "How can we expect to keep you safe if you won't stay out of sight?"

Doc Simpson held up a hand. "I'd like to hear what Amelia has to say."

She took Gabriel and held him close as she repeated her story. "I can't hide out here forever. Even if I try, how long before Vern finds me? I want to walk proud and show off my beautiful son." The fight left her as quickly as it had come. "What will he do?"

They all knew she was referring to her husband.

Doc puffed out his cheeks. "I can't say for sure what he might do, but I agree that you can't hide forever."

Colton balled his hands into fists. "I don't trust Vern."

"Nor do I," the doctor assured him. "Amelia, you have to leave the man once and for all, and live your own life."

"How can I do that? I have to be able to support myself and my child. Besides, he won't let me go that easily."

"True. But once you've made the decision, the sheriff will have to convince Vern to honor it. You'll certainly need a means of support." The doctor studied Amelia then shifted his gaze to Rebecca.

Colton watched him closely. What did the man have in mind? He didn't have long to wait for his question to be answered.

"The mayor and the selection committee have been looking for staff for the orphanage."

"Are you saying I might get a job? I can cook," Amelia said. "And I like children. But what about Gabriel? I don't want to leave him with someone else."

"Are you committed to going through with this? Leaving Vern and not letting his anger make you change your mind?"

Amelia looked down at her son for several seconds then raised her face.

In her countenance Colton saw a depth of determination and stubbornness he'd never seen before.

"For Gabriel's sake, I must and I will."

"Then let me look into things and see what I can come up with. You're absolutely right. Sooner or later you have to come out into the open and confront Vern. But perhaps it's best if you lie low for a few more days. I'll check on him and assess his mental state. If we can approach him when he's sober, we might have a chance at having a reasonable conversation."

Colton kept his opinion to himself, but he doubted Vern would be reasonable after learning that Amelia meant to leave him—and take his son, to boot. The man had a very deep streak of meanness in him.

He wondered what Rebecca thought of all this.

She didn't look his way. Instead, her gaze rested on Heidi, who had listened to the whole story, her eyes wide and staring.

He could have slapped himself. The child should not have heard all this, but the adults had forgotten she was there. He reached for her, but Rebecca beat him to it and drew the child to her lap. She wrapped her arms about Heidi and held her tight.

When she finally lifted her head, Colton saw that her eyes were almost as wide as Heidi's. What was she thinking to look so frightened?

Rebecca knew Amelia and the doctor were right. Amelia deserved the chance to raise her son openly. They'd just have to figure out how they could make that happen without putting anyone at risk.

A little later the doctor left and Colton went out to do chores, taking Heidi with him.

Mr. Hayes looked around at those who remained in the room. "We will miss the young fella, won't we, Mother?" Mr. Hayes rose and limped to the stove with very little effort. He filled his cup with tea, then carried it back to the table.

Rebecca watched him. She realized something she'd subconsciously noted before. "Mr. Hayes, it seems to me you don't appear nearly as crippled when Colton isn't around."

He winked at his wife. "I let Colton think I need his help more than I do."

Rebecca looked at Amelia to see if she understood what he meant, but she shrugged.

"Why would you do that?"

"For Colton."

Mrs. Hayes nodded agreement.

"He blames himself for my injuries. Helping me is his way of making up for it so I pretend I am worse off than I am."

Amelia sat across from him and gave him some hard study. "So how bad off are you?"

"I can't walk very far. Don't suppose I could ride a horse, which I miss like nobody's business. But I can get around the house just fine." He leaned closer as if to share a secret. "When Colton's in town, I go outside and walk around. It's helping me get my strength back."

He could do so much more than Colton knew. Was it really fair to make Colton continue to pay? Again Rebecca sought enlightenment from Amelia.

She lifted her eyebrows in silent agreement with Rebecca's assessment. "Why is Colton to blame?"

Mr. Hayes let out a long sigh. "He's not. No more than I am. He called out to the Thatcher girl. The cows were edgy and they stampeded. That much was his doing. But I was adjusting my hatband and didn't have my mind on the job or I would have been alert and seen the cows getting restless. If I'd had my wits about me, I wouldn't have taken a nosedive." He shrugged and looked sheepish.

The look Amelia gave her uncle would have made Rebecca squirm. It had the same effect on Mr. Hayes.

"Don't you think it's time to stop such nonsense?"

"But Colton—"

"But Colton is a big boy. Don't you think he can handle not having to play nursemaid to you two?" Amelia rumbled her lips. "Seems to me you've hog-tied him, deprived him of a future." She blinked as if she'd spoken more harshly than she meant to, then rushed on. "But you've done the same to yourself. The only way you can get out and enjoy the outdoors is to wait until Colton's not here. That's just plumb foolish."

Rebecca couldn't have said it better.

But if Mr. Hayes's injuries were bearable and if the new medicine helped Mrs. Hayes, then neither of Colton's parents would need him. And if Amelia took the baby and lived in town...

Seemed there'd be no need for Heidi's help.

Or the presence of a city gal with little proficiency in farm life.

Talk that evening centered on where Amelia might live. Would she live at the orphanage or elsewhere? How would she take care of herself and little Gabriel and what might Vern do? Thankfully, Heidi played outside with the cats and didn't hear the conversation. Rebecca wished she could avoid it, as well. Every word was another board nailed to a wall, boxing her in until she felt she couldn't move.

Except a move was inevitable.

After they went to bed, Heidi crawled close. "Is Amelia going to live in town?"

"She wants to."

"Will I have to go, too, or can I stay here?"

Rebecca wrapped her arms about the child. She had hoped Heidi had not picked up on the air of change and uncertainty in the house, but she should have known better. Heidi was far too astute to miss it. "I don't know what's going to happen. I'm glad Amelia is going to stand up to her husband, though. I don't know what decisions will have to be made in the next few days, but whatever unfolds, you and I will be okay."

"I hope I can stay here. I could help Mr. and Mrs. Hayes."

"I'm sure they'd like that, but we'll simply have to wait and see."

"I know we can live here because Colton said we could." And she turned to her side and fell asleep with Colton's promise to comfort her.

Rebecca wished she could feel such assurance, but things had changed.

One thing hadn't changed, though, and that was God's care. *Show me where You want me to be and what You want me to do.* She added a thought, but didn't think it was an appropriate prayer. *Help Colton love me.*

On the trip to town the next day, Colton seemed interested only in the growing crops beside the trail.

At the orphanage, the work kept her mind occupied. She made note of the final little things she needed to buy for what would be the girls' dormitory. She needed to be in control of something, if only making notes on a piece of paper.

Done, she went to the store to place her orders.

As she stepped from the store, a man lurched into her path. Vern Hicks. Drunk. He squinted at Rebecca.

"Ya seen my wife?"

She scrambled for an answer. She was no good at lying and he'd likely guess the truth if she tried. "I thought Amelia went to Kansas to see her sister."

"Yesh." He staggered away a step then turned, the movement causing him nearly to fall. "When did she go? Shouldn't she be back by now?" Every word was exaggerated as he tried to form it in his brain and then get it out his mouth.

She backed away from his rank breath. "I have no idea what her arrangement was. Now if you'll excuse me." She tried to slip past him, but he fell into her.

"Some wife," he muttered. "Gotta beat her to keep her in line."

Mr. Gavin stepped from the store and pulled him off her. "Vern, you need to go home and sober up."

"I'se sober as a jug—a ju—"

"A judge. I know." Mr. Gavin guided him in the general direction of the Hicks house.

"She's avo—vo—" He swallowed hard. "She's keeping away. If I find her—" He shoved Mr. Gavin. "Leave me alone. All of you leave me alone. Or do you wanna fight?

I'll fight ya. Any day. Come on." He swung his arm and almost fell.

Mr. Gavin simply stayed out of his reach. "Go home, Vern."

Vern staggered away, muttering angrily, "When I find her, I'll learn her a lesson."

Mr. Gavin shook his head. "I hope Amelia stays safe in Kansas. Vern is one mean drunk. He's even meaner when he starts to sober up."

Rebecca hurried back to the orphanage and sank onto the bench Amelia had used just a few days ago.

Colton stepped into the room. "Is something wrong?"

"Vern was outside the store, drunk and making threats against Amelia." She shuddered. "How is Amelia going to live in the same town as him?"

He sat beside her. "I'd feel better if she stayed hidden on the ranch. But you saw how stubborn she is."

"What if she moved away?"

"He'd track her down. And in another town she wouldn't have me and everyone else in Evans Grove to watch out for her and help her." His fists curled. "No one is going to stand by and see him hurt her or Gabriel."

Rebecca thought of Mr. Gavin stepping in at the store. She knew he'd do the same for Amelia. But none of them could protect her in the privacy of the Hicks home. "I wish—" She couldn't even say what she wished for. To wish Amelia hadn't come back was purely petty. To wish things hadn't changed was pointless. To hope for Colton to give her a reason to stay—well, that she could wish for.

But only Colton could make her wish come true.

Ted joined them. "Miss, we can build frames for the beds if you show us what you want."

"I'll come right away." She spent the next two hours discussing the size, number and placement of beds in both the girls' and boys' quarters, as well as a hundred other details.

They moved on to the smaller room between the two dorms—the room where the director would sleep. Two other small bedrooms separated the boys' dorm from the girls'. Rooms for additional staff. As they studied the room, a plan began to form.

She went in search of Colton to tell him about it. "If Amelia lived here, she'd be safe."

"How?"

"The children would warn her if Vern showed up. There are older boys coming from Greenville. I hope they can get an education while they're here. But educated or not, these are street children, as Miss Ward so often points out. They're little scrappers. They know how to deal with the challenges of the streets. They'll know how to provide a modicum of protection for Amelia. When they aren't here, other staff will be."

"Children shouldn't be expected to protect adults."

"I'm not suggesting that they confront Vern or get involved in a physical altercation, but these kids are wily. I think they can outsmart a drunk."

Colton still looked dubious. "It's better than any other idea we've come up with." He popped his fist into the palm of his hand.

Pleased with her idea, happy that Colton seemed ready to consider it, Rebecca said, "Then I'm going to suggest to Pauline that she offer Amelia the position."

"Do you suppose we can keep her presence at the ranch a secret until the orphanage opens?"

"I think it would be best, but it will take a lot of talking to convince Amelia. She grows more and more restless with each passing day. And she's a stubborn Hayes."

He opened his mouth, preparing to argue, then laughed. "Sometimes it's good to be stubborn."

She tapped her finger to her chin. "I'm trying to recall a situation where I could agree." Finally, she shrugged, prompting him to chuckle. "I'm going to check if Pauline is at town hall."

"I'll come along and add my support to your request."

She thought to tell him she didn't need his help, but in truth, she did. Pauline might well have all sorts of reservations about hiring a woman with a child and a troublemaking husband. So together they crossed through the town square. The hackberry trees filled the square with patches of shady invitations. Beneath one, a bench had been placed. Rebecca would have enjoyed sitting there sharing Colton's company. But he hurried onward toward town hall.

Pauline sat behind a big desk, Curtis Brooks nearby. A stack of papers lay before them, but their attention did not appear to be on the documents.

If Rebecca wasn't mistaken, Pauline looked more startled at the appearance of two other people in her office than she would have expected. Did she resent their intrusion?

"How may I help you?" she asked.

Colton pulled two chairs close to the desk and nodded for Rebecca to speak. She explained her idea.

As expected, Pauline raised all sort of questions. "Can we hope to keep Vern from being involved?"

Again, Rebecca explained how Amelia would not often be alone at the orphanage.

"I don't like to put the children in danger."

Rebecca sat back. "Is Vern more than loud and argumentative?"

Pauline nodded. "He's unpredictable."

Curtis had been listening to the discussion. "If I may, Pauline?"

"By all means."

"It seems to me that a woman in her position needs a hance to get free of her husband. If we enlist Mason's help, s Rebecca suggests, and alert as many people as we deem ppropriate, then surely she deserves this job." He turned to Rebecca. "From what you say, it would appear she is well qualified."

"I believe she is. In fact, I would appreciate her help now, ut I realize it's best for her to remain hidden on the ranch intil she moves into the director's room."

"I know her well enough to feel comfortable giving her he position without an interview." Pauline nodded.

Colton thumped his fist on the desktop. "We'll keep Mason informed of developments."

Curtis nodded. "By all means."

Their business satisfactorily complete, Rebecca and Colton left town hall. Miss Ward marched by, thankfully without noticing them.

They hung back until she turned the corner out of sight.

Rebecca sighed. "Is it just me or is that woman always urking about?"

"She's always lurking. No doubt making sure the town is perating according to her standards."

"And hoping to find it isn't so she can fuss about it."

Colton chuckled. "She needs a different hobby."

They returned to the orphanage, and he began helping uild cupboards in the kitchen, while she went to work making more lists.

Her job here would soon be over. She'd done everything he'd planned to except find a home for Heidi. For a few days he'd hoped the Hayeses would come forward to officially ake her in, but now it seemed she would stay at the orphange. It certainly made sense for Heidi to go with Amelia. She could help with the baby. She would be closer to school. She would be surrounded by her friends.

Everyone's life seemed to be sorted out satisfactorily.

Except Rebecca's.

But she had her duties back in New York. That had to be enough.

Chapter Seventeen

Three days later, Amelia watched as Colton and Rebecca prepared to leave for town. "I wish I didn't have to stand around and wait."

"Only a few more days." They'd told her about the position and she had embraced the idea.

Rebecca sat beside Colton in the buggy, quiet as if lost in thought. Or distancing herself from the community.

"I suppose—" He couldn't bring himself to finish the thought. *I suppose you'll be planning to return to New York now that the orphanage is nearly finished.* "Wyatt will soon return." He'd sent regular telegrams informing them of his progress.

She nodded. "In yesterday's cable he said the judge was due to arrive in two days—that would be tomorrow. He expected the judge to order the release of the boys he found in the Colorado mines."

"There will be some small details to finish on the orphanage, but the boys' dorm is done."

"The ladies' society is making quilts for the beds. The curtains will be hung today."

"Your job will soon be finished." He swallowed back a lump of despair. "You should be proud of yourself."

She studied him unblinkingly and without a smile. "I am."

Would she take advantage of the opportunity he'd provided and say her job had just begun? That she saw herself as part of the community, the ranch and—dare he hope—his life?

She seemed very interested in the horse pulling them toward town. "I hope my father will be pleased."

His shoulders sank. That was her answer, then. It mattered more what her father thought than what he thought. Or wanted.

Good thing he'd never voiced his longings. He stuffed them into the depths of his heart.

Shortly after they arrived, a group of ladies descended on the place. He recognized many as those who had taken in the other orphans Rebecca had brought to Evans Grove. Holly and Charlotte were among them. Their arms full of material and bedding, they trooped upstairs. In a few minutes the buzz of female conversation and laughter drifted to the kitchen, where Colton and Ted continued to work. Rebecca had suggested a long table with benches for the children and Ted constructed one while Colton made a worktable for the kitchen. He wondered if Rebecca's hands would ever touch the surface as she rolled out pie crust or kneaded bread.

Only, it wasn't at this table he longed to see her. It was at the ranch.

With determination, he settled into the rhythm of work, hoping the labor would clear the foolish daydreams from his head. Toward noon, the women trooped back down the stairs and left for their homes.

Rebecca followed, her face glowing with joy. "The boys' room is ready. It looks lovely. The women are going to prepare quilts for the girls' dorm now."

"I want to see." He followed her back up the stairs. Cots stood along one wall, facing the windows that allowed a view of the street. Colorful quilts covered each bed, and beside each cot was a narrow set of shelves that the men had built. They'd also constructed a chest to go at the foot of each bed for personal belongings.

"It looks very welcoming," he said. The newly hung dark green cotton curtains would shut out some light. He went to one window to check how easily they pulled back and forth. A block away, the church steeple stood like a beacon. The trees in the town square waved their green heads. On the ground below, one of Ted's helpers cleaned up debris. A rider approached on horseback.

Colton leaned closer to the window. "It can't be."

"What is it?" Rebecca joined him.

"That's Pa's horse. And that's Pa!" He could barely get the words out. "He can't ride."

"But he has."

"There's something wrong."

He crossed the room in long strides and descended the stairs in three steps. He flung himself out the front door and raced to his pa's side. Seeing the pain on his father's face, he reached up to assist him. "Let me help you down."

"No time. No time. You got to get to the ranch right now."

Rebecca caught up to Colton, her face emotionless but her eyes wide. "Mr. Hayes, what is it?"

"Vern. He's at the ranch, drunker than a skunk. And waving a sidearm. Threatening to shoot everyone in sight."

Colton's heart kicked with the power of a raging stallion. "Where's Ma and Amelia and the children?"

"He's got them all in the kitchen, waving a gun at them."

"Pa, give me your horse and I'll take care of Vern."

"I ain't getting down until I'm back home. I can still take care of my own." He reined out of reach. "Might need some help, but I'm not in my grave yet." He flicked the reins and trotted away. "Best get going or I'll have to handle this myself."

Colton headed for the buggy before he finished.

Ted stood in the doorway, clearly having heard the whole conversation.

Colton called to him, "Go find Mason and tell him everything."

He jumped into the buggy and grabbed the reins. Rebecca planted her hands on the other side.

"I'm coming."

"Best you stay here." There could be shooting. He didn't want to worry that Rebecca might be in the line of fire.

She pulled herself up to the seat beside him. "There is no way I will stay in town and twist my hands waiting to hear if some mad drunk shot you or the others. I'm going."

He didn't have time to argue. He had to get back before Pa did. He had to save his ma from harm. And the others. Poor Heidi. She'd had enough bad things happen in her life without a drunk wielding a gun.

His chest muscles tightened until he could hardly breathe. If Vern hurt anyone… Blood drained from his face and settled in a thick lump in his heart. If something happened to any of them—

He gritted his teeth. He should have seen this coming. Done something to prevent it. How could he have failed everyone?

"How did Vern learn that Amelia was at the ranch?" Rebecca's words were jerked from her as she clung to the seat, hanging on as the buggy raced toward home.

Colton had to loosen his jaw to answer. "I don't know."

"God preserve them." Rebecca practically shouted the words to be heard above the rattle of the ride.

They slid around the last corner and headed for the house.

Pa rode beside them. Colton couldn't imagine the pain this frantic pace was inflicting on his injuries.

They reached the yard and Colton sawed back on the reins. Best if they didn't race up to the house, announcing their arrival. Two riders caught up to Pa. Mason and Bucky Wyler, who helped Mason when it was called for. The man was steady and a crack shot. Colton couldn't ask for anyone he'd sooner have on his side in this situation.

Colton jumped from the buggy before it stopped moving and raced for the door. Mason and Bucky dismounted at a run and followed suit.

Mason held up his hand, signaling them to stop. "Let's be careful. Vern is drunk and unpredictable. If we can approach without him hearing us, we have the element of surprise on our side. Most likely, he'll turn to the door when I throw it open so everyone stand back."

Colton looked back to the buggy. He meant to signal Rebecca to stay put, but she was at Pa's side, helping him to dismount. He couldn't get her attention without calling out and that would alert Vern if he hadn't already heard them approach.

"Ready?" Mason asked.

Colton nodded and the men crept toward the house. Colton strained to hear any sound from inside. Some sign that the occupants were safe.

A muted scream jerked through his senses and gave his feet wings. It had the same effect on Mason and Bucky.

Heidi's cat raced past his feet, streaking for the barn.

A cow mooed, the contented sound such a marked contrast to Colton's heightened tension that it jarred his nerves.

Two feet remained before they bombarded the door. Two feet before he could rescue those inside from an angry drunk. At least the scream meant someone was still alive.

Thunder drowned out all other sounds. All other thought. Colton didn't bother to look at the sky. It was clear.

It was not thunder that battered his eardrums but a gunshot.

Had Vern shot someone?

Colton no longer cared for caution or surprise. He shouldered the door open and burst into the room. The smells of sulfur and fear filled the air. In a heartbeat he took in the situation.

Ma sat on her cot, clutching Heidi. Both were as pale as an old sheet. Only Heidi's brown eyes gave her face any color. Amelia held little Gabriel in one arm. She clutched the back of a brown wooden kitchen chair with her other hand, her knuckles shiny white marbles. She stared at the floor, her mouth working soundlessly.

Colton jerked his attention to the floor and the source of guttural grunts. Vern wrestled with someone.

Mason scooped up the gun from near the stove, grabbed the collar of one of the combatants and dragged him from the melee. Colton lifted Vern by the front of the shirt and shook him hard. "You crazy drunk. How dare you venture into my house and threaten my family. I ought to—"

"Easy, Colton," Mason warned.

Rebecca helped Pa through the door. He hobbled over to Ma and sat down, pulling her into his arms.

Rebecca hurried to Amelia. She pried Amelia's clenched hand from the back of the chair and pushed her onto the seat.

"Now, who is this young man?" Mason asked.

"Jakob!" Heidi broke from Ma's arms and threw herself at the young man. Her sobs filled the stunned silence.

Mason released Jakob so he could hold and comfort his sister. "So you found her? We wondered how long it would take."

Colton studied the boy. Tall and lanky. Longish light

brown hair that curled about his head. Jakob measured the situation with brown eyes so like Heidi's there was no mistaking that they were brother and sister.

Mason took Vern and shoved him into a chair. "Vern, you've crossed a line here. You can't use your fists or your gun to control people."

Vern, somewhat sobered, scowled at Mason. "She's my wife. I tell her what to do and nobody better interfere."

Amelia finally found words to fill her empty mouth. "Vern, I am leaving you."

"That old biddy said you planned to. Said you thought you could walk out on me and get a job at the orphanage."

Colton leaned close. "What old biddy? Who told you?"

"Miss Ward, of course. That bird knows everything going on in town. Thought you could hide my wife from me, did you? And that baby? She says he's mine."

The color drained from Amelia's face. She swallowed hard, then faced her husband with boldness. "He deserves better than you for sure."

Vern surged to his feet and reached across the table toward Amelia.

Mason shoved him back. "Bucky, take him to town and lock him up." He glowered at Vern. "Enjoy your stay in my jail. It will be temporary until you get transferred to a bigger one. I expect the judge will send you away for a good long time."

Dirtying the air with his curses, Vern was dragged from the house.

Mason pulled out a chair and sat down. "Jakob, I'd like to hear what happened."

"I been looking for my sister." His speech revealed a stronger German accent than Heidi's. "I promised our *mutter* and *vater* that I'd look after her—that is why I ran away." He looked at Rebecca as if begging her to understand. "I had to make sure she was okay. That people weren't being unkind to her." He touched his face as if thinking of Heidi's scars. "If she was unhappy, I figured to take her and go west, where we could live on our own."

Heidi's gaze shifted from adoring her brother to giving Rebecca a pleading look.

Did she want to go west with Jakob?

Colton got the sinking sensation that everyone he cared for was about to leave him. Except his parents. He'd have them for a few years yet. The thought normally consoled him, but today it failed to do so. For a few weeks he'd shared his life with a woman and children. He'd known family. And something more. But words to describe it eluded him at the moment.

Jakob continued, "I found her here and she was so happy I decided to move on. Figured I'd write her from someplace farther west and tell her I was okay. I was headed down the road a spell when that man rode past. I was walking in the field so he never seen me. I didn't like the look of him so I waited and watched. He barged into this house with a gun in his hand. Then that man—" he indicated Pa "—rode away so fast I knew there was something wrong. I had to make sure Heidi was okay. And everyone else. Took me a few minutes to get back here, then I peeked in the window and seen that awful man waving his gun around and threatening the ladies. I sneaked in the other door."

Colton couldn't remember when the door in the parlor room had last been opened.

"He never seen me. All I had to do was tackle him down."

Mason narrowed his eyes. "He could have shot you or one of the others."

Jakob smiled confidently. "I knew enough to get his hand first and make sure a shot wouldn't hurt anyone." He nodded toward the ceiling.

Every pair of eyes followed the direction he indicated and saw the hole overhead.

Mason chuckled. "You're a smart fella."

Jakob grinned at Heidi. "Not so smart that my little sister couldn't trick me. I can't believe you got the other children to help you so a family would take me. You knew I didn't want to be separated from you."

"But no one wanted me. I didn't want you to be sent back to New York."

The adults exchanged glances. They knew now that no orphans would have gone back to New York. If Felix Baxter had had his way, though, they might have ended up in his clutches.

Colton studied his parents, still sitting on the cot with their arms around each other. "Pa, I can't believe you rode to town. How did you manage to get away from Vern?"

Pa got the look of a guilty child. "I was outside when he came. I heard him. He's not very subtle. I heard him yelling at the women, and when I saw he had a gun, I knew I'd need help. I'm not as agile as that young man."

"But to saddle your horse and ride to town— Pa, it doesn't seem possible." Certainly people did amazing things under stress, but this was beyond Colton's imagination.

His parents exchanged a long look. Pa nodded. "I guess it's time to fess up. I've been getting around pretty good the last while. Today I had decided to try riding. Already had the old nag saddled when Vern showed up."

Colton's jaw dropped so far he thought it might have come unhinged. He worked it back into place and swallowed hard. "Pa?" This didn't make sense. He sought Rebecca's gaze, hoping for enlightenment. She and Amelia darted a quick look at each other.

When she lifted her head, he saw guilt and apology.

"Everyone knew this but me?"

"He's getting better," Heidi said, full of staunch loyalty. "That's good, even though he kept it a secret, isn't it?"

Mason pushed to his feet. "I need to get back to town. Jakob, perhaps you'd better come with me. I'll find you a place to bunk."

Colton pushed aside his confusion. "He can stay here with his sister."

Heidi sprang to Colton's side and hugged him. "Thank you so much." She danced across the floor. "I'm so happy to have Jakob back."

Colton headed for the door. "I've got chores." He stopped, glanced at Rebecca. "I— You—" He shook his head. He had to think.

"I'll help," Jakob said.

Colton needed time alone to figure out what to do, but he couldn't refuse the boy. "Come along, then."

Pa got up, too.

Colton sprang forward to help, then stopped himself. He didn't know if his help was needed anymore. Seemed he'd been blind as to what his role was.

"I'll take care of the chickens," Pa said.

Colton nodded and the three of them crossed to the barn.

As he fed the horses in the barn and slopped the pigs, all the while explaining his actions to Jakob, he tried to shepherd his thoughts into some semblance of order.

He soon discovered that Jakob was quite capable and left him to finish the barn chores. Pa headed to the house with a basket of eggs.

Now was a good time to check on the rapidly growing corn crop and Colton slipped away. But he paid scant attention to the size of the plants or the moisture condition of the soil as his thoughts scattered like hail.

Heidi had Jakob. Amelia had a place at the orphanage. Seemed Pa didn't need him nearly as much as Colton had thought. He floundered. Who was he? What did he want? What was he supposed to do if he wasn't worrying about the needs of others?

Rebecca. Her name lit up his mind with the light of twenty bolts of lightning.

But he had no reason to ask her to stay at the ranch. Gabriel had a mother. Heidi had a brother. Ma had Pa.

If he let Rebecca return to New York, he would have no one. But what could he offer her to compare with a thirty-room house?

Two crows flapped overhead, squawking as if scolding him.

He stared at the birds as they passed.

He had one thing to give, something he'd been denying for almost as long as she'd been staying at the ranch. He loved her.

He studied the notion. He was a strong man. A man used to caring for others, protecting them. He loved his parents. He loved Gabriel and Heidi. So why couldn't he simply walk up to Rebecca and confess his feelings? But he couldn't. Something dark and wide made it impossible…the difference between a poor rancher and a rich, city girl.

He kicked at the dirt on the edge of the cornfield until he'd dug a good-size furrow. He had nothing to offer her except a loving heart. How did that compare to what she had in New York?

Amelia waited until Jakob and the men departed, then burst into tears.

Rebecca rubbed her back. "Shh. It's all over. He'll never hurt you or your son again." He'd go to jail for a good long spell.

After a few minutes, Amelia quieted down, sat up and

wiped her eyes. "Heidi, your brother is very brave and very smart."

Her eyes gleamed with pride. "I know."

Rebecca was happy things had worked out for everyone. Jakob and Heidi reunited and had perhaps learned that nothing was so bad if they were together. Amelia was free to pursue a fear-free life with little Gabriel. Colton's parents were learning the benefits of remaining independent as long as they could—especially now that his ma's new medication seemed to be working well. Since she had begun taking it, Mrs. Hayes had more energy and far less swelling in her legs. Certainly they would appreciate Colton's continued help, but not as they had in the past.

And Colton didn't need help from a city girl.

She would not dwell on what she couldn't have. Instead, she would rejoice in what the community and she had accomplished. "I think we need to celebrate the way this day has ended. Let's make the meal special."

The others immediately agreed and sprang into action. Mrs. Hayes said she would make the meat loaf that her husband had always said was his favorite. Amelia promised another chocolate cake. Rebecca volunteered to make creamy mashed potatoes, which she knew was popular with everyone.

"What can I do?" Heidi asked.

"What's one of Jakob's favorite dishes?"

Heidi grew thoughtful. "Some I don't know English names for." Then she brightened. "Potato dumplings. We always had them at Sunday dinner."

Rebecca lifted her hands in defeat. "Amelia?"

She shook her head.

They all turned to look at Mrs. Hayes. "Child, do you recall how your mother made them?"

Heidi drew her eyebrows together in concentration.

"Mashed potatoes and flour. Mama let me help. We squished the potatoes and flour together and then I made tiny snowballs. Mama said they had to be pea-size. Then we boiled them. Yummy."

Mrs. Hayes nodded. "Mrs. Kruger made something like that. I think we can manage."

Mr. Hayes returned shortly, as did Jakob, who stood awkwardly at the door.

"Sit, boy." Mr. Hayes waved him to a chair. "Looks like we are in for a feast."

"It's a celebration," Heidi said, brushing hair from her face. The movement smeared flour across her cheek.

Jakob laughed as he wiped the flour away. "You're getting more on you than in the food."

Rebecca tried to keep from looking at the door. Where was Colton? She'd thought her heart would burst from its mooring earlier when he bolted into the house following the gunshot. Not until she saw him holding Vern, breathing normally and not bleeding from any wound, did her heart settle into place again.

He returned in a little while, looking pleased with the sight before him. "Smells great in here."

"It's a celebration," Heidi announced.

"And what are we celebrating?" He grabbed her hands and danced her around the table.

She giggled, but managed to get out the words, "I'm celebrating finding Jakob."

"Seems as if he found you."

She giggled some more.

Amelia grinned at them. "I'm celebrating my freedom. Tomorrow I am going to town to see the orphanage and learn about my new job."

Colton released Heidi and went to his parents. "Ma and Pa are celebrating feeling better. Right?"

His pa clapped him on his back and his ma patted his cheek.

Heidi studied Colton. "What are you celebrating?"

Colton grinned from one to another. His attention rested a moment longer on Rebecca, or so she thought. "I'm celebrating that everyone is safe and sound."

She shifted her attention back to meal preparation.

Now that everyone was safe and sound, where did she belong? She knew the answer. Nothing had changed. Her place was back in New York.

Why, then, did that feel like a prison sentence?

The meal was lovely. Jakob praised Heidi for the dumplings. Said they were the best he'd ever tasted. Colton insisted he tell them how he'd found Heidi.

"I just kept looking." He ducked his head and ran his finger around the rim of his empty plate several times. "Miss Sterling, you know the orphans that were placed in Greenville from the groups that came through before ours?"

What had he discovered? "Yes. What about them?"

"You know they aren't there?" The look he gave her revealed his concern. "I think that man—Mr. Baxter—sends them to work in mines and stuff. He's not a nice man."

"We found that out. Someone is tracking them down right now." She told him about the new orphanage in Evans Grove. "It's kind of you to be concerned for them."

Several times throughout the evening, Rebecca caught Colton studying her with a great deal of interest. Twice he started to speak to her. Once he got as far as suggesting a walk, but each time she pretended to be distracted by something.

She did not want to provide an opportunity for him to explain how she was no longer needed.

Tomorrow would be soon enough. After she'd had time to get used to the idea and pray for God's strength to deal with it.

In truth, she would never get used to it. It had been relatively easy for her to forget Oliver. Why, she couldn't even recall his face any longer. To her shame, she knew she'd never loved him. Had only wanted to please her father. What a silly reason to enter a marriage.

But having her pride hurt when he eloped with another woman would surely be an easier pain to bear than leaving Evans Grove. And even the thought of saying goodbye to Colton forever made her heart feel as if she'd breathed in fire.

She managed to keep busy until Heidi's bedtime and hurried after her, even though it was early. They prepared for the night, then climbed in beside each other.

Heidi faced her. Even in the darkened room, Rebecca could see her happy smile.

Heidi patted Rebecca's cheeks. She'd miss those gentle touches. But she'd miss the child even more. Thankfully, it was too dark for Heidi to notice the tears stinging Rebecca's eyes.

"I'm so happy," Heidi said.

Rebecca hugged her. "I'm glad for you."

"Remember when I cried because I didn't think I'd see Jakob again?"

"Yes, I do." There'd been a few teary sessions.

"You said I could trust God to provide what I needed. Remember?"

"Of course." She had wanted to give the child something to hold on to.

"You warned me that sometimes God allows things that seem hard to help us grow strong. Since then, I've prayed for God to make me strong, but I never stopped missing Jakob. I guess God thinks I'm strong enough for now." She sighed deeply. "I'm glad."

A few minutes later Heidi's measured breathing indicated that she had fallen asleep.

Rebecca stared into the darkness. It seemed as if she was going to have to trust God herself, even when things were hard. She would need to be strong. Stronger than she'd ever thought possible.

Chapter Eighteen

The next morning Amelia and the baby accompanied Rebecca and Colton to town. At Heidi's request, she and Jakob remained at the ranch, where Mr. and Mrs. Hayes welcomed their company.

Rebecca was no more prepared this morning to hear Colton explain why she was no longer needed at the ranch than she had been last night. Amelia's company and questions provided a buffer for her.

They arrived at the orphanage and she escorted Amelia upstairs.

Amelia fairly glowed with excitement. "I can't thank you enough for hiring me for this position. I am going to love working here and caring for the children. It's like a dream come true."

Rebecca smiled, though her heart felt like a lump of clay in her chest. "I'm glad." She led Amelia toward the boys' dormitory. "The ladies have done such a nice job of decorating." She stepped into the room and gasped.

The shelves were all overturned. The beds stripped of their new quilts. The bedding lay in a heap against the far wall.

A rat had been nailed to the wall, its throat slit, and blood

ran down the wall to stain the quilts. A scream pushed pas
her teeth and filled the room. Bile burned up her throat.

She backed up, pushing Amelia from the room, an
slammed the door.

"What's wrong?" Amelia asked.

Rebecca rolled her head back and forth. She couldn't fin
her voice.

Colton burst up the stairs. "Did I hear you scream?"

Still unable to speak, she waved toward the room.

He edged past her, his eyes full of curiosity. He steppe
into the room and made an angry sound. "I thought this wa
over." He didn't sound as surprised as she expected. Rebecc
signaled Amelia to wait as she inched inside.

"This has happened before?"

He yanked the rat from the nail and tossed it out a window
"Not like this." He told her about the dead rat hanging in th
orphanage and the one on the pump at the ranch.

"But why? How could anyone be so mean as to ruin th
prepared room?"

"I think it's meant to be a warning." He seemed distracte
by the streak of blood on the wall.

"What for?" Then she realized what he meant. Horro
widened her eyes. "Someone is this opposed to the orphan
age? Miss Ward?"

"I can't believe she'd do this. It's disgusting. And thi
takes someone who doesn't mind getting her hands dirty."

Rebecca gave a mirthless chuckle. "That would exclud
Miss Ward."

Colton sprang for the door. "Did you check the othe
rooms?"

"No." She followed hard on his heels.

Amelia glanced over his shoulder and saw the damage
Her expression hardened. "Did Vern do this?"

Colton grabbed her shoulder. "This had to happen after th

vorkers left yesterday. By then Vern was in jail, so it can't
e him. Take the baby downstairs. And be careful."

He and Rebecca crossed the hall to the girls' room. He
eld her back as he examined it, then lowered his arm to let
er in. The bedding was torn off three beds. No other dam-
ge had been done.

"It looks like the culprit was interrupted."

Rebecca's knees turned to rubber and she sank onto the
earest bed. "But who could have done this?"

Colton sat beside her, put an arm about her shoulders and
ulled her close.

She barely restrained herself from burying her face against
is chest. In a few more days, such comfort would be unavail-
ble to her. "I feel like I've been touched by something evil."

He tightened his hold on her. "I'd hoped whoever it was
ad given up."

"The orphans will soon be here, but they won't be safe
vith this sort of thing going on. What are we going to do?"
he sat up straight, letting his arm slip away. It left her weak
nd frightened. But she would not let fear or inexperience
top her from creating a safe, welcoming environment for
ie children Wyatt would soon be bringing. "Maybe we can
et a trap."

He turned to consider her full-on. "What do you have in
iind?"

"I don't know if it will work, but what if we clean this all
p, soak the quilts and make all the beds again? If this per-
on is set on destruction, won't he return, most likely after
ark, to finish the job? You said yourself that he must have
een interrupted before he could destroy the girls' room. We
ould wait and catch whoever is responsible for this."

"It might work, but *we?* Sounds a little dangerous for both
f us to stay."

She rose to her feet in a way she hoped communicated her

determination. Silently, she thanked her mother for lesson in hiding her emotions. "This orphanage is my responsibil ity until I turn it over to Amelia. The idea to trap the culpri was mine. I will be part of the plan."

He shook his head, prepared to argue further, but Re becca spoke again.

"We'll enlist Mason's and Bucky's help. Besides, we hav no guarantee that it will succeed."

He studied her a full, long minute. "I don't suppose there' any point in saying no."

"Not really. Now let's get to work."

They recruited Amelia to help. The bloodstained beddin was soaked, scrubbed and hung to dry. Like flags of chal lenge to whoever had done this.

The beds were remade. The rooms tidied.

Several hours later, Rebecca surveyed the rooms. "We'r ready."

Colton had slipped away to consult Mason, and the had agreed it would be best if Rebecca, Amelia and Colto headed home as usual. Bucky would watch the place unti dark, then they would all slip into the building under cove of night.

On the way home, the adults agreed that they would tel Colton's parents the truth about what they were doing, bu they'd tell Jakob and Heidi only that they had business t attend to in town.

Rebecca had to force herself to sit calmly through th meal and tend to the various chores around the house whe her nerves jumped and her limbs twitched. She had neve done anything like this before, and she was both nervou and excited.

Colton fought an inner battle. He wanted Rebecca to sta home with the others, where he could reasonably hope she' be safe. But he wanted her at his side, too. He couldn't have it both ways and eventually decided to follow his heart, rather than his head. He smirked in the dark. As if telling her to stay home would have done anything but instigate an argument.

He sat beside her on a bed in the boys' dorm. Mason waited in the girls' room and Bucky sat in a corner of the kitchen. The culprit would have to be a shadow to enter without someone noticing.

She leaned close. "Isn't this exciting?"

Her breath caressed his cheek, filled him with longings to the center of his being. Would she stay in town if he asked her to? He let his dreams gallop apace. If she did, he could see her every day...or at least often. He could court her. They could grow close, share dreams and wishes...

A sigh filled his thoughts. What was the point in dreaming?

He turned, caught her chin in the dim light coming through the windows so he could speak close to her ear. "This person is dangerous. I should have left you at home."

She turned and their cheeks brushed. He closed his eyes, caught her shoulders, telling himself it was only to steady her, but his arms crept about her and he held her gently, his heart so full of longing he couldn't breathe.

"I wouldn't have stayed."

He righted his thoughts as best he could. But he could not think of a reply other than to tip his head to hers, their foreheads touching. It wasn't his imagination that she sighed and lifted her face slightly.

As if asking for a kiss?

A sound came from downstairs. Like someone stepping on a loose board.

He tightened his arms around Rebecca. Had the culprit slipped past Bucky? Was he outside the door? Though he hated to do so, he eased his arms from around Rebecca and tensed, ready to spring into action.

She grabbed his hand and squeezed.

They sat tense and alert. The silence filled his ears, the only sound his own careful breathing.

A crash from downstairs brought them both to their feet.

Colton's heart thumped against his ribs. "What was that?" No need to be quiet with the noise below.

"Got me someone," Bucky called.

Holding Rebecca's hand, Colton rushed from the room. Mason headed down the steps ahead of them. He lit a lamp and they stared at the man Bucky held with an arm twisted behind his back.

"Let me go." The prisoner twisted and fought Bucky.

"He's just a boy," Rebecca said.

The lad looked to be about fourteen, about Jakob's age. His dark eyes glinted with anger.

"A dangerous boy." Wyatt snapped on handcuffs. He and Bucky held him on either side. "Another dead rat." The carcass lay two feet away. "What were you planning this time?"

"Let me go." He squirmed so much that both men clamped down on him.

"What's your name?" Rebecca asked.

"What does it matter?"

Ignoring Colton's restraining hand, Rebecca stepped forward. "Let me help you. I am an agent for the Orphan Salvation Society."

The boy snarled. "Know all about them. Don't need their kind of help."

Rebecca glanced over her shoulder toward Colton and mouthed the words *Felix Baxter?*

He understood her message. Had this boy been victimized by Baxter?

She turned back to the boy. "I know some bad things have

happened to children placed by the Society. We only recently discovered the truth. We're doing our best to remedy the situation. That's why we've built this orphanage."

The boy growled, "I know all about orphanages. Hate 'em." He shot a look to the ceiling. "Mean to warn the others to avoid this place."

"But why? We only want to help. Give the children a safe place."

"I heard that song before, lady. I ain't about to believe it twice." He fought his restraints.

"Settle down," Mason said. "You aren't going anywhere except to jail."

"Were you involved with Felix Baxter?" Rebecca asked.

"Not me."

"Then what are you so angry about?"

The boy glowered, but Colton wondered if he detected a sheen in his eyes. "I got my reasons."

"I'm sure you do, but maybe we can help you."

He snorted. "It's too late for anyone to help me."

"Surely not. If you have a friend or relative in Mr. Baxter's clutches, he can be rescued. There is a man finding orphans. He'll bring them here, where I guarantee they will be safe. If you tell us who—"

"Lady, I said it's too late. He's dead."

Rebecca fell back a step. Colton caught her and steadied her.

"Dead?" Shocked hollowed out the word. "Who was it?" Her voice grated from her throat.

"My little brother." The fight left the boy so quickly that he sank toward the floor, and Mason nodded to Bucky to let go but stand by in case he tried to run.

Rebecca sat beside the boy, her legs tucked to one side. "I am so sorry to hear that. I wish I could have arrived in time to stop it from happening. What was his name?"

"Kenny. He was only eleven. Baxter sent us both to a farm. The owner was cruel. I tried to protect Kenny, but in the end I failed." Challenge flared in his eyes. "I don't aim to stand by and see a bunch more kids treated the way we were."

"Nor should you." Rebecca's agreement with him deflated his anger. "I feel exactly the same way, which is why I personally took on the challenge of seeing that the orphans will have a safe, happy place here. This man—" she turned to Colton "—is a good friend of mine. He helped build this place."

The boy nodded. "I seen him."

A *friend?* Somehow the word lacked warmth. He wanted so much more, even though it was out of reach. A vast chasm separated them. It was not just a matter of who she was or the luxuries she was used to. His own dark walls held his heart tight. Could he look after her, protect her? Or would he fail as he had with his parents?

"His cousin Amelia is going to run the home. She's a kind and brave woman. The whole town is set on taking care of the orphans."

The boy studied Rebecca, shifted his gaze to Colton. His expression clearly indicated that he wasn't about to trust any of them.

Rebecca touched the boy's arm. "My name is Rebecca Sterling. What's yours?"

The boy looked at Rebecca. He must have seen something he liked. "Sam Johnson."

"Sam, I'm glad to meet you."

Colton held back, knowing Sam wouldn't accept any kindness from the men at this point.

"I'd like to help you." Rebecca spoke so gently.

"What could you do?"

"Get you a safe place to live."

"I ain't living in no orphanage ever again."

Colton stepped forward. "Sam, you're a big, strong boy. And resourceful, as we've seen. I know of a farmer or two who would welcome a boy like you."

"I done seen how a farmer welcomes boys."

"Not all people are cruel. I know lots who aren't. Do you like cows and horses?"

"Lots better than weeding turnips."

"I know a man who runs a herd of horses and is always looking for someone to help with them."

Eagerness flared in Sam's eyes, but he quickly tamped it down.

Mason nodded toward Bucky. "We'll be taking him to the jail now." They helped the boy to his feet.

Rebecca sprang up. She turned to Colton, grabbed his arm and looked up into his face. "Jail is no place for a boy."

"Won't hurt him none," Bucky said as they headed for the door.

"Colton, stop them."

"I doubt it's safe to turn Sam loose. Besides, as Bucky says, it won't do him any harm." He hated the idea as much as Rebecca did, but letting the boy continue on his vendetta was not the answer. "Sam, I'll be by in the morning. We'll talk."

Rebecca waited until the trio was out the door before she rammed her fists on her hips and glowered at him. "How can you stand by and let them do that?"

"Do you really think Mason will let any harm come to the boy? Or that he would tolerate my interfering?"

She spun away. "There must be something we can do."

He followed her. "Maybe a night in jail will give him time to consider his options. I fear if he continues to let anger rule his actions he will end up in jail for more than a night."

She whirled about. "How many more are there like him and his brother?"

The agony in her voice ached through him. He opened

his arms and she readily came into his embrace. He held he
close. "We've done all we can to help them."

She stilled in his arms. "I pray Sam will accept your offer
She leaned back and smiled up at him. "Thank you for it."

Her smile smoothed the sharp corners of his insides th
had been built there with Sam's story. "You're the one wh
got through to him."

She sobered. "It's so dreadful."

He couldn't bear to see her troubled expression. He pulle
her closer, relishing the comfort she took in his embrace.

A few minutes later they headed home. All the way sh
talked about Sam and the others like him, words racing fror
her mouth. He helped her from the buggy, holding her lor
after her feet rested solidly on the ground.

She laughed softly. "I really am a force to be reckone
with."

"I'd say so. Your job here is just about successfully con
pleted."

Her smile fled. "I hope my father will appreciate all I'v
done." Her sigh came from deep inside. "He's expecting m
home soon."

Colton backed away. Her constant reminder of her plar
to return to New York rebuilt the creaking walls in his hea
with double strength.

Chapter Nineteen

Amelia adjusted a quilt on one of the cots in the boys' dorm. "Things have worked out well for everyone. Praise God."

Sam had accepted Colton's offer and had gone to work for a nearby rancher.

"Not that there aren't bad things in life." Her expression clouded. Rebecca wondered if her thoughts had slipped back to Vern.

"Like what these poor children had dealt with." She straightened and her mouth grew stubborn. So much like Colton. "With God's help I will do my best to make their lives here pleasant."

"I know you will." Rebecca could leave with her conscience clear that she had done well as an OSS agent. However, the thought provided scant comfort. She wanted to stay. To belong. Not just in the community, but in Colton's heart.

She had no one but herself to blame for thinking it could be different. From the start, people in the community had made it clear that they expected her to leave.

She didn't belong here. That knowledge festered inside her.

But she had her life to return to. And, God help her, she would face it with newfound grace and courage.

"I'd like to go through the kitchen again," Amelia said.

They descended the stairs. Ted, Colton and two other were putting the final touches on the shelves and furnishing The wooden table had been sanded and oiled to a glowin finish. Benches offered seating on either side of the table. Th kitchen cupboards provided adequate storage, and a thick topped worktable would allow three or four women to wor together. Rebecca could envision the room finished, childre clustered around the table, chattering happily.

"I want to go over the list of supplies you have and se if there is anything that needs to be added." Amelia studie the kitchen as if seeing it occupied.

With no desire to face Colton, Rebecca turned to the roor that would serve as a front room or a library—basically, a all-purpose room. Unfurnished at the moment, she though of putting in a couple of sofas and some big chairs where th children could curl up and read. Another table for homewor And a piano. She doubted the town would consider it neces sary, but she could imagine the children learning to play c someone coming in to entertain them.

She would give them a piano as her present when she lef

Her ribs tightened like a fist, squeezing her heart so eac beat was painful. Clutching her middle, she staggered to th window and looked out at the street, the town square. Cha lotte and Sasha walked through the grove of trees.

Rebecca had been instrumental in making sure that chil had a home.

Her only failure had been Heidi.

The pain in her chest deepened until she wondered ho she didn't bleed from her pores. She loved the child. Ha dreamed of keeping her, even if she had to return to Ne York. Now she must relinquish her, because Heidi woul be staying here. She would be near her brother. Rebecc couldn't be happier for the child, but oh, how she'd miss her sweet presence.

Almost as much as she'd miss the town. Her new friends.

Somehow she must keep from adding Colton to the list of things she'd miss, for she feared any more pain would tear her asunder.

"Rebecca." Colton stood in the doorway.

At the sound of her name on the lips of the very person she was trying so desperately not to think about, Rebecca's heart refused to keep beating.

He took a step forward, hesitating.

She couldn't answer. Couldn't think. Her brain thundered with lack of oxygen. One thought surfaced. She would not faint.

She forced her ribs to lift and sucked in air that steadied her.

"A lot of things have changed."

This was it, then—the moment when he told her that she was no longer needed, that it was time for her to go. She could not bear the apologetic tone of his voice. But she lacked the power to walk away.

He closed the space separating them, one slow step at a time. She couldn't watch, so she kept her gaze focused out the window as she counted his steps. One. Two. *Oh, please, hurry and get this over with.* Three. *Stop. I don't want to hear it.* Four. *I will survive. I will survive.*

Although she looked out the window, nothing registered.

Five. He was at her side. She closed her eyes. To her dying day the scent of fresh-sawn lumber would bring back every detail of her stay. But mostly she'd think of Colton.

Thankfully, she would have little reason to be around newly cut wood.

"We have company," he muttered. "I wonder what they want."

Did she only imagine that he sounded disgusted? She opened her eyes to see who he meant. Pauline, Mason and Reverend Turner were at the front door. Already the door opened and they stepped inside.

"Hello? Colton? Rebecca?" Pauline called.

"We're in here." Colton strode to the hallway to greet them.

Rebecca forced in two deep breaths to still the pounding of her heart and followed.

"There you are." Pauline nodded a greeting.

Mason and the reverend also greeted her.

"After what Vern Hicks has said about Beatrice—the way she told him where to find Amelia and put all of your lives in danger—we have decided we must confront Beatrice." Pauline was the spokesperson for the trio. "She has put people at risk. She simply must desist."

"We all agree," Mason said.

"We want you to come with us so she can apologize to you," Reverend Turner said.

"Me?" Rebecca squeaked out the word.

"You and Colton." Pauline was quite adamant.

"We'll come." Colton answered.

Rebecca didn't want to confront Miss Ward, but she lacked the strength to argue, so they trooped from the orphanage, turned right and marched down First Street to Victory. Like a parade, they turned left and continued onward to the hotel. Pauline led the way, pulling Rebecca at her side. The men followed.

Rebecca would have preferred to be at the back of the entourage, but walking at Colton's side would have made it impossible for her to be calm and collected. From past experience, she knew that she must be when facing Beatrice Ward.

They marched up the steps and walked single file through the door into the lobby.

Beatrice looked up from an armchair, where she was reading. She saw them flank each other and fear flickered through her eyes, replaced almost instantly with defiance.

Ned Minor stood behind the desk, as curious as the farm cats.

Pauline spoke to him. "Ned, would you give us some privacy, please?"

Ned reluctantly slunk away and closed the office door with a click.

Beatrice jumped to her feet with an agility that surprised Rebecca. "What's this all about?"

Pauline, still the spokesperson, answered, "I think you know. You have opposed the orphanage from the start and gone out of your way to destroy and discredit the Orphan Salvation Society's work. But your interference in sending Vern after Amelia was more than opposition. It was dangerous."

Beatrice bristled. "Vern had a right to know where his wife was. I'm not responsible for his getting drunk before he went out there."

Mason sighed heavily. "You should have known he'd do something violent. It's the way he always deals with things."

Rebecca thought she detected a flicker of regret before Beatrice sniffed. "I had no idea what he would do. I merely knew that his wife was being considered for a role running the orphanage, and thought he'd prefer to have her running her home, as usual."

Pauline sighed. "You endangered half a dozen people just to prevent the orphanage from having a director? Beatrice, this must stop. Your opposition to something the community is committed to is, at the very least, a cause of division."

"I'm entitled to my opinion."

Reverend Simpson stepped forward. "Beatrice, I don't believe you meant for things to get out of hand the way they did. Why not apologize for your part in the events and then move on as a supportive part of the community?"

Beatrice sniffed extra long and hard. "I cannot support bringing those ruffians to Evans Grove. Haven't we dealt with enough already? The flood. Homes and businesses damaged. Hasn't the community allowed enough street children into our midst? Against my advice. Mark my words. We will yet rue the day. Now if you'll excuse me…" She retrieved her book and, with head held high enough to brush the cobwebs from the ceiling, marched up the stairs.

Rebecca stared after her.

Pauline shook her head. "That woman refuses to change."

"As long as she isn't directly responsible for any more dangerous incidents," Mason said, "I don't care what she thinks about how the rest of us choose to live."

Reverend Turner held his black bowler hat to his chest. "We could all live with her attitude if she wasn't so intent on making us adopt it."

Colton simply stared, then said, "How hard is it to apologize? Even if she wasn't responsible for how Vern acted, at the very least, she told him Amelia was at the ranch, and that deserves an apology." He looked at Rebecca, his eyes as dark as a forest floor. "Things might have turned out a lot differently than they did."

Rebecca, trapped in the softness of the forest, nodded. No matter what happened, she would forever be grateful that no one had been hurt, both when Vern stormed into the ranch house and when Sam sneaked into the orphanage.

They trooped out the door.

Pauline escorted them back to the orphanage. "I want to talk to Amelia."

Pauline and Rebecca spent an hour with Amelia double-checking supply lists.

"It sounds fine to me," Pauline finally said. "Amelia, do ou have someone you'd recommend as a cook?"

"I haven't given it any thought. This whole thing is new ɔ me. What would you suggest, Rebecca?"

Rebecca jerked. "I'm sorry?" It had taken only a glance ut the window, to where Colton spoke to some of the men, ɔr her thoughts to slide sideways.

"I wondered if you had anyone in mind as cook."

She shepherded her mind back to the duties at hand. "It ɲight be nice if we had an older woman. A grandmotherly igure, perhaps." She'd seen how much Colton's parents of-ered Heidi. "But I don't know of anyone who would fit that escription."

"I do," Amelia said. "Mrs. Aarsen."

Rebecca tried to think if she knew the woman. Seeing her ɔnfusion, Amelia explained. "She's a dear Dutch woman ᴠho lost her husband a few years ago and her only son in the ᴠar. She lives on what's left of their farm. She's hardwork-ɲg, practical and kind to the core."

Pauline tapped her chin. "I wonder if she would agree."

"She might be glad to be surrounded by a different kind ᴏf family." Amelia appeared eager for the woman to be given chance.

Pauline didn't consider the idea long before she made up ɪer mind. "Rebecca, why don't you write a letter to tell her ᴃout the job and what it involves? Ask her if she's interested. 'll arrange for someone to deliver it to her while I'm at the tore placing this order."

Rebecca gladly took on the task. She'd done her job. Done ɪerself out of a place in the community. The walls of the or-ɸhanage seemed to mock her. She couldn't abide to stay in ɪe building where all she had to do to see Colton was look ᴏut the window. Or look at signs of his workmanship and emember his strong hands doing the work, and the glory of

the earlier days when they had worked side by side. "I'll g
to Holly's for paper and ink." She fairly flew down the street

Colton tried to keep his attention on the construction o
kitchen cupboards. The orphanage would soon be done. The
orphans would be arriving. The community was prepared
to welcome them. Amelia had determined to start a life fo
herself and Gabriel. Heidi would stay with her. Everything
seemed to be falling into place.

He shifted his focus back to the shelf that would hold
dishes. He should be happy, but instead, his insides twitched

Why couldn't he rejoice that they'd met every goal?

Because it wasn't what he wanted. He wanted—

He drew up hard and stared into the empty cupboard, see
ing nothing but the glaring truth in his heart.

He wanted Rebecca to stay. Wanted her in his home, car
ing for Heidi and more. So much more. He'd asked her to
stay for the children's sake, but now that excuse was gone
The only reason left was the echoing cry of his soul. He
loved her, but he could not tell her so. Oh, he could ask her
to stay, given any justifiable reason, such as the children, bu
he couldn't bring himself to say he loved her.

He didn't deserve love.

He didn't deserve love because he'd caused pain for both
his parents. Love did no harm. But was he responsible? Ba
bies came when they came, sent by God. Accidents happened
Certainly he'd played a role in Pa's accident, but ultimately
was he to blame?

He set his hammer aside and mumbled, "I got something
to do." With hurried feet, he fled the building, jogged across
the street and found a bench sheltered by trees in the town
square. He slumped to the wooden seat and buried his head
in his hands.

Oh, God, help me sort this out.

Colton sat back and stared at the leafy branches above his head.

His parents loved him. They'd never blamed him for their ill health, though Pa admitted that he thought Colton needed to take care of him out of guilt.

Guilt! Was he going to carry it the rest of his life? Let it steal the joys of the present?

Guilt was a heavy burden with harsh chains.

Love was a freeing joy. A gift from God. His for the choosing.

Oh, God, forgive me for letting guilt be my motivation when You offer forgiveness and so much more.

His life was a gift from God. As was the love he had for Rebecca. Time to tell her how he felt and give her a solid reason to stay in Evans Grove—or, more correctly, at the Hayes ranch.

Thank You, God.

Grinning widely, he headed back to the orphanage.

He would declare his love for her. They would work things out.

He half stumbled. What if she didn't share this wonderful, amazing feeling?

How could that be possible? The power of it should fill everyone in the world with a smile and a song.

Moderating his smile, he returned to the kitchen and the work that remained to be done.

Amelia wandered in with Gabriel in her arms. "I'm excited about this job. It's a chance for a new life."

He grinned at his cousin. "You deserve a second chance."

"Thank you for not saying *I told you so.*"

He knew she was referring to his warning against marrying Vern, but pretended otherwise. "Why would I say that?"

She patted his arm. "You wouldn't because you're far too

nice." She tipped her head and studied him long and hard. "You deserve your own happiness. I hope you get it."

They considered each other. She didn't say anything more. She didn't need to. They'd known each other far too long for words to be necessary. But he had to conceal the depth of his feeling until he spoke to Rebecca and knew her answer to his offer of love. He dared not hope beyond that. He turned away and picked up a piece of wood, though he had no idea what he meant to do with it. "I'm glad you're free of that man."

"Me, too. Before I forget, I don't plan to return to your place. I've got my own home. And for the first time I can go there without worrying about the mood Vern will be in when he returns."

So he'd have Rebecca alone on the way back to the ranch. He hummed under his breath as he carried the scrap of wood to the pile at the back of the lot.

He glanced at the sky. Two more hours and he could confess his love.

He watched for her to return, impatient for a glimpse of her.

She dashed up the street and into the front door as if there was an emergency.

He hurried to the back to see if she was hurt.

She sat at the table with Amelia across from her. "There's been news from Wyatt. The judge has ordered the orphans from Mr. Baxter's orphanage be released to Wyatt's care. He says he'll have them here Monday."

Amelia sat back. "It's finally time."

Colton stepped out of sight. Once the orphans arrived, her work would be done and she would begin her preparations to leave. He'd hoped for more time for her to get used to the fact that he loved her before he had to worry about her going back to New York. How long would she need?

He'd soon know, because in a little more than an hour, he would take her home and bare his heart to her.

As he stood in front of the orphanage, he saw the afternoon stagecoach rumble up to the store and stop. Two people got out. He recognized the one man returning from business in Newfield. The second man was a stranger. A tall man with a fine-looking top hat and a black suit jacket who walked as if he owned at least half the sidewalk.

Colton watched until he disappeared into the store, then shrugged and returned to his thoughts. To help pass the time, he reviewed every move, every gesture, every touch that gave him hope his love was returned.

Realizing that he was staring at the orphanage with a wide smile on his lips, he turned to look down the street again.

Pauline escorted the tall stranger toward the orphanage. Colton's smile flattened and his eyes narrowed.

He dashed through the back door and reached the kitchen just as Pauline and the stranger came through the front door. Rebecca glanced up, and he noted the exact moment she saw the man. Her blue eyes widened, then she bolted to her feet and raced into his arms. "Father."

Colton stared at the man. He'd removed his hat to expose silver hair. His face revealed his years and yet he was handsome, with the same blue eyes as his daughter. As the man hugged Rebecca, those blue eyes studied Colton, measuring him. Colton drew himself up tall and met the man look for look. He might not be city stuff, but he wasn't ashamed of who he was or what he did.

But would Rebecca see it that way? Would she feel she had to choose between the two of them? And if she did, which would she choose?

Rebecca clung to her father, finding comfort in his sheltering arms. She wouldn't have to deal with the future alone.

She could now face Colton, hear his words that she was no longer needed and not drown in her misery. But why was her father here? Had he come to check on her?

She pulled from his embrace. "Why have you come?"

"In response to a letter from Mayor Evans, whom I learn is this woman."

"A letter?"

Pauline nodded. "As grateful as I was toward the anonymous donor who funded the rebuilding of the school and building the orphanage, I wanted to be able to thank him directly. I figured it had to be your father. Who else could provide that much money? So I wrote and thanked him."

Her father gave Rebecca his most demanding look. One that had the power to make her agree to anything. Though she was so confused it failed to impress her this time. "Father, you?"

"Not me. Unless you committed me to something without asking."

"Of course I didn't."

"Normally I wouldn't have thought so, but from Mrs. Evans's letter, it seems you've been behaving very differently from how I would have expected."

Whatever Pauline had said about her, Rebecca would not shrink from the criticism. She'd made plenty of mistakes, especially in the beginning when she didn't understand the strength of this community and how people pulled together... but she was still proud of what she'd accomplished. "What did she say?" She might as well know the worst.

"Besides thanking us for our generosity, she said you've been an example of kindness, community spirit and endless enthusiasm for helping the children. Apparently, you have been a most welcome addition to the whole community."

Rebecca blinked. "She said that?" She turned to Pauline. "You said that?"

"Why wouldn't I? Every word is true, as everyone knows." Amelia nodded.

Everyone but me. She'd thought they couldn't wait to get rid of her.

Her father continued, "It sounded so different from the daughter I put on the train back in April that I had to come see for myself."

"If the funds didn't come from you, then who sent them?" Pauline tapped her chin in concentration, then confronted Rebecca. "Are you sure you don't know?"

"I don't. I'm sorry."

Pauline's mouth pursed into determination. "I won't rest until I get to the bottom of this mystery. I don't like not having every *i* dotted and every *t* crossed."

Mr. Sterling looked intrigued. "Exactly what did the note say?"

Rebecca thought a moment. "Besides how the money was to be used, it said, 'There is no better gratitude for an act of kindness than to pass it on.'"

Pauline gasped. "No." She pressed splayed fingers to her chest. "It can't be."

Amelia edged Pauline toward a bench, where she sat down, her eyes wide, her mouth open, but no sound came out.

Rebecca knelt before her. "What's wrong?"

Pauline sucked in air and pulled herself together. "Have you ever heard that exact saying before? The one in the letter?"

"I don't think I have."

Pauline sent an inquiring glance to Amelia, Rebecca's father and then to Colton, who hovered at the doorway. They all shook their heads.

"Well, I have. It was my husband's favorite saying. He learned it from his best friend in the army. After my husband saved his life, his friend lived by it. My husband mentioned it a number of times." She tipped her head, considering something. "It can't be. His name wasn't Curtis. It was Charlie." She looked surprised as she considered the information. "That was only a nickname, wasn't it? Oh, how could I have overlooked it? He once said those exact words, but we were arguing and it never registered." She jerked to her feet. "I must find him and talk to him."

Rebecca and Amelia stayed on either side of her in case she got wobbly.

Father fell in behind them. "This might be interesting."

Colton joined the second parade of the day. "Mr. Sterling, pleased to meet you. I'm Colton Hayes."

Father didn't slow his steps. "Hayes? Isn't that where my daughter's been living?"

"It is."

"Humph."

Rebecca refused to look over her shoulder at either of them. They both had her so confused that she didn't know which way was right and which was left. So she faced forward and marched straight ahead.

"Curtis will likely be at the hotel," Pauline said.

So again they paraded up the street, through the wide door and into the lobby. Curtis saw them approach and stood.

Ned rested his elbows on the desk.

Pauline shot him a look.

"I know. A little privacy. I'm leaving." The door shut rather loudly as he stepped into the office.

"Curtis Brooks, I'll have you know that thanks to you, I've made a fool of myself by writing this fine man—" She paused to introduce Rebecca's father. "I mistakenly thought he was the anonymous donor. He is not. I suspect you already know that—because I suspect that you yourself are the donor. And I believe there's something more you've been keeping from me. Something about my husband and your acquaintance with him. Am I right?" She crossed her arms and waited.

Curtis puffed out his cheeks. "Robert wrote me a letter when he knew he was dying." He pulled it from his pocket and handed it to Pauline. "He asked me to take care of you."

"Why not tell me that when you came? Why pretend you were only here to supervise the loan money from the bank?"

He looked embarrassed. "It's all in the letter…" When Pauline simply glared at him, he continued. "Robert didn't think you'd accept help if I offered it directly. He told me I'd have to find a way to help you and the town without your realizing who was responsible." He offered the letter again. This time, Pauline took it and began to read.

Rebecca figured she read it at least twice.

She folded the pages, inserted them in the envelope and handed the letter back to Curtis. "So you're here out of obligation? You're simply passing on gratitude?"

"At first that was all it was. But I soon came to respect the townspeople as they pulled together. I grew fond of them." He closed the distance between himself and Pauline. "I grew particularly fond of one of them." He took her hands and rubbed his thumbs across the backs of them.

Amelia cleared her throat. "I think we're done here," she said, leading the way outside for everyone but Pauline and Curtis.

In front of the hotel, Father took Rebecca's hand and tucked it around his arm. "Why don't you show me around this little town?"

"We'll go to the orphanage." Amelia took Colton's arm and led him away.

Rebecca allowed herself only a second to stare at Colton's departing back. She didn't realize how much that glimpse revealed until Father shook her gently. "Seems like they're fond of each other."

"They're cousins." She would say nothing more. "Come, I'll show you through town." They walked through the village green, stopped in front of the town hall, passed Pauline's house and reached the schoolyard. "Holly lives here." She paused long enough to introduce her friend, then they retraced their steps to the other side of town, past the jail where Amelia's husband awaited the judge's arrival, past the grain mill now again in operation. She told him what other businesses and homes had suffered damage in the flood. She pointed out homes where children from the Society were placed. "Many of them are out of town." Laughing, she told him about some of the fiery town meetings. Finally, they reached the creek. "It's hard to believe it flooded the town this spring."

"This trip was good for you. You'll be a real asset in New York. An efficient hostess, but also a person with well-formed opinions. I'm proud of you."

She watched the water gurgle past and assessed his words. She had grown, matured. She had become confident and sure of herself. She had fallen in love with a big-footed cowboy. Unless she put words to her newfound maturity, it would be wasted. "Father, I would never dishonor you. You know that, don't you?"

"You've always been a dutiful and obedient daughter."

She sent up a heartfelt, silent plea for God to guide her words. "I will continue to be obedient." She faced him knowing her eyes begged for understanding. "But I'm asking for you to grant me permission to stay in Evans Grove."

He studied her, his expression inscrutable. "It's because of Colton Hayes, isn't it?"

She nodded.

"Has he said he loves you?"

"No, Father," she whispered. She hoped against hope that he did, but she must face the possibility that he did not. "Bu even if he doesn't, I want to stay." Her voice grew strong and sure. "I have found something here I never knew in New York."

"What is that?"

"Friends, acceptance, community. And purpose. I can do things here that really matter."

Father pulled her against his chest. "I don't want to lose you."

"You won't. The trains will continue to run both ways."

"So they will." He sighed deeply. "If this is what you truly want, if you're convinced it will make you happy, I will not stand in your way."

"Thank you." She kissed his cheek.

"Promise me one thing."

"If I can."

"You'll come home if things don't work out."

"I promise."

Chapter Twenty

Colton swallowed back his disappointment as he drove home alone. Rebecca had said she would stay at the hotel with her father. He should have found a way to speak to her earlier. Now it was too late. Her father had come for her, and she would return with him.

At the ranch he had to answer a hundred questions about why Rebecca and Amelia weren't with him.

When Heidi learned about Mr. Sterling's arrival, she jerked forward on her chair. "Did he come to take Miss Sterling back to New York?"

"I expect so."

Heidi clutched Jakob's hand.

Colton slammed his fist on the table and bolted from the house, his long strides eating up the distance until he reached the spot on top of the hill.

Normally he would find peace and contentment there. But no longer. He remembered Rebecca sharing the place, admiring the wildflowers...

He could not let her go. She belonged here. She belonged in his family. More, she belonged in his heart. She'd always be there, whether or not she believed it. She was capable, generous, kind—just what the community needed. And what he needed more than he could begin to measure.

He'd petition her father for permission to ask her to be his wife. If she said yes, they'd sort out the details, such as his parents, after that.

His heart alive and well again, he did the chores. Jakob joined him and did more than his share.

The next day he saddled his horse. It would be good to ride again, rather than take the buggy.

Jakob followed him to the barn. "Tell me what needs doing and I'll do it. I need to work."

"I don't mind if you enjoy your time with Heidi."

"No. No. You not understand. I *need* to work."

"I see." The boy was almost a man. And likely used to being treated like one. Of course he needed to feel useful. "I haven't had time to check the fences for some time."

"I can do it."

"Thanks. I appreciate that. Supplies are in the tack room."

As Colton rode to town, he rehearsed what he would say to Mr. Sterling. He meant to find the man and speak to him at the first opportunity.

He'd expected to see Rebecca and her father at the orphanage, but they weren't there when he arrived. Amelia sauntered over an hour later, but still no Rebecca. A horrible thought shattered his peace of mind. "Did Rebecca and Mr. Sterling leave town?"

She shrugged. "Not that I know of. They are likely lingering over breakfast."

He considered marching over to the hotel and confronting the man there, but they needed to speak in private. So he stared at the orphanage. The walls said nothing.

Ted looked up when Colton walked around the corner. "Almost finished here. A coat of paint is all that's needed."

Colton nodded. He should be glad. The farmwork had been

neglected too long. But he couldn't be glad. Not yet. Not until he opened his heart and confessed his love.

Not until his love was returned.

He charged from the yard and headed toward the hotel. He would wait. A few minutes later Mr. Sterling stepped from the hotel. He stood on the front step, leaning back on his heels to study his surroundings.

Colton watched for Rebecca to join him, and when she didn't, he crossed to the man's side. "Sir, may I speak to you?"

"Certainly."

"In private." He indicated the town green and the man nodded. They crossed to the grove of trees. Colton drew to a halt and faced the man squarely. "Your daughter has become a valued part of the community."

"So I understand." He watched Colton with the same steady expression Rebecca gave him when she didn't want him to know what she was thinking.

Taking courage from the echo of familiarity, Colton continued, "She's more than that, though. I've enjoyed her stay at the ranch." His rehearsed words sounded pitiful in his ears. "What I'm trying to say is I've come to care for Rebecca. I'd like your permission to ask her to be my wife."

The man nodded slowly. "I see. And what do you have to offer her?"

"I'm just a rancher. Not even a big one. I have a house. Small."

"That's all you can give my daughter?"

Colton drew himself up tall. It gave him courage to realize he had a couple inches on the man. "No, sir. What I will offer Rebecca is my heart. My love. My fidelity. My loyalty. For as long as I live."

Mr. Sterling clapped Colton's shoulder. "No more and no less than she deserves. You have my blessing to ask her." He strode away, leaving Colton with his heart thumping madly. Now he only had to convince Rebecca of his love.

She stood on the hotel step watching her father approach. Mr. Sterling said something to her and waved her toward Colton. She nodded and crossed the street toward him.

"Father says you have something to say to me."

He nodded, his mouth so dry he couldn't speak. Not that he intended to say anything in full view of anyone who cared to look. He offered his arm, and she tucked her hand around his elbow. The warmth of her touch set his pulse racing. He led her to the center of the square, where the trees were thickest and where a bench waited. They sat side by side, her hand still resting on his arm. He pressed it close. Where he wanted to keep it as long as they both lived.

"Rebecca, I know your father has come to take you home."

She murmured something that was neither agreement nor argument.

He faced her, studied her watchful blue eyes, drank in her beautiful skin, her golden hair, her slender neck, her kissable lips. "I could never get tired of looking at you." His voice grew husky.

Her pink-china cheeks made him realize how bold his words had been.

"Rebecca, I am nothing but a big-footed cowboy. I don't have a thirty-room house." He shook his head. He didn't mean to focus on his deficiencies. "What I'm trying to say is I don't have a lot to offer, but I love you and I always will. Marry me, please? Make me the happiest man in Nebraska, in the world. I can't promise you riches, but I can promise you my undying, unending love."

Her smile filled his heart with sunshine and hope. "I can't think of anything more precious than that." She searched his eyes, shifted and studied his chin. Her gaze came to his mouth and stalled there.

He lowered his head, ready to accept her silent invitation to a kiss.

She touched her fingers to his chest. "Let me finish. I wondered if you would find me worthy. After all, I'm a spoiled, city girl. Before I came to stay at your ranch, I was totally unprepared to take care of a ranch home." She ducked her head. "I'm not sure your parents approve of me."

He laughed. "They've grown fond of you." He tipped her chin so he could look into her eyes. "I love you and that's all that matters to me. Not your qualifications. Besides you're a quick learner. You've proven that you are capable of anything you put your mind to." He watched her, wanting to know how she felt.

She brushed her fingers down his cheek, the stubble making a rasping sound. She stroked his chin then pressed her fingers to his lips. "Colton Hayes, I love you."

The words he longed to hear. He dipped his head and claimed her mouth. She leaned into him, offering her lips, her heart, her love. Her arms stole around his neck and she held him tight, as if she never wanted to let him go. He eased them to their feet so he could wrap her close and hold her next to his heart where she belonged. Where he belonged.

Epilogue

A month later

The street in front of the orphanage was crowded with people. In the park, tables had been set up.

Colton pulled Rebecca to his side. "How does it feel, sweet wife, to see the culmination of everything you came here to do?"

She leaned her head against his shoulder. Her love for him had grown so strong it seemed to root her and fill her and bless her. Not a day passed that she didn't thank God for bringing her to this place. "It feels good, but it was a community effort. And you had more than a little to do with getting the orphanage finished."

They were jostled aside by Liam chasing after another boy.

"Where's Heidi?" she asked.

"Over there." Colton pointed to the girl, who was playing with Sasha and several other children. "And Jakob is nearby. No one will make cruel comments to her while he's there."

Rebecca and Colton smiled at each other, silently sharing their secret.

Another wagon rumbled down the nearby street and drew

to a halt. The Holland family jumped down with Friedrich, the boy they had taken in.

"Looks like the whole community is here," Colton said. "Just like at our wedding."

"Father insisted he must give the sort of wedding that would make my mother happy." At first he'd wanted her to return to New York to be married, but she had convinced him that a wedding there would be a society spectacle, while in Evans Grove it would be witnessed by people who had become like family to her. He had relented and said they would put on a wedding that would leave the community happy for weeks. "I can't help but think that this event is of far more significance to everyone than our wedding was."

He chuckled. "Except for you and me. That was the best day of my life, and I don't mean because of the fancy food your father had shipped in or the beautiful lace-covered dress you wore. I mean because you and I became one for the rest of our lives."

She smiled, knowing the fullness of her heart showed in her eyes.

"No regrets?" he whispered.

"None."

"Not even having to share our home with my parents?"

"I couldn't manage without your ma's help and instruction."

"No regrets about Jakob and Heidi living with us?"

She nudged him gently in the ribs. "You know my answer. You just like to hear it. I think a home should include everyone who belongs in the family."

"I love you, Rebecca Hayes," he whispered.

"Shush. The speeches are about to begin."

Curtis Brooks and Pauline Evans stood in front of the orphanage and signaled everyone to quiet down. Then Curtis spoke. "It is with great joy that I officially open the orphanage and welcome the last of the Greenville orphans." He waved to the four children Wyatt had brought back two days ago. In total, eighteen children had been rescued. Everyone clapped. "Thanks to Wyatt's hard work and God's all-powerful hand, each child has been delivered from slavery."

Wyatt, at Charlotte's side with Sasha in front of them, lifted his hat in acknowledgment.

Curtis continued, "There has been much discussion regarding naming the orphanage. I felt it should bear Pauline's name. She was adamant that it bear my name. We were at an impasse."

People chuckled, knowing Pauline did not give up any fight easily.

"However, we have reached a very suitable arrangement." He pulled Pauline to his side. "I'm certain my feelings for this woman will come as no surprise to any of you. Thus it is with great joy I stand before you and say she has agreed to be my wife."

The crowd erupted into cheers and whistles.

Curtis smiled, then again signaled for quiet. "Hence we both get our way in naming the building The Brooks Orphanage." He and Pauline exchanged serene smiles. Then he turned to cut a red ribbon across the front door. "I declare The Brooks Orphanage officially open."

People clapped and cheered.

Curtis handed the scissors to Mrs. Aarsen, who had readily agreed to become cook and housekeeper.

"Now let's enjoy the feast the ladies have prepared. Reverend Turner, will you ask the blessing on our gathering?"

"I wish to say something." Miss Ward joined Pauline and Curtis.

Rebecca knew she wasn't the only one to bury a groan. Couldn't the woman let one single community event pass without attacking the orphans and the orphanage?

Beatrice twisted her gloves into a knot and cleared her throat twice. "I wish to publicly apologize to Rebecca and Colton and to you, Amelia. I have been remiss in my opposition to this work." She indicated the orphanage. "Everyone deserves a second chance. I hope you can all find it in your hearts to forgive me." She rushed through the crowd. When she reached Mr. and Mrs. Hayes, they stopped her and insisted she remain with them.

The reverend stood before them. "Beatrice, I'm sure I speak for everyone present when I say that was a truly humble apology and we extend our forgiveness. What matters is a spirit of unity and cooperation in our community. Thank you, Beatrice. Now I'll say grace."

As soon as he finished, lines formed to pass the laden tables.

Rebecca and Colton made their way to Beatrice's side.

Rebecca held out her hand. "No hard feelings." She was sure that even without active opposition, Beatrice would do her best to keep them all on their toes. Maybe that wasn't such a bad thing. With her determined attention to every detail, problems could be found and solved—together, as a community.

Colton also shook her hand. "Apology accepted."

She nodded and joined the line by the food tables.

Colton shook his head. "What came over her?"

His ma chuckled. "Pa and I remember what she was like when she was young. We simply reminded her of some of the things she'd done. Made her recall how generous people were to forgive her and give her a chance to do better."

"What did she do?" Colton asked.

Pa shook his head. "The past is past. Let's leave it that way."

Colton and Rebecca glanced at each other and decided to

let it go. Whatever Beatrice had done, the Hayeses weren't about to say anything.

"Mother and I have an announcement," Mr. Hayes said. "We've decided to move into town."

"But, Pa—"

"Hear me out. Amelia's house is empty. She'd like to have us live there. Your ma is feeling much better with that new medicine Doc Simpson gave her. We've discovered how much we enjoy the children and we'd like to help Amelia with them."

Colton looked stunned. "You've made up your mind, haven't you?"

His pa nodded. "It's time for things to change."

"Of course."

Rebecca understood it was hard for him to release his responsibility, but as his pa said, it was time.

His parents walked away.

"It's going to be fine," she assured Colton.

Before he could reply, Jakob and Heidi sidled up to them. Heidi's brown eyes were dark with worry.

Colton caught the girl's hand. "What has you so anxious?"

"Do we move into the orphanage today?"

Rebecca caught Heidi's other hand and pulled her close. "You and Jakob won't be moving into any orphanage."

Jakob's hands rested on his sister's shoulder. "I do not understand."

Colton pulled the letter from his pocket. "We've been given permission to adopt both of you, if that meets with your approval."

Heidi threw herself into their arms. "It does. Doesn't it, Jakob?"

Jakob's face was wreathed in a wide smile. "I'd say it does." He stuck out his hand to shake with Colton, but Colton pulled him close and hugged him, pulling Rebecca into the same embrace.

"Our own family." Heidi's voice was muffled by the press of bodies around her, but she sounded supremely happy.

Rebecca cupped Jakob's head and pulled his face close to kiss his cheek. She smiled at Colton.

"We are family, blessed by a loving God."

His answering smile signaled agreement.

* * * * *

Dear Reader,

I've always wanted to write a story about an orphanage, so what fun to be in on the ground floor—literally—of building an orphanage and rescuing a number of orphans. I got to design it to suit me, and even got to furnish the rooms. I have to confess that the rooms remind me of an orphanage my husband and I visited in Brazil many years ago when we went there to adopt a daughter. Hence, this story has a lot of personal elements to it. Even the heroine strikes a personal note. She is a rich socialite who was unsure of her strengths and abilities. I've never been rich or a socialite, but I have struggled with insecurities. Still do.

I hope you find some personal truth for yourself in this story. I'd love to hear from you if you do. You can contact me at linda@lindaford.org. For updates on my stories (and my life) check out my website, www.lindaford.org.

Linda Ford

Questions for Discussion

1. Rebecca believes it is her duty to obey her father. What is right about this? What is wrong?

2. Rebecca has neither lived in plain circumstances nor been independent. How well do you think she handles this?

3. Why is she afraid of her growing love for Colton?

4. What emotion keeps Colton from being free to love Rebecca? Is his reason/emotion based on good motives?

5. What do you think of how the community is handling the orphans? Could they do better? How?

6. Why is Beatrice Ward so opposed to the idea of the orphanage? Does she have valid arguments?

7. It is never revealed exactly what the Hayeses said to Beatrice to make her change her mind. What do you think it was?

8. Was Mr. Hayes correct in pretending to be more crippled than he was? How did you feel when you learned the truth?

9. Do you think Rebecca will be an asset to the community? What about Colton's parents? What do you see them doing once they leave the ranch?

10. Do you think Colton and Rebecca have a true faith in God? What makes you answer the way you do?

11. What do you see happening to the orphans in the orphanage? Will Beatrice Ward's predictions come true?

12. If you could write the next few chapters in Rebecca and Colton's life, what would they include?

13. Is there a spiritual lesson in the book? What is it?

14. What is your favorite scene in the book? Why?

The pavement outside the Kansas City airport radiated heat
even though the sun had already sunk below the horizon.
Tate held his seven-year-old daughter's hand a little tighter
and squinted against the dying sunshine to read the sign
hanging overhead.

"That's it down there," he said, pointing. "Baggage
Claim A."

Lily Farnsworth was the last of six new business owners
to arrive, each selected by the Save Our Street Committee of
the town of Bygones. As a member of the committee, Tate
had been asked to meet her at the airport in Kansas City and
transport her to Bygones. With the grand opening just a week
away, most of the shop owners had been at work preparing
their stores for some time already, but Ms. Farnsworth
had delayed until after her sister's wedding, assuring the
committee that a florist's shop required less preparation than
some retail businesses. Tate hoped she was right.

He still wasn't convinced that this scheme, financed by a
mysterious, anonymous donor, would work, but if something
didn't revive the financial fortunes of Bygones—and soon—
their small town would become just another ghost town on the
north central plains.

Isabella stopped before the automatic doors and waited

or him to catch up. They entered the cool building together. A pair of gleaming luggage carousels occupied the open pace, both vacant. A few people milled about. Among em was a tall, pretty woman with long blond hair and und tortoiseshell glasses. She was perched atop a veritable nountain of luggage. She wore black ballet slippers and white nit leggings beneath a gossamery blue dress with fluttery leeves and hems. Her very long hair was parted in the middle nd waved about her face and shoulders. He felt the insane rge to look more closely behind the lenses of her glasses, but f course he would not.

He turned away, the better to resist the urge to stare, and canned the building for anyone who might be his florist.

One by one, the possibilities faded away. Finally Isabella ave him that look that said, "Dad, you're being a goof again." he slipped her little hand into his, and he sighed inwardly. urning, he walked the few yards to the luggage mountain nd swept off his straw cowboy hat.

"Are you Lily Farnsworth?"

To find out if Bygones can turn itself around,
pick up LOVE IN BLOOM
wherever Love Inspired books are sold.

Love Inspired **HISTORICAL**

Former gunslinger Hunter Mitchell wants to start his life over
with his newly discovered nine-year-old daughter—and his best
chance at providing his daughter a stable home is a marriage of
convenience to her beautiful and fiercely protective teacher.

Charity
HOUSE

The Outlaw's Redemption

by

RENEE RYAN

Available July 2013.

When helicopter pilot Creed Carter finds an abandoned baby
on a church altar, he must convince foster parent
Haley Blanchard that she'll make a good mom—and a
good match.

Baby in His Arms

by Linda Goodnight

Available July 2013
wherever books are sold.

www.LoveInspiredBooks.com

LI78